RUNE KINGDOM

UNCOMMON WORLD: NORTHERN ISLES

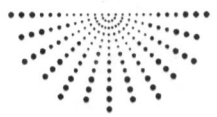

ALISHA KLAPHEKE

Text copyright © 2018 by Alisha Klapheke
Cover art copyright © 2018 by Dan Van Oss

Library of Congress Cataloging-in-Publication Data
Klapheke, Alisha
Rune Kingdom/Alisha Klapheke. —First edition.
Summary: When a woman's mother is chosen as a human sacrifice, she risks her entire people to raise a new kind of magic and rebel.

❀ Created with Vellum

THE ANGRY MOUNTAIN

ALTAR MOUNT

JARL'S STEAD

ICE WINE VINEYARD

LINDEN LOWS

N
W · E
S

— SNOWFALLEN —

Magic and blood. Blood and magic. My mind sang a twisted song with the two words. Were they as linked as we thought?

A very dangerous idea sparked to life inside me.

Standing in knee-high snow, surrounded by grapes like jewels, I carved another Cold Weather rune into a vineyard post, wishing I could magically call a freeze like *he* could, like Fellriki the Protector, the powerful leader of our isle, could. The lines and curves of my magical carving glowed silver. A small, but obedient wind tossed a chill over the vines and tugged at the braids above my ears.

A tiny snow bunting chirped, white and black feathers ruffled with the sudden change in temperature. Tucking my carver under my arm, I whistled softly and scooped him up. A tuft of stubborn winter grass held onto a pine near the vineyard's border. Gently, I settled the bird into the yellow growth and tried not to feel sad that he was so afraid of me and my magic. I only wanted to be strong so I could protect those who weren't.

The cold my rune called up was enough to discomfort a bunting, but nowhere near enough to freeze the grapes. My parents ran the most prestigious ice wine vineyard in the Northern Isles. We should've had a frosty harvest yesterday and already been crafting the ice wine. Winterskvöld was almost here. If the weather wouldn't cooperate, we'd lose our place on the council here in Snowfallen.

I squeezed the wooden shaft of my carver, frustration boiling out of me. I was surprised the snow didn't melt around my feet. I'd been born with the need, the longing, the want for control within my homeland. I refused to live without it. I would not obey rules that my family hadn't helped create. I hardly even followed the ones we did.

The bladed end of my carver reflected the shy winter sun. The rays were too weak to give me any strength. Sun was the answer for most of us who worked magic with the symbols we carved—the *lykill*. But almighty Fellriki lived in a cave on the mountain and he used blood instead of sun for his magic. No one questioned it. No one used blood themselves. My parents would be appalled I was even thinking of mimicking the all-knowing Fellriki. I eyed the fine steel of my carver, the blade's viciously sharp edge. My dangerous idea flared to life again.

It might work.

If Fellriki used blood to do what he did, maybe I

could too. Even if it was blasphemy. I'd never been one to follow the rules.

I lifted my sleeve, my skin nearly as pale as the snow.

Everyone else—magic-wielding *seithr* and regular humans alike—had already gone into their nearby houses to rest. Even Mother and Father were headed that way. We'd been trying our magic to bring the deep freeze all day. Father's voice tangled with Mother's as they left me. They were too riled up to notice I was hanging behind.

Father coughed and wiped his nose with the back of his sleeve. "If we don't harvest tonight—"

"We still have another day." Oh Mother. Always the calm one.

"But if we're late to offer, the jarl will drop us from the council." The jarl was our version of a king.

"Not necessarily."

Mother was wrong. Our family would lose our seat at the jarl's side if we didn't make the wine in time for the Winterskvöld festival.

I slammed my carver's end into the snow and ice.

What if the jarl gave our seat to another magic family, or worse, a regular family who had no *seithr* blood—no magic blood? The jarl loved those cattle keepers. Like they were some kind of adorable pet or like they were somehow braver for living a life without seithr magic. If I had to bow my head to some cow herder, I'd explode. It would all be over. Death for the most promising youth in Snowfallen.

The steel of my carver's blade blinked the sun back at me.

It might work.

My carver was sharp enough. I'd choose pain over shame any day.

I flipped the length of yew wood. Steel whistled through the air and caught against my forearm. The blade bit into my flesh, and I fought to stay quiet as blood poured into the snow at my feet. It hurt more than I'd guessed.

"Bryn!" Father's boots crunched across the snow as he ran, leaving Mother standing with her mouth open.

Turning the blade to the earth and ignoring the pulsing pain in my arm, I shaped the Cold Weather lykill —the same magic symbol I'd used on the post—into the bloody ground.

I held my breath, ready for a storm of sleet or a bright gust of frigid air off the fjord. But all I got was another steady, cold wind. Nothing more than I'd managed before the blood. Fellriki claimed to need blood to protect Snowfallen from storms and famine and all sorts of horrors.

He lies, my mind whispered. *Fellriki lies.*

Father grabbed my hand. "What are you doing?"

I raised my chin. "I wanted to know if we could use blood. Like him."

Mother ran up and pulled me to her. "Daughter. That isn't how it works. You know that."

No one challenged Fellriki and his demands for human blood. How would I know our magic and his worked differently?

My cut burned as I breathed in the smell of pine and barley cakes on Mother's bluehare cloak and held her tighter, gripping my carver against her back.

4

"I'm fine," I said. "Now let me go. I'll ruin your cloak."

Wearing the rare fur, she looked perfect, every bit the rich woman she was. We looked very fine side-by-side. Strong mother and strong daughter. Pride rose in my chest. There was nothing wrong with being proud of one's appearance. Wasn't that black and white bunting proud of its feathers? It was only natural to want prestige and finery. I wanted that and more.

Father cupped my face gently. "We'll get the freeze."

Doubt and fear glazed his eyes, and I wished I could swallow my pride and hug him like I did when I was young.

A familiar twisting feeling heated my middle. It burned inside me when I pushed forward during moments where most people would bow down. "And if we don't?"

He ran a hand over his silver-black beard. "We may lose our council seat…"

"Will Fellriki punish us?" The image of empty wine bowls flashed through my mind.

Mother's gaze flew to Altar Mount, beyond the jarl's farmstead and the center of town—Snowfallen's beating heart. "Hush, daughter."

I heaved myself away from them, pressing my sleeve against my wound to close it.

Father followed, his voice gruff. "Let's get that cut clean so your Raven can tell you about his latest song."

"Rafn is here?"

Mother nodded and took a length of linen from her belt—the stuff we used to tie up errant vine branches—and helped me wrap my cut.

A dark shape loped out of the pressing house carrying two large bottles. A sensation like feathers falling trailed down my chest and stomach. Seeing me, Rafn stopped, tucked the wine against the stone wall, and made his way over the wagon-rutted path that ran the length of the vineyard. His black hair fought the braid work on top of his head, several chunks freeing themselves to move in the wind. He'd shaved the sides clean to show off his new inking. Giving me a tentative smile, he ran a hand over the raven and skull artwork that marked him as a cemetery singer, a singer for the dead.

"Greets, Bryn."

Before this summer, he would've called me by my nickname, Starling.

"The inking looks good on you." My cheeks heated.

He almost smiled, just a flash of teeth showing between his lips. Then he saw my arm and his face fell. "What happened?"

"It's nothing," Father said.

Rafn met my gaze with a silent question.

"It's nothing," I echoed.

My parents left us, stomping away and muttering about me as Rafn eyed my injury.

"Really, Bryn. What did you do to your arm?"

I snorted and worked my sleeve down. "You wouldn't get it."

"Because I'm not a seithr?"

Gods. He looked so offended. We'd done nothing but snip at one another since the summer. I still had no idea what had happened to change him. He'd always been a bit stiff, but now the only thing that made him smile was his work.

"Look," I said, explaining. "I cut my arm to see if blood would get our Cold Weather lykill working better. To bring a freeze for the grapes. It didn't work. Not even a little." I looked to Altar Mount, as if I could see the hooded figure of Fellriki there with his white carver and heavy cloak. "Fellriki says he has to have blood. If it's so important for his magic, why didn't it do a thing for mine?"

"That's blasphemous."

"I said you wouldn't get it." I started toward the house. Why did I start these conversations? They always ended like this. I was the only one in Snowfallen that dared question Fellriki.

He hurried to catch up. "Do you want us to turn into that?" He threw a hand toward the distant sweep of black rock that had been people and buildings until the mountain erupted when Mother and Father were my age. Fellriki had stopped the next eruption after that, and ever since, Snowfallen had worshipped him as a god.

I whirled to face him. "Why would bringing a freeze for ice wine work so much differently than controlling storms and the mountain and all that? Magic is magic." My heart beat in my ears. My arm hurt and I couldn't stop picturing the blade coming down on my throat instead of Grandfather's. "I think Fellriki takes the blood sacrifice just to keep us cowed."

Rafn paled. "Please don't let anyone hear you say that."

A laugh shot out of me. "I'm frustrated, not stupid. I

like my tongue in my mouth, not on the jarl's chopping block."

"Fellriki gives us everything. Good harvests. Protection."

"I'm well aware," I mumbled, placing my gathering basket inside the door of the pressing house. We'd have to go spar at the field soon—part of the Winterskvöld celebration—and I wanted to fill up with Mother's food instead of the Raven's stiff rhetoric.

"I'm starving," I said. "I'll see you at the field."

Rafn grabbed my sleeve. "Hey." His eyes were soft. "I'm scared too. About the sacrifice."

He was such a good person. He wasn't a seithr, and he didn't have much clout, but he said the things others didn't. Not like me—he didn't voice arguments—but he exposed his less-than-powerful feelings. True feelings. It was brave, really, admitting to fear.

But the thought of Fellriki's blade wasn't my main concern.

"I'm not scared of dying, Raven. I just don't...I don't want my life in someone else's hands."

Rafn's brow furrowed handsomely. I sighed and warm air clouded the space between us. My heart tapped against my chest, and I touched Raven's hand for a second. His skin was smooth and rough at the same time. A scar marred his first finger. He'd nearly cut it off last year, catching it between the anchor's rope and the boat's side during a wild day sailing to the end of our isle to explore.

"Thank you though," I said. "For admitting that. After sparring, why don't we scale the low cliffs? Like we used to. Well, if I'm not harvesting... We can spy on the next isle over."

His face dropped into its new normal—an emotionless wall. "I have to work with Father."

And this was what I'd been dealing with since summer. Any sort of chancy behavior and he was out. No fun anymore for Rafn and me. "Fine. Well, I suppose I'll see you at the field."

"Yeah." His face lightened a little, but his shoulders were still tense. "Find me, and we'll go a round."

After he gathered his wine bottles, I watched him weave through the gates and scanty pines to the road, his words jumbling around inside me, heavy and sickening. It was too bad there was no lykill for making a friend bleed his secrets. I was certain I could fix him if I only knew the problem. I missed his true smile—the one that made anything possible. Somehow I would bring that smile back to our lives. If anyone could do it, it was me.

CHAPTER TWO

The jarl's sprawling farmstead was empty as a sand-scrubbed skull. Cows, their brown eyes wide and clueless, stood unmilked in their wattle fences. As I ran a hand along the woven branches, the animals stepped back, wary of the magic in me.

"Don't be afraid." I offered a hand and one plodded forward.

The cow's hide was soft under my fingers. The animal's warmth spread into my hand and made me feel less alone. If only I could properly explain why I felt the way I did, maybe then someone would understand my ferocity and drive. I longed to be the mother bear of this isle and its people, to keep them safe, my claws at our enemies' throats.

The scent of heated metal flowed from the open door of the blacksmith's forge and into the air as I walked.

Between the turf outbuildings, I worked my way down the split logs lying across the mud, heading toward the steeply pitched roof of the jarl's house and the training field beyond.

I removed my bluehare cloak. One of the jarl's workers hung it on a peg pounded into the house's outside wall. Spotting my fair-haired friend Ulla, I raised a fist. Her wide cheeks lifted into a grin. A thin line of blood divided her heart-shaped face as she bumped her shield against another fighter's short sword.

Mother and Father were talking and gesturing to the jarl, who ran a hand down the five braids of his beard.

Mother should've helped Father braid his beard into four to show our rank, but she wasn't into that sort of thing. She smiled at me behind the men's backs, and I waved, showing her that I wore the new ring she'd given me.

At the weapons stand, I dodged the shield-maker's little boy and the jarl's youngest as they wrestled. The smallest knocked into a bucket holding spirit of salt. I grabbed the back of his longshirt before he fell into it.

"Watch it," I said, pushing the boy safely away and screwing the lid onto the stuff. "Some idiot left this thing open. See this?"

The boy eyed me, then looked where I pointed, at the three-colored circle on the bucket.

"It's a *ridgrasil*. A warning. Spirit of salt will take the rust off your sword, but it'll also take the skin from your hand. Don't be stupid like the fool who left the lid off."

The boy grinned and ran away.

I nabbed a sword with a grubby hilt and there was my friend Ulla coming at me with a wild smile and an axe.

"Defend yourself!" she shouted.

Dropping the sword, I threw my carver up and caught her blade before it could touch flesh, the strike making my hand and arm buzz.

I laughed. "At least let me get ready."

"Would an Invader allow you to get ready? Or a war party from another isle? Hm?"

Smirking, I swung low to slice at her knees. The edge whispered over her leather breeches. "That would've been it for you if this thing was properly sharpened."

She bowed, shield and axe extended. "Your win, friend."

We started up again, her taking the brunt of my blows with her shield. The Protection lykill on my carver brightened as Ulla came down with the axe. The symbols made her strike go slightly right, allowing me to hit her axe-hand with my carver. She shouted and dropped the weapon to the muddy grass and ice-clumped snow.

"Witch," she said wryly, glaring at me with deep blue eyes. According to Rafn, her pronunciation of the southern lands' slur was spot on. I'd heard it a few times during the trip to Silvania. That Kinneret woman from Jakobden had said it with a wry smile. She had a touch of strong magic herself, it seemed.

"Brute. I'm thirsty. Come on."

I led her to the spring that bubbled from the jarl's land. As we drank our fill of water chilled by the glacier beyond Snowfallen, I watched Rafn fight the jarl's eldest, Jakob. Rafn was tall, but Jakob towered over him like a ship's mast.

When Jakob whipped his axe at Rafn's head, I thought perhaps this was the last time I'd see him breathing. But

Rafn, hair waving like black flames on his head, ducked and came up under Jakob's third rib with a blunted spear he shouldn't even have been using so close to his opponent. I shook my head and Ulla snorted.

Ulla, Rafn, my most timid friend Liv, and I were born one right after another. All under Din's Feather—a string of tiny stars that hung above the horizon during our birth month. When we were still toddling around in homespun baby dresses, everyone called us the hatchlings. Rafn's name meant Raven. Ulla was the Eagle. And Liv. Though she had the typical seithr features that spoke of her power—feathered eyebrows and a silver seithr streak running through her chestnut hair—she pretty much embodied a pea finch, all darting eyes and hopeful for any crumb of love from anyone. Me, I was the Starling. It fit, I guessed, with my mostly black hair and penchant for aggressiveness.

Ulla lifted her eagle beak of a nose and eyed Rafn as he continued sparring. "He doesn't look like a fighter. But he's actually pretty good." She raised her voice, eyeing his intricately decorated cemetery singer clogs. They were caked with black mud. "If he wore decent boots, he might win more than one fight in a lifetime."

"I heard that," Rafn said loudly as he dodged a strike. He wiggled a foot behind him before going after Jakob with a turning back kick.

"Ooo, our dark Raven has a sense of humor." Maybe there was still a chance to get our old Rafn back.

Ulla slurped more water and whispered, "You going to bed him?"

Heat raced up my neck. "What? No."

Ulla shrugged and stood, wiping her axe on her belted longshirt. "I think you want to see if you can crack that hard surface of his."

I did. But not until he made the first move. I wasn't going to risk being made a fool of. "I do not."

Ulla leaned down, her nose close to mine. "You do."

"And you," I said, "smell like *fiskibollur*."

She patted her flat stomach and tucked her axe into the tie at her belt. "Fish cakes are good for you. Ate ten this morning."

"Ugh. Ten? Where do you even put all that food?"

"Into my big, amazing brain so I can outsmart my clever seithr friend," she said.

I thumbed the shape of an Uncross lykill in the air, out of her field of vision. "Just try."

The rune worked its magic and her axe's tie came undone from her belt. She yelped as the weapon conked the toe of her boot.

"Witch," she snarled, grinning.

"Brute," I shot back.

Liv ran up, her braids in a tiny crown. "Greets," she said quietly, checking that her hair was still in place. Only Liv would wear it like that on a sparring day.

Ulla threw an arm around Liv's shoulders. "Good day! As usual, you are accidentally late to training. Nice work."

Liv made a little noise like a laugh, and I rolled my eyes.

"You are a seithr, Liv. Act like one. You don't have to put up with her." I rubbed my fingers together for warmth and tsked at Ulla.

"Yes, you do," Ulla said.

I gave Liv a look. "You're not going to get any better if you never practice fighting, Pea Finch."

"You're right," she said. "You're both right. About everything."

Ulla blew out a breath that smoked like a sleepy geyser in the freezing air. "Ugh. Why do you always agree, Liv? It's so boring."

Liv bit her bottom lip. "But you *are* right."

Ulla made a noise like a sheep bleating. I knocked her blonde head with my carver. Ulla was right, but Liv was a hatchling and there was no call for insulting one of our own.

Jakob leaped into a fighting match with the butcher's grown daughter and son, his voice rising in a prayer to Fellriki.

I wondered what would happen if we decided not to give up someone for the sacrifice this year, not to bow down to Fellriki.

"Let it go, Bryn," Ulla said, gazing appreciatively at tall Jakob while she chastised me. "I don't want to have to sneak you into the South. Their boys are too tiny for my taste."

A few steps away, Rafn drank from the spring, the muscles in his arms turning under his thin, sweat-dampened shirt.

Wiggling her nearly invisible, blonde eyebrows at me, Ulla grabbed Liv's sleeve. She dragged her toward another sparring match, leaving me alone with the Raven.

"Want to fight?" I asked him, spinning my carver and widening my stance.

Rafn's eyes glittered as he wiped his mouth with the back of his hand. "Let's."

Holding his spear like a carver, he brought the top end down at an angle toward my temple. I blocked the strike with my carver, flipped my weapon, and smacked him in the knee.

He made a noise and winced, his face vicious but somewhat teasing too.

A grin tore at my cheeks as I swung at his other knee. He leaped high and popped me on the shoulder with his spear's back end. I grunted and let the small pain drive my hands to move faster, the blade of my carver arcing toward the side of his neck. A neck I'd rather kiss than injure. Not that I'd tell anyone that.

Rafn spun away and breathed out in a rush. A swirl of incense came off him, a scent that marked him as a cemetery singer as much as his inking did. I inhaled, and he hit me in the back, his spear jarring my spine just a little. I bent and pretended to be more hurt than I was, hiding my smile.

He leaned in, checking on me, his voice truly worried. "That wasn't too rough, was it?"

I slid my carver behind his ankle and shoved him with my shoulder, throwing him to the mud. An exhale opened his mouth, and he lay, defeated. I spun my carver and set a foot on his stomach.

"Don't underestimate me." I smiled to take some ice out of my words.

He stared up, his gaze drifting from my boots, my

breeches and dress, to my neck and cheeks. "I don't know how anyone could."

To hide how much I adored all this, I turned and headed for the spring. No need to let him know how much he affected me. Not unless he could let go of whatever was bothering him so much.

"Bryn!" Both my parents shouted and nodded toward the jarl's oldest daughter. They wanted me to spar with her.

Rafn took off, and I tried very hard not to enjoy the sight of his lanky, broad-shouldered form fading into the crowd. It might never work out for us. My knees were shaking, so I grabbed the spring's marker stone when I bent to drink so I wouldn't land on my bum.

An impression marred the back of the rock.

I maneuvered around the wet growth until I could see the other side. The impression was faded, hardly noticeable, but it looked a lot like a Growing lykill with its two slanting lines. But what was the circle that surrounded the bottom half of the symbol?

My parents called for me again as Ulla and Liv walked up.

I pulled Liv around to see. "What does this look like to you?"

"A Growing rune, maybe?"

"But what about that circle?" My mind wheeled around the possibilities. "That's a lykill we don't know. That's new."

"New?" Ulla kicked at the marker.

"Not new. I mean, it's one we don't use. It's old

probably. Liv, what do you think? Is it a magical symbol or not?"

"I don't know. It's really hard to see."

"I'm going to draw it. In the dirt. What if it's some seriously powerful lykill? What if there are more?"

Ulla rubbed her hands together. "I love it when she gets like this."

The Finch frowned. "You're already such a strong seithr. Why bother with it? You might get in trouble.

The magic families here in Snowfallen had a collective knowledge of many lykill—also called runes. We used them for everything from keeping bugs out of our food to driving away illnesses or increasing our physical strength. Many said the magic in our blood came from a group of people with fully silver hair. The strangers joined up with the settlers here and told tales of a silvery fog that could give magic or take souls. The stories said a lost isle called Ayarazi holds the original source of the magical mist.

The sailor I had met in Silvania—Kinneret Raza—had found that isle. Now, I wished I'd made time to question her about it. Of course, it was obvious that woman hated my people, so she probably wouldn't have told me anything useful. Kinneret's anger at how Snowfallen treated those who didn't grow properly had shaken me. Really, that was when I first began questioning some of our traditions. It was both a scary and a fascinating road I'd started down. I knew if I ever bore a child like that Oron fellow, that I would keep him and get him sailing. I wouldn't leave my child on the rocks, no matter what challenges he faced.

"The jarl is looking over here," Liv said, breaking into my thoughts. "So are your parents."

"They probably want to talk about the ceremony." I felt sick.

As the eldest child in last year's tribute family—we'd given up Grandfather—I had the honor of reading the message Fellriki sent naming the sex and age of the next sacrifice. Men between forty-five and sixty. Or women fifty-nine to eighty-nine. That sort of nonsense.

With my boot, I edged snow away and started the lykill.

Liv looked ready to vomit. "I wish you'd go to your parents. Can't you just enjoy things the way they are?"

She sounded like Father. "I could be content," I said. "If I were strong like Fellriki."

"You'd be a fearsome thing." Liv's voice was a whisper.

Ulla grinned. "She'd be perfect."

"Power demands sacrifice," Liv said. "Could you take blood?"

"Maybe I wouldn't need to."

Liv and Ulla traded looks.

Ulla ran a hand over her head. "You might want to keep that between us hatchlings."

The finished rune sat in the muddy ground, doing nothing.

I fisted my hands. "Why don't we go to the lair tonight and look around for things like this?"

When they agreed, I gave each of their arms a squeeze and started toward my parents.

Yes, I could keep my thoughts between friends. And maybe I could settle down. If our vineyard got the freeze and my family kept our place. My parents did look fine and powerful in their bluehare cloaks, keeping the jarl himself company.

We were gaining ground in Snowfallen. If we managed this harvest as well as the ones in the past, Mother would be in line for a council seat herself in the next year. That would set me on my way to being a leader. Who knew? Maybe the jarl's children would prove to be weak or have some terrible accident that made it impossible for them to rule. Of course, I didn't *really* want that to happen, but if it did, well, with both parents on the council, I'd be in the running for become jarl myself someday. One person's tragedy could often be another's victory. No reason to ignore the good that came from the bad. And I'd be especially powerful if I could find some ancient lykill no other seithr knew. That would definitely impress the council, seithr and non.

"That's a mighty grin, daughter." Mother took my hand and ran a finger over the ring she'd given me last moon. The wine-colored stone, wrapped in threads of silver, had been in our family longer than anyone could remember.

I nodded respectfully to the jarl and he responded with a dip of his head. "Life is ripe with possibilities, Mother."

CHAPTER THREE

That night, while most of the village gathered in the meeting house, Ulla, Liv, and I hiked the wind-scraped incline to the abandoned house we'd claimed. Cut from the turf, the house we'd adopted sat on a treeless cliff, a spot where salt and wind wouldn't allow anything to grow except rough grasses.

The man who'd built and lived in it had been sacrificed when we were children. Though he'd suffered from a mysterious pain in his hip most of his life, he'd been a well-respected cemetery singer like Rafn and his father. The man had collected all sorts of things. Odd bits of writing, plant and insect specimens, smooth stones from deep water, and items whose purpose remained a mystery.

No one else in Snowfallen was interested in the far-off house, so Ulla, Liv, and I had deemed it ours. We called it the lair. I liked the fact that it pushed back at our childish bird nicknames and made us sound more like vicious beasts.

In the past, Rafn would've joined us. Not now. The thought tugged at my chest.

Holes in the walls, shelves, and buried casks made certain a day at the house was never without its small surprises.

Inside, Liv rifled through a basket near the hearthstones at the fire in the middle of the room. She lifted a smooth stone and held it to the flames' light. Squeezing it once—I knew she wanted to keep it but was afraid it was wrong—she returned it to the basket, humming happily, and went back to searching for items with old languages written on them. Once, she'd found a poem about a man made of swamp water and river plants. It had been scribed on white crystal, the ink rubbed into the markings was barely visible after sitting for who knew how long. Liv had poured over it for hours.

Ulla stood on tiptoe beside a splintered shelf. The man who'd owned the place must've been seriously tall to have a spot Ulla had trouble reaching. She sniffed at a bunch of dried, sweet *ilmreyr* grass and smiled.

I poked at the fire and the barley cakes I was cooking up for us. I wanted to rummage too, but the cakes weren't finishing as quickly as I'd hoped. So far, we hadn't found anything remotely resembling a lykill and I didn't know how long I'd be able to stay away from the vineyard. "Come on flames. You're lazy as Atli." Liv's brother was the worst kind of layabout.

The cakes near the coals were hot to the touch. I

sucked a burned finger and inhaled the woodsmoke and bready scents of the lair, trying to throw off my snarling mood. I rubbed a spot on my backside that was sore from sitting on one foot.

Ulla sniffed and frowned, her stomach growling. "You burning your cakes, Starling?"

"Why? You interested in kissing them better, Eagle?" I shook my rear at her.

She snatched up one of the small rounds of bread and threw it at me. "Sea slugs for brains."

Liv looked up from her hunt. "Same color. Brains and slugs."

I grinned. "Brains and slugs. Sounds like the boys we have to choose from."

Ulla grabbed another cake and took a bite. "I disagree. There isn't any slug built like Jakob. And give Rafn a year or two and he'll be more than a nice voice." She leaned behind me and whispered at Liv. "Not that Bryn hasn't noticed."

"Shut it, you two," I said.

"These cakes aren't so bad." Ulla took another. "Maybe it's your special Bryn venom that makes them taste so good."

Liv's eyes sparked. "If we eat enough, will we learn to scowl like you?"

"Ha. Ha." I handed her a barley cake. "It takes years of daily practice to achieve this." I pointed at my face and gave them a good one.

Ulla threw herself on a pile of furs beside me. "I prefer fists to frowns as my weapon."

"Oh, but a great sneer makes a wound no herb can heal," I said.

"Haven't you seen Jakob's left cheek? No pretty plant is fixing that scar. He'll think of me every time he sees his face in the water until the day Rafn sings his death."

"No wonder he goes to sea every chance he gets," Liv said.

"Think he fancies me?" Ulla asked.

"Maybe," I said. "You might try smelling more like goat. They say he's overly fond of visiting the cow shed."

Ulla barked a laugh and hit me in the arm. Liv covered her face, though I could see her shoulders shaking as she went back to poking around the hearthstones.

She reached under a rock colored by years of black smoke, then sucked a slow breath. "Ooo. A nice, little box."

I leaned in to look. The container was made from very dark wood like the ones that held the jarl's best books.

Turning the box over, she ran her fingers over the carved surfaces and whispered to herself. With the lid worked off, I could see a slim roll of something. Liv set the box between us, removed a scroll, then unrolled it. Her finger traced her bottom lip and her eyebrows drew together as she read silently. After several lines, her hand stopped moving and her chest froze in a held breath.

"I found something," she said.

I doubted it, but maybe.

Ulla crossed her arms. "If it's another ode to the

swamp man, go ahead and keep that to yourself, Pea. We'll manage somehow."

"This is different." Reverence hummed in Liv's voice.

We shuffled around, Ulla cramming her cake into her mouth. Liv held out the rolled length of vellum, the calfskin a buttery yellow. With careful fingers, I smoothed it out on a flat hearth rock.

A simple drawing decorated the center.

My heart jumped.

Though it was more rustic than the ones we used now, the design was clearly a ridgrasil—a circle divided into three triangles, one red, one gray, one silver. The ridgrasil was a warning of bad luck, danger, the unknown. It was similar to the one that marked the spirit of salt bucket on the sparring field, the stuff I'd kept the boy out of earlier.

The language surrounding the warning symbol was obviously ancient.

"Can you translate it?" I asked Liv. Only she and Rafn were into this sort of thing.

"The cadence will be off...the rhyming..."

I blew out a breath. "It's fine. Go on."

She nodded. *"The Silver lives open for all seithr to see. For the wine, for the herbs, and...to the family. The Redbook was...,"* she looked up. "I'm not sure about that part. I can't quite make out the last of that sentence." I motioned for her to go on. *"...the Graybook sleeps with a long-dead master; the Lows hide it from...ignorant minds."* Liv paused. "Then there is something about simple magic, beasts, and maybe...heat or cold or...Oh! It's the elements. Then it goes on...*Many lost blood and kin...keep the red, gray, and silver from seeing sun together again.*"

"What does that mean?" Ulla asked.

"It's talking about grimoires." I stood, drumming fingers on my carver. "Books of lykill, of runes. It has to be. One book about simple magic, another book is a bestiary, and a third book is for the elements or something like that. But which is which?"

Liv held the writing up to the fire and squinted at the lettering. "We should put it back. Or even burn it." She eyed the ridgrasil.

I tapped my carver. "Why would this be marked in warning?"

"Umm, because lykill can be dangerous?" Ulla shrugged.

"Fellriki's are," Liv said.

"It's a strange word, ridgrasil," I said.

"It's close to the old word for those sea snails people used to use for dye." Liv held up the dyed hem of her dress. Dark blue ships sailed along the edges. "The little striped ones. Greyridsils."

Ulla clicked her tongue. "Oh yeah those colorful little snails are delicious. My aunt used to make a stew out of them."

"Ugh. Gross. Can we focus, please?" I traced the sharpened blade of my carver, careful not to cut myself. "Ridgrasil. Liv, what is the root of the snails' name?"

"I think it's derived from their color. They're mostly gray, but with silver and red stripes. Greyridsils."

"Gray was gray. Rid was red. Sil was silver. So if we use that line of thinking to study the name of our warning ridgrasil, we could say it means Red, Gray, Silver too. So maybe…Silverbook. Redbook. Graybook. Silver. Red. Gray."

Ulla wiped a hand over her face. "Are you going to make a point?"

It had to be related somehow. Maybe this was where that practice had started, the circle's first warning. "They wanted us to be wary of the grimoires. Redgraysilver. This is where the ridgrasil started, with this warning about the three books being together."

"Oh," Liv said, her fingertips grazing her bottom lip in thought.

"Whoa. The words do slur together. But the writing isn't even true, is it?" Ulla pulled her sleeves higher. "You seithr don't even have a Silverbook. Do you?"

Liv shook her head, her lips moving in silence as she translated the old writing.

"Maybe we did. Once." I gripped my carver. The magical lykill carved into the wood pressed into my skin. "Do you realize what this means?"

Liv swallowed. "That there are more lykill than any of us know. And the runes are written down somewhere."

"If no one found and destroyed it yet, the Graybook is buried in the lows. Linden Lows. It has to be. The writing said it lies with its master there."

"What runes does it explain?" Ulla leaned over to look at the words.

Liv silently read the scroll again. "The writing doesn't say exactly."

"If we found the Gray," I said, "no matter what it

holds, we could be the most knowledgeable seithr in the North."

"Except for Fellriki," Ulla said. "Because he's part god."

"Except for him." A plan began to sprout in my head.

I was very glad Rafn wasn't here to guess what it was. If I could get my hands on an entire book of runes that no other living seithr knew, my family's place in Snowfallen would be secure forever. Ice wine or no ice wine. I'd never have to see worry grow lines in my parents' faces. I'd never have to fear the jarl or the council. We would run this place. Perhaps I wouldn't even have to fear Fellriki. A buzzing filled my hands and I flexed my fingers. That would be true freedom.

"Ulla. Liv. I'm going to find that grimoire."

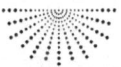

CHAPTER FOUR

All night I dreamed of tattered books and a fire that burned through me but somehow didn't hurt. The morning sun glimmered around the slim cracks of our house's one window, set high in the wall. My mind snaked around various possibilities. If I could find the Gray grimoire in the cemetery where Rafn lived in Linden Lows, I could rival Fellriki. I wondered what he would do if I showed everyone he was just another seithr like the rest of us magic workers. A smile as sharp as a knife's edge cut across my mouth.

In the morning, I left the warm furs of my bed, dressed and grabbed my boots, and stumbled my way to a stool near the firebed.

Dressed in blacks and greens for the Winterskvöld, Mother handed me a wooden bowl of oatmeal with a half spoon of butter. "Did you forget it's a festival day, Daughter? Why are you up so early?"

Day Two of the festival and everyone's mind was on

gathering food and drink offerings for Fellriki's Demand at Altar Mount. Today we would learn who might die for the sacrifice.

But my mind focused on the Graybook.

"Is the oatmeal good?" Mother asked, giving me a smile.

The wind had reddened her cheeks. I knew that pain. I grabbed my face cream from my curtained bed space and handed it to her. She needed to look her best during festival days.

"Thank you, Daughter." She rubbed a bit on each cheek.

"What did the jarl say about the ice wine not being ready for the Demand?" I made quick work of my oatmeal as she scraped the pot and filled a bowl for Father.

"As long as it's ready in time for the Presentation, he said it'll be fine."

She eyed my purple cloak, but thankfully, didn't push me to change into the somber green and black one. By now, Mother knew how to choose her battles. She knew I had my white woolen longshirt on underneath. Even I knew that wasn't negotiable today.

"The temperature is almost low enough," she said. "We'll harvest, then you and whomever you choose may bring the bottles to the Altar Bowl. Take it up right after the feast tomorrow, all right?"

That was an honor. I'd make sure everyone heard about my role to play. I nodded. "Did the jarl seem angry?"

"Yes. But he didn't mention the council seat. I

convinced him there was no reason to get his feathers ruffled." She winked.

"You are a wonder." I kissed her beeswax and lavender scented cheek. "I'm so glad I don't have some idiot for a mother."

She laughed and spread more of my cream over her face. "You never answered *my* question about why you're in such a rush this morning."

"I'm going to meet Rafn. We're going to walk together to the Demand."

She gave me a slitted glance. "Remember what I taught you."

I flushed, knowing exactly what she meant. "We're just walking."

But despite my logical retort, my mind went along with that very specific thought trail.

Before I'd even shut the door behind me, I imagined Rafn's hand curled around the nape of my neck, warm and strong. His body—wide shoulders, half-lidded eyes, sharp hipbones—heavy on mine somewhere in the pines with crushed ferns beneath us.

I should've been pining—*ha ha*—over Jakob like Ulla did. He was the jarl's son and more powerful. But Rafn looked like he'd walked right out of a saga-song, with his jet hair, darker skin, and mysterious eyes. His mother had been from another isle and her blood gave him such a unique look. I couldn't help but want him. He was a rarity. Special. Different.

It was so strange to imagine things like this about Rafn. He'd been my friend forever. And now, with his weird change of attitude, he was as accessible as an icy peak in an avalanche.

I shook my head to clear it of the Raven's lips, fingers, breath. I couldn't be drooling over him like an idiot when I was supposed to be prodding his brain for information about the dead master of the Graybook.

LINDEN LOWS WAS the oldest saga cemetery in Snowfallen. Stone walls like crumbling castles fortified the dead's homeplace. There didn't seem to ever have been a plan to the boneyard. One roughly square area bled into two more that had offshoots of their own. Cairns were everywhere on the snow-choked grass, stones piled in small circles, great heaps, and tidy rectangles. No discernible path led through the graves, and I had to wander with the whispers of ghosts pushing this way and that.

A stone higher than even Ulla's father's head marked the entrance. Blood red images of men and women in long boats, their oars near swallowed by stylized waves, covered the marker stone. I liked it. It reminded me of the songs Rafn sang about back when our people sailed to other lands, conquering and bringing back silver. He hadn't shared one of those songs since summer. They used to be his favorite.

Deep voices came from the keeper cottage—Rafn and his father Benedikt. I rapped on the door and Rafn answered wearing nothing. Well, nothing on his upper body. I blamed Mother and her attempted lecture for the way my heart listed like a storm-tossed ship.

"Oh. Sorry. Hold on." He grabbed his shirt and pulled it on.

I'd seen Rafn without much clothing. We used to swim in the fjord on hot days. But it had been a while. He was more man than boy now. I wished his shirt had been a little more out of reach.

I cleared my throat. "I need to...ask you something." Great start, me. Very clever. "I thought we could walk to Altar Mount together."

"Come in for a minute. Okay?" He opened his mouth, then closed it.

"Right." I walked up to his father, who was working at the table while Rafn disappeared behind a hanging curtain, maybe to put on more layers for the cold day.

"Greets, Bryn," Benedikt said in his rocky voice.

His eyes narrowed in concentration as he stirred something foul-smelling in a small, black bowl. The Deadbook lay open behind him on a smaller table. It looked so old sitting there. Like the oldest thing in the world with its tattered vellum edges and the fading ink of ancient lettering.

"I'm cleaning the older pages," Benedikt said, even though I hadn't asked.

"Good."

He stopped and looked at me. Then flashed a white-toothed smile like a wolf and went back to work. I was fairly sure Benedikt didn't trust me. He was a smart man.

I leaned toward the Deadbook, eyeing the simplistic drawing of a snow-covered forest. What if there was something in there about the Graybook and its master?

"May I?" I made a page-turning sort of motion over the book.

Benedikt's lips bunched. "Are your hands clean?"

"Other than that manure I helped shift this morning…"

Rafn tugged the curtain back. One arm stuck out from a furred vest. "Bryn." His tone weighted my name, like the sounds alone could sink the word to the sea's bottom. "Father. Let her look, please." Giving me a glare, he disappeared again.

"All right then," Benedikt said.

I slipped a finger under the winter forest page and turned. More of the old language. No images. The next page showed a black sea and a pale boat fighting its white-tipped waves.

"What is this about?" My breath moved the flame of a beeswax candle beside Benedikt and his little bowl.

"It's about a seithr and his non-seithr wife who were caught in a storm," Rafn said, suddenly at my ear. His breath was warm.

I shivered. "What happened to him?"

"He wasn't a sailor, but he managed to get his wife to the safety of another family's boat before theirs was crushed on the shore's rocks." Rafn slid his Winterskvöld robes on. Cemetery singers had to wear the solemn green and black to remind everyone of who we'd lost to sacrifices in the past. "This lettering details a song about his bravery."

"Where is he buried?" I asked.

Rafn pushed a short, black braid off his forehead. His hairline had a small peak that pointed toward his face and made him look different from anyone else in Snowfallen.

I thought again about his mother and where she was from. She'd died when we were still very young, but I remembered very clearly how Rafn looked when he cried. I'd stared and stared at him, his hunched shoulders, the glistening tears raining down, barely visible on his cheeks as he bowed his head and his mop of black hair hung forward. Mother had put a hand on my back and told me to let him be. It was one of the few instances I had obeyed without argument.

Rafn touched the top right side of the page briefly before going back to lacing up the top of his longshirt. "Do you see this marking?"

It looked like a mistake. Just a small dot inside what appeared to be a brown stain. It was all very faint. The book nearly brushed my nose as I studied it.

Benedikt's hand snaked between Rafn and me, and went flat against my shoulder. "Don't blow your damp breath on it now, please."

I gave him a look, but nodded, straightening.

Rafn sat on a stool, tossed the ends of his robes aside, and slipped his clogs on. In stunted lettering, the cemetery singers' oath curled around the shoes' arches and onto the toes.

We shield those who shielded us.

I shook my head a little, wondering what pulled people into being singers. It seemed such a dull duty, bemoaning historical events in the frost-blue grass and long sweeps of snow. Rafn used to dream about sailing to other isles, even to the mainland to visit different people and see their strange culture.

When we were little we tried to make wings out of Benedikt's discarded pelts. Rafn always wanted to fly over the mountains. "I wonder what we'd see first," he'd said in his cracking ten-year-old voice.

"The brown is Linden Lows," he said now, bringing me back by pointing at what I'd thought was simply a water stain. "The black dot marks the gravesite."

"So this"—I pointed to the squiggly part on one side—"is the sea cliff."

Rafn mumbled a *yes* around a bite of dried fish.

"So our brave, albeit unwise, sea-faring seithr lies near the entrance to the Lows," I said.

Rafn and Benedikt were giving me twin stares of unhappiness.

I held up my hands. "It's not all right to say he was unwise? Since when do seithr sail out without someone who knows the waters?" We weren't exactly known for our sea-worthiness. The first time I was on a boat was during my trading trip to Silvania just recently. We seithr let the other folk work the ocean waves. Our magic liked the land.

Benedikt sniffed, insulted. I bit my lip to keep from laughing. He was a fantastically ennobled curmudgeon with his inks and books and important calling in life. "You should go on to the altar," he said smartly. "I need to finish up."

Rafn closed his eyes and shook his head, silently swearing at me, I was fairly sure. "We will leave you your peace then, Father."

Rafn nodded toward the door and I led him into the morning's lightening blue-white. Churned earth and decay perfumed the air and washed the cottage's bitter ink and incense from my nose.

"I wish I could've looked at the Deadbook a little longer," I said.

"Why?"

"I was only curious." And wondering if I could knock Fellriki off his pedestal a bit by finding the Graybook. Not that I was going to tell him that.

"You've never cared before," Rafn said. "And after the jokes you've made about what I do…"

Guilt pricked my heart. "Raven. I'm sorry. You are amazing. And it is important that you and your father keep a record of our histories. Forget the Deadbook. I don't need to see it." My guilt didn't let up. Although I meant my apology, I also knew that playing nice and acting like I didn't need to see the Deadbook would work in my favor.

Rafn ran a hand over the bones inked into the skin above his ear. "Look. It's…why don't you come by after Winterskvöld is over. I'll take you through the best parts." He looked almost shy. "But only if you promise to keep your jokes to yourself."

"Jokes?"

He raised an eyebrow. "Brynja. Outside your own ego, you take nothing seriously."

"Excuse me?"

"You don't. You… Listen, we can argue after the Demand. And look at the book."

If I showed too much interest, he'd sniff me out. He'd

know I was up to something. "Fine." He was wrong about me. I took a lot things very seriously. My family. Friends. And the ability to live my life the way I chose. Yes, I was quite serious when necessary. I was always serious about power.

ALL OF SNOWFALLEN made their way along the winding path to Altar Mount. The wind gusted up from the fjord and raked nails over any exposed skin.

We hatchlings hung back from the crowd. Well, all except Rafn, who was being such a good boy and leading the pack toward the slaughter.

A wild goat scampered away from our noise and Liv slipped on an especially icy patch. She leaned toward the cliff's edge as Ulla and I grabbed for her. I caught her dress with my free hand. Ulla leaped, got a hand behind her, and shoved Liv to safety in a lithe move I never could've accomplished.

We helped Liv into a crouch so she could catch her breath, but she stood quickly, her eyes alight.

"I'm fine," she said, her words shaky.

Ulla curled her fingers around Liv's carver. "Good thing, Pea Finch. I'll take this and you focus on your feet."

Her carver should've helped her place her feet. I wanted to tell her so, but I also didn't want her to die. No lykill in the world could fix you after falling from this kind of height.

Ahead, a wooden bowl that could've held five of me collected snowflakes. Beside it, the altar stood. Blood stains had turned the stone nearly black. A deep shudder started in my gut and traveled all the way to the crown of my head.

Aside from the pines shushing in the wind, there was silence, heavy, almost tangible. Darkness lurked at the base of another mountain butted against this one. I eyed it as we approached the bowl.

Fellriki could be here already and we'd never know.

As everyone gathered in a half moon shape near the Altar Bowl, I tugged at my white woolen longshirt and watched Ulla take her place beside her towering parents. She and her mother gave the jarl a foul look. They'd never seemed to like him. Liv stared toward the darkness beyond the altar, her face smooth as the fjord on a summer day. I wasn't sure what kept her calm on Demand day. Innocence? Faith? Rafn bent his head like he was already praying. He looked almost happy. Yes, he was definitely playing the good boy role. And I would definitely have to do something about that. His spirit was too daring and interesting to wither away under his father's watchful eye.

Why was I the only one who saw the Demand for what it was? Why wasn't I caught up in fervor for Fellriki anymore? I had been. All my life, I had been. Raised with stories about how Fellriki came out of his chosen solitary life in the mountains and saved Snowfallen from the last eruption, I used to pray with all my heart and sing the songs at the top of my lungs. But now, I was pulling away, tearing my view of the world, ripping it little by little away from what I'd been taught. Only threads remained, and truth showed clear and bright past their frayed ends.

I blamed it on one person. Kinneret Raza, the sailor I'd met in Silvania. Her brazen questions about the Northern Isles had shaken me to the core.

Mother poked me a little and I looked to the jarl. The ceremony was about to begin.

Soon, we would have a very good guess as to who would die on the altar.

The jarl's blond-gray hair curled around his silver circlet and his eyes were as blue as the fine tunic and cloak he wore. The only thing that marked him as a former warrior was the nose, bent to one side during his legendary battle with Invaders when he was a youth, and the faint scar like a spear under one cheekbone. Now, he was like our king, second only to Fellriki, our Protector.

"Our Protector tells me the angry mountain stirs," the jarl said.

What? The mountain was going to erupt again? I swallowed around a jagged lump in my throat and gripped my carver hard enough to bring pain.

The jarl sighed. "Snowfallen could perish in fiery rock and choking smoke. Our Protector will call up a very special group of chosen. It is paramount that we obey him in word, deed, thought. Remember to pray to him, to ask the heavens to give him strength."

Everyone but me nodded and whispered prayers. What a herd of sheep. They weren't even asking for proof or about the special group of potential sacrifices. I had to speak up. If an eruption was imminent, we had to make preparations beyond hoping Fellriki would save us.

Then the jarl looked to me. Before he could tell me to step forward and do my job as eldest of the last tribute family, I moved away from my parents and raised my voice.

"We gather on this day of thankfulness," I said, the words so familiar that they meant little. "And celebration to offer our blood to our protector, Fellriki. Man in the hill. Hand of strikes and shield." I picked up the small Blood Bowl from the altar and lifted it.

Why wasn't I stopping to ask a question? Surely the jarl wouldn't kick Father off the council for one question.

Father gave me an approving nod. Rafn and Ulla joined Liv in staring toward the dark recess in the mountain pass—a path above our heads but still visible.

He was almost here.

Magic hummed from the shadows, buzzing under my skin. Wind curled through my braids and pinched my scalp with frozen fingers. I turned to look at the icy rock face of the mountain.

A hooded figure swept into view.

I shivered hard, nearly dropping my carver. I gripped it tightly and raised my chin.

Fellriki's midnight cloak rippled in heavy waves. His carver shimmered silver as he tucked it under his arm.

Gods, he was glorious. Kind of old, but still, glorious. With every shudder of my heart, I wanted more and more to be him. A better version of him. Smarter. Kinder. More cunning.

He lifted his hands, then spread them wide, and one of his tiny hanging dragons bloomed from his clasp and into the air. The charcoal-colored creature settled into a wind current, then soared down, like ash falling from the sky, until it perched on my outstretched arm. It licked its snout with a forked tongue and eyed me with far more intelligence than anything that small should possess.

My blood careening through my veins, I removed the tiny slip of the parchment clutched in its small claws.

This writing would tell us what we all wanted to know.

The creature flew off, its wings flapping against my face. I untied the thread holding the parchment in its roll. My knees wobbled. My parents reached for me, but I took a breath and stood on my own.

I unrolled the slip and read aloud. "The chosen will come from women aged thirty through fifty years and men aged twenty through thirty years."

The parchment, the expectant faces, the tables and bowls, they seemed suddenly far away.

But the ages, they were too young. Normally he chose old people. I wasn't in the chosen group. Or my friends since we were just shy of twenty. Not Father. He'd seen fifty-two years...

Mother smiled at me. "It will be fine."

My stomach dropped.

Mother was in that group.

"No." I grabbed for her as she stepped into the center of the gathering and Father yanked me back, his fingers angry.

Ulla and Liv stared at me, fierce and concerned.

Rafn's chest rose and fell, and he met my gaze, his eyes closing briefly. I couldn't hear him, only his lips moving told me what he said. "Be strong," he whispered.

I jerked free from Father, but held my ground. I was already strong. I was just angry. But this didn't mean

Mother would definitely die. It was only a possibility. We had the tribute last year—Grandfather had given his life —and Mother was one of the youngest in the chosen group, besides the jarl's son Jakob. Fellriki always selected the eldest in our jarldom, sometimes the diseased. This had to be wrong. It had to be a mistake.

I leaned toward Father, who watched for the jarl's signal to begin the singing.

"He can't take her, right?" I hissed. "He won't take from the same family twice, will he?"

"We were blessed last year Daughter. We would be truly blessed to be chosen again. There are no cowards in our family."

His voice didn't even tremble. He smiled.

How had I ever been like them? How did I ever think this was all right?

The jarl stepped forward, his face moon-white. "We honor those who may give their blood to protect the rest."

"We honor them," everyone echoed. Their heads swiveled to look at me.

I handed the Blood Bowl to the jarl. All of the chosen held out their forearms.

My teeth clattered together as the jarl slid his dagger across Jakob's skin, catching the red stream in the bowl. He moved to Mother. Her eyes were steady as she nodded to our leader. The steel cut into her flesh and she jerked just a tiny bit before the blood began to flow.

My mother had a wound because of Fellriki.

And later, she could be killed, her throat cut on his command by the jarl's knife.

Her smile and sharp mind and strong arms taken away from me.

I swallowed bile and stepped back to stand behind Father.

Once the Blood Bowl was filled, the jarl spread the viscous fluid along the lip of the giant Altar Bowl. The jarl's wife poured in two handfuls of coins. Liv's parents lowered bottles of the late summer wine their family had been in charge of harvesting at our vineyard. Rafn and his father Benedikt gave up a leather-bound book, some historical text that took years to pen. Ulla's family offered a fine shield with brass rivets and bright green paint that cost more than they could trade for in two years.

When each family had given their best, everyone crossed their arms to take the hands of those on either side. With the fire stakes burning and snaking around us, the singing began.

"Down down comes the Demand.

We will fulfill it.

We will fulfill it."

Mother and Father's hands gripped mine and I tried to pull away. I caught a glimpse of Liv's brother Atli's right hand. He'd blasphemed against Fellriki once and now he was short a finger, thanks to the jarl. He'd only been nine at the time.

The circle turned, faster and faster, as we raised our hands higher and higher.

"Here, here comes the rain.

He will give it.

He will give it.

Out, out with our blood.
We will bless it.
We will bless it.
Up, up to his sky.
He will take it.
He will take it."

The song took on a fevered tone, rising like fire, our throats burning.

"High, high the crops do rise.
Calm, calm the weather sighs.
Full, full the sea bears fruit."

Then all grew silent and we dropped our hands to our sides.

We whispered, *"With the blood, with his strength, we thrive, alive."*

Mother's heartblood wouldn't color the altar.

I would make sure of that.

Somehow, some way, I'd show everyone that Fellriki wasn't worth the Demand, that he was just another seithr and a sick one at that.

I was going to find that Graybook and knock a surprised Fellriki from his high place.

Even if it killed me.

CHAPTER FIVE

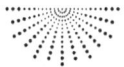

We were harvesting as quickly as we could. The moon was falling and dawn was only four hours away. Mother had been right about the temperature, but soon the sun would stretch over the snow-tipped mountains that cradled us and strike hard at the vineyard. I couldn't stop glancing at my parents as I plucked frozen cluster after frozen cluster, gently dropping the grapes into the basket at my chilled feet. The candle tied to my head dusted yellow light over the ice covering both my gloves and the fruit.

My heart was about as cold as the weather. The warm reverence I'd once had for Fellriki had completely iced over. I'd been over it and over, untangling the ways he toyed with Snowfallen. If he really needed blood, why didn't he ask for volunteers? The old people would do it. Or if he wanted someone in particular, why didn't he simply choose one person to die and be done with it?

Why pick a chosen group for sacrifice and drag the torture on? It was such a power play.

And I did not like being played.

Father practically ripped a bunch of grapes from the next row over. "The dead visited my dreams last night."

Ghosts bled into seithr's dreams once in a while to give us information. I remembered the only visit I'd had. Mother had finished singing the lullaby *Lost Ones*, and I'd drifted away. The lullabies were meant to help young seithr commune with the dead. Before I could dream fully, a feeling like being underwater overtook me, and a gray face materialized in front of a tree made of smoke. Though the spirit hadn't spoken with words, I'd understood her intent. It'd been a promise of sorts. The ghost told me that in a moment when I felt I couldn't move, I would move nonetheless. The message was rather vague, but at least it held positivity to it.

Mother put a hand on Father's shoulder and his breath puffed white as he looked at her, his dark eyes blazing. "Any prophecies?"

"Not anything exact. Just a warning for upheaval in the year to come." His eyes glazed a little, and he swallowed, his throat jerking.

Mother touched his cheek, then went back to harvesting.

I shook my head and lifted my full basket onto my hip. One of the basket's woven grapevines snapped and pinched into my woolen dress.

Liv came up beside me, also carting frozen grapes.

I leaned close as we crunched through the snow. "I'm sneaking into the cemetery."

She squeezed her eyes shut for a second. "I think you should talk to your mother about what you want to do."

"So she can tie me to the house like a disobedient mule? I'd be better off to try Father."

"Will you?"

"No. He'd growl along with me, but he'd never act on his anger. He just enjoys the growling. I'm done with that. I want to bite."

Liv made a withering noise and sucked her lips into her mouth. She set her basket on the ground and grabbed my arm. "Benedikt is rarely in the cemetery now, but you'll never get around Rafn."

"Are you actually arguing with me? Growing a spine at last?"

She glared.

"No, it's good," I said. "I'm all for it." I pushed past her. "But it's misplaced. I'm going to do this whether you like it or not. I'm not going to let Fellriki jerk us around anymore. You don't have to help, but I will find a way to get my hands on that grimoire."

I turned and she was still standing there like an ice sculpture.

"You're not going to tell on me, are you?" I asked.

She wilted a little. "Of course not."

"Then get word to the Eagle if you two want to come along. I wouldn't mind the company."

The sour odor of old grapes and wet stone hit me as I swung open the press house's wooden door. I emptied my basket into the crusher, Liv doing the same.

Father, Mother, and Liv's older brother, Atli, tromped in behind us and lowered their larger baskets to the floor to wait their turn with the crusher. As the rest of our workers and Liv's family unloaded the last of the grapes, Liv and I headed to the one small window to shake out our gloves. I walked past Atli, and he stuck a foot out, tripping me. To catch myself I put out a hand.

It was sort of an accident that said hand socked him in the eye.

"Watch yourself, Starling," he said, pushing me off.

Father cranked the crusher and the first batch of bruised grapes fell into the vat. Fresh juice scented the cold air.

"Why are you always bothering me?" I asked. "Are you so smitten that you can't stand not holding my attention, donkey?" He seriously had the biggest ears ever.

"I'm sure that's what you dream of, but sorry, no. I'm only here to remind you that you're a short, little seithr, who will only ever be a short, little seithr. You walk around like you're next in line to be jarl." He laughed and his donkey ears jiggled. Or maybe that was my imagination. Either way.

"More likely me than you."

"Unless Fellriki keeps killing your family off," he whispered. Then he burst out laughing. "Gods, I'm funny."

I popped my neck, my rage building. "A real kick in the tail, you are."

"Atli!" Liv's eyes were bigger than Ulla's fists. "What if someone hears you?"

But I could push Atli's comments aside. I had everything planned out. When Fellriki arrived at Altar Mount for the Presentation, I would have the Graybook.

I would use some forgotten lykill to humble him in front of Mother, Father, and the jarl. And Rafn. Everything would change then.

Atli's laughs dropped off. He pointed at me. I hated it when people did that. "You're up to something." Getting close, he breathed into my face.

Liv tried to pull him back, but he shoved her away. Everyone else was busy running the rest of the grapes through the crusher and didn't notice our trouble.

"I heard you," he said, "whispering with my sister."

I snatched his finger and bent it backward until he jerked it away. "You're short on sleep, donkey," I said over the sound of more grapes being smashed. "Why don't you go find a spot in the barn?"

An ugly grin tugged at his muzzle. His hand slid down my shoulder and touched my breast. "If you join me in the straw, I might just keep your secret."

I dug my nails into his hand and ripped the worthless weight of flesh off me. He howled and a few heads turned our way.

"Touch me again, and I'll deliver that hand back to you minus its fingers."

"Bryn!" Father waved me over.

Atli swore at me as I left Liv to scold him.

I brayed loud, ignoring everyone's confused looks.

Father shook his head, but put a hand on my back and let it drop. "You and Liv, put on the wine boots. We need your young, small feet first. We have a lot of very frozen grapes in there."

I nodded, and after Liv's parents dislodged the crusher from the vat, my friend and I climbed the short stairs and heaved ourselves into the vat. Our dresses were tied high, right at our thighs. The soft, frostdeer leather boots were loose on my feet, though I was nearly too old to be doing the job. *Big as a bug,* Mother always said. I always tried to stand very straight to be seen as taller than I was. The wine boots slid up and down my heel as I held onto Liv's hand and stomped. When my toes tingled and threatened to go numb, I waved to Liv's mother, who always lit the candles on the table next to the vat.

The flames' scents of sweet *ilmreyr* grass, white *aetihvonn* flowers, and violet wood cranesbill petals floated around the press house. I took up my carver and drew a Warmth rune in the air. The candles' fire bent toward me. The magic pulled heat from the candles, and the warmth coursed across the short distance and flowed into my feet.

"Not too much now," Father said. "Don't melt the grapes."

Liv and I nodded. My feet ached and pinched as the half-frozen boots slid around. We began to sing the pressing song.

"Sweet grapes, give us your red heart
Fine grapes, release your essence,
With our magic we rooted you to the earth
We etched our lykill into your posts
Brought energy into your vines
Sweet, fine grapes give us your red heart."

It wasn't a particularly pretty song, but Mother and Father smiled at one another as they lifted their voices along with the rest of us, and I couldn't help liking it. It was a fire in the hearth, a warm blanket, Mother's hand on my back. It was as familiar as the worn threshold of our turf roof house.

The juice flowed, red and strong, over the white leather boots. The special leather was taken from frostdeer—the tiny, less magical cousins of the legendary *hreinin*.

The men helped us out of the vat, and since he was the closest in age to us, Atli had the job of removing our wine boots and cleaning our feet with the ceremonial oil. He did so quickly with his sister, mumbling the required words about duty and blessing. But when he came to me, his hand slithered up my calf.

"One more inch and..." I bared my teeth.

"Bryn," Mother whispered as she upturned a harvest basket and set it on a shelf carved with the three prongs of the Preservation lykill. The symbol would keep most of the mice away. "Be quiet and holy during the cleaning. Atli, be wise. I'm making the meal for everyone after this. Including your portion."

I saw a little of myself in Mother's wicked grin.

The Raven burst through the door, the rising sun behind him. My heart fell over a rib and pushed into another. His festival robes pooled at his feet and his furred collar blew up at the back of his neck.

"Apologies," he said in his lilting voice. "But I wondered if you needed any help. I know you don't have much time."

Rafn looked from Atli—who'd once again grabbed my leg—to me, a flicker of something going over his face.

His long fingers, knuckles punching at skin, gripped the edge of the door.

"Thank you," Father said, beginning to pace. "I think we have it under control. You should get some rest, Deadsinger."

Pulling my toes back, I shot my bare foot at Atli's face. The ball of my foot knocked him in the chin, and he grunted.

From the door, Rafn gave me a heavy look and left. Something fluttered in my stomach.

The Finch crossed her arms and whispered, "Deserved," at her brother, who was still rubbing his face.

Thunder grumbled in the distance and Liv gripped her gloves tightly in one hand. She was surely thinking the thunder was related to the angry mountain.

Atli stood. His nasty tongue touched his bottom lip. "You sure about not coming to my bed? Those who fight well also—"

"There might be a surprise in your bedding tonight, Atli." I shifted my hips. "You'll just have to wait and see."

I ignored Liv's clueless look.

There would be something in Atli's bedding tonight all right, but it wouldn't be me. Something a bit more... slimy. A sea slug would do nicely.

AFTER A VERY LONG DAY, I set to my night's work. With the sea slug where it would do its simple work, I waited until everyone was asleep and hurried through the wind toward Linden Lows.

The sea spray flew an impossible distance to lash my

cheeks and hands. I'd forgotten my mittens and the cold spirits were trying to persuade me to go back home and hide under the turf roof with the goats and my parents.

It wasn't going to work.

I put a hand on the Protection rune on my carver. The lines and starbursts glowed like the winter night lights, then faded. The spirits might not want me to raise their fellow dead man, but it had to be done. First, I had to actually find the Graybook's master. That involved sneaking the Deadbook out from under Rafn and his father's noses.

At the towering hulk of the crossroads stone, Ulla chewed a long piece of grass and mumbled something to Liv, who earlier had been at the jarl's farmstead to trade some of our unused grapes. I made eye contact and veered right.

Ulla laughed. "Oh, she's wearing her solemn anger face."

Liv followed with quick, light steps.

"If you can't be serious about this," I said, "go home."

I loved joking around as much as the next person, well, as long as the jokes were nicely sharp, but this was no time for laughs. Ulla must've reluctantly agreed, because she kept her mouth shut the rest of the walk and listened as I explained what Rafn had told me about the Deadbook.

"So the top corner basically has a rude map?" Liv stopped to scratch her ankle, then scurried to catch up.

"Yes. But we'll have to somehow find the right page. And that book is written in at least two different old languages. I don't know how difficult this is going to be."

Ulla flipped her axe. It spun, caught the moonlight, and she grabbed the hilt easily. "You can be pretty quiet when you want. You can sneak into the cottage and nab the Deadbook. Then we have until sunrise to leaf through the thing."

"I'd thought you'd do the stealing." She was way more coordinated than me.

"You're the one for that job. If I get caught, I'll just make things worse by hitting someone. You'll intimidate them into believing whatever story you come up with."

"Fine. I hope Rafn and his father sleep like their neighbors."

"That would make it easier." Ulla tossed her knife up and caught it. "Are you ever going to tell us what you plan to do if or when you find the Graybook?"

"I want to do something to the food offering. Something that'll humble Fellriki in front of everyone and show he is just another seithr like Liv or me."

"We could do that without finding long lost runes," Ulla said. "How about just pissing on it or replacing it with goat dung?"

Liv covered her mouth. "Oh gods. This is so not a good idea."

"No, we need something more...horrifying," I said.

"What do you have in mind?" Ulla asked.

"It depends on which grimoire the Gray is. Elements or beasts."

Liv whimpered.

"Either way, should be interesting." Ulla rubbed her hands together.

"Yes," I said. "I hope Fellriki is so interested, he chokes on it."

Ice and small pebbles crunched under our feet, and soon we passed into the blue grass and heaped snow of the cemetery.

Beside the singing post—the gnarled trunk of an ancient ash tree, charred by Din himself one thousand years ago—Rafn sang.

My chest tightened. He was supposed to be asleep.

CHAPTER SIX

Rafn's voice rose into the whipping wind. Low. Deep. Strong. Like a current no one's boat could fight. I shivered in its decadent wake.

"He seems like a seithr when he sings, doesn't he?" Liv asked in a hush.

He didn't look like a seithr though. Lit by the ghostly moon, he looked like his nickname. Raven, black bird of the gods, calling to the spirit world. His thoughts and words flew above the oblong marker stones and the cold ground. They soared beyond the cliffs and beneath the blue-black sea, then under the rock cairns of the graves. Goose flesh crept along my arms as his song recalled the deeds of those buried in Linden Lows.

"Rest spirits and dream of your glory.

Gruall the Great, your wide hands pulled down the Invaders' ships, brought them into the sea to die, to breathe only water and think and plot no more.

Your strong hands parted the wildest of waves and cupped

their ill-begotten hulls and dragged their war-lusting hearts down, down, down. You saved your Snowfallen people. You held the shores secure, the shores of Bull and cliffs of Gyrfalcon. The caves echo your deeds as we do, in hollow notes that respect the gravity of your accomplishments.

Know that in your last days, when you hid in the sea cave by the black coast, we revered you. We sent ice poppies into the tides for you, to please you, to bring scent and life to your final heartbeats."

He closed his song with a bowed head, and my heart surged, aching at the power in his singing and pulling me toward him. He could've been a living lykill, drawn in deep, strong strokes, his passion for the past coiling around him in curved lines and artful circles. The embodiment of our culture, full of solemn rituals to the moon and magic, dances that mimicked the sun's sweep through the sky, of placing family and courage above all.

But also a culture that bent to Fellriki.

Joy flitted off my shoulders.

Unhitching his lanky frame from the singing post, he came toward us. My thumb rubbed across the Protection lykill on my carver and I sucked a breath. He'd never been my enemy. But my intuition was right. He held the Deadbook under one arm and I knew he wouldn't let me use it the way I needed to.

"Greets," he said. "What are you all doing up?"

"Greets, Raven," Liv said in a birdlike chirp.

Ulla jerked her chin at him. "Just looking around." She unabashedly leaned over to admire his backside.

I had to think fast. "We couldn't sleep. I thought

maybe you could show us the Deadbook like you said you would."

His eyebrows furrowed. "Now?" He looked up at the moon, then cocked his head at me. "I've never known you to skip sleep."

"Can we see the book or not?"

"What are you up to?"

Ulla scowled. "What are you, her father?"

Rafn set the Deadbook on the cairn behind him and crossed his arms. "Do I look like her father?"

Ulla grinned, then pursed her lips at his bare forearms. "No, you definitely do not."

I waved my hands. "Listen. Raven. This is not a big deal. We're just bored and couldn't sleep and thought maybe it'd be interesting to see the book. What's the problem? We have a right to see it, don't we? As people of Snowfallen?"

His eyebrows lifted. "Spoken like someone who is definitely, absolutely up to something."

I gritted my teeth and pulled my cloak back into place over my shoulder. The wind had kicked it off and my dress and linen shift weren't nearly enough to hold off a chill.

Rafn's gaze traveled from my leather boots, up my dress, all the way to my silver and black braids. He frowned at the braiding pattern, as if he could see the back of my head, that I'd woven my hair into three stars to ward off evil. If we got far enough, if we found the grave, I wanted all the magic I could muster.

"My father doesn't want me to speak to you. Thinks you're dangerous."

No surprise there. "He is asleep. We'll be quiet as the dead." I smirked at him and he glared. "Come on, Raven. We used to do things like this every night. Now, all you want to do is—"

"Fine," he said, turning.

Giving one another a nod, Ulla, Liv, and I trailed him into the keeper cottage.

It was too dark to see a thing, so he lit a candle that made him glow like a ghost. We gathered around the table, and I turned the book toward me before he could take over.

"Anything in particular you're looking for?" Rafn asked. He glanced over his shoulder in the direction of where his father slept behind a curtain. Snores rumbled around the room.

"No," Liv said too quickly to sound genuine.

I squeezed my eyes shut for a breath, then opened them to find Ulla leaning back in Benedikt's chair with an arm slung over her bent knee. "Anything really horrible in there? Anything...dangerous?"

That was better. He'd believe a comment like that from Ulla.

Rafn turned to the first page and pointed at charcoal colored lettering. "Of course. It's the Deadbook, not granny's recipes." The shapes looked like a skeleton's finger bones.

Liv pulled the book toward herself. "What writing is this?"

Rafn peeled the book out of her grip. "Please. Be respectful. This is the oldest saga we have. It sings of a woman who gave birth to an evil spirit that haunts the highest mountains."

I wanted him to flip past this story because it didn't have the ridgrasil symbol. But maybe I needed to pretend at caring, so he'd let us keep looking. "What kind of spirit?"

"A beautiful, female spirit with a hollow back that sucks the life out of men. A *huldra*."

Ulla folded her hands behind her head. "I've heard some still roam the highest elevations. Maybe one will take Atli."

"She'd spit that foul thing back out," I said.

Liv sighed, but kept staring at the page. "I wish my brother would take up wandering." Wandering consisted of traveling beyond our shores in an effort to gain knowledge and insight. It was a way of life no one in Snowfallen had chosen in years and years.

"Maybe some other culture would view his... personality as acceptable," Liv added.

"Doubt it," Rafn said. His words were fairly venomous.

"What do you have against him?" I asked.

He seemed to shake something off before replying. "I don't like how he treats you," he said quietly.

"Our Starling can handle him," Ulla said.

"She shouldn't have to."

"Eh, I'm still here," I said. "Can we get back to the book?"

Liv nodded and pointed to the writing. "What language is that?"

"It's what we call the sea's words." A dreamy look

poured over Rafn's face. "The language of those who first sailed here and settled."

Ulla rested her elbows on the table and made a noise. "How do you even read that? It's barely there."

Rafn frowned. "It is, sadly, very faded. My father is trying to clean it, but the solution we use to revive the hawthorn ink we use today doesn't work on the ink they used here. We don't even know what it is."

"I bet it's bones and ash," I said.

"A good guess. But it wouldn't have lasted this long. Unless they included some other ingredient…"

I started to flip the page, giving Rafn a look to ask permission. He tipped his chin, and I turned until I saw a flash of color.

"Ah," Rafn said. "The ridgragsil. I've seen this page. I've always wondered why it comes with the warning. It's only another saga about a seithr."

My pulse leaped in my throat. I leaned closer, studying the markings.

"What is going on here?" a deep voice said behind us.

Benedikt threw his sleeping space's curtain back. The metal rings screeched along the pole. He took two steps that felt more like ten.

"Set the book down, children," he said.

Really? Children? We were nearly eighteen.

"Go home, girls," Benedikt said. "Rafn, I'm surprised at you. Do you not take your calling seriously? I thought you did. Especially after our talk. This is unacceptable. The Deadbook is not something to be poked and prodded, laughed over, for those lacking the discipline to sleep when they should."

Rafn's eyebrows pinched together, and he swallowed. "Forgive me, Father. They were only curious. But you're right." He clenched his jaw and stared at me hard enough to leave bruises.

Benedikt blew out a loud breath. "Son, you and I will talk about this further in the morning. A good thrashing might remind you of your status. Now, to bed. All of you. If I see you again this night, girls, or any other, I'll talk to your parents about it."

Rafn closed the Deadbook gingerly as we hurried from the cottage.

The door shut soundly behind us.

"Now what?" Ulla asked.

"I can't believe we got the Raven in trouble." I headed for the front of the cemetery, Liv behind me.

"Yeah, I bet Benedikt can thrash like the best of them when his dander is up," Ulla said.

From the fire in his father's eyes, I knew Rafn wasn't going to have a pleasant morning tomorrow. "We need to find the Graybook. Tonight. Benedikt will stalk this place like a wolf from now on."

Liv's round eyes reflected the moonlight like a cat's as she surveyed the sprawling cemetery grounds. "How will we find it? This place…"

"The grimoire will be bursting with magic," I said. "We'll feel it, Finch."

"So the book will give off energy like a lykill?" Liv asked.

"It is filled with them. So yes."

"You don't have to snap at me, Starling," Liv said quietly.

I sighed. It was like she ignored all her brains when it came to magic. Figuring grape to wine ratios was no problem. Reading through pages faster than a seastinger zips through water, easy. But anything related to her being a seithr and she was all biting lip and tentative hands.

Stepping high to keep snow out of our boots, we rounded a pitted stone wall. Liv and I held our hands and carvers out to feel for sleeping power.

Ulla leaned on another tall marker stone and eyed the black artwork that twined around its head like a crown. "The person buried here might be pretty important." She jabbed a thumb at the stone. "He had like fourteen swords."

"Steel weapons do not a seithr make." I gave her a wry grin.

Another barrier of rock and white winter moss herded us into an even larger section of the boneyard. The cairns here lay side by side, foot to head, with no room for us to step except to set foot on the dead. The wind dipped from on high down and whistled in my numb ears. My eyelids closed, and I dragged them open again with an iron will.

After combing more and more graves, Ulla groaned. "I need sleep."

"Me too." Liv pulled her cloak tighter and tugged at a boot that had slipped as we stepped between the markers as best we could.

"Let's meet after dark tomorrow and come back," Ulla said.

"Rafn and his father will be on the lookout. You know this," I said.

Ulla led us toward the entrance.

I turned and looked out over the Lows. It was just so, so big.

Ulla pulled her cloak tight. "Freezing to death won't help us find it."

"Good point," I mumbled, my breath coming out in puffs of white.

At the split, Liv and I raised a fist to wish Ulla farewell.

"After dark tomorrow. After the celebration," I said, my carver cold in my hand.

"After all that dancing you're going to do with the Raven." Ulla shimmied her hips and kicked up a heel.

I stopped walking and turned. "I'm not dancing."

Liv slowed and came up beside me. She and Ulla traded a look.

Ulla tilted her head. "Fellriki isn't going to choose your mother. Not after taking your Grandfather last year."

"You don't know that," I whispered, hating how I sounded.

Liv hugged me. I tolerated it because she meant well. Too bad hugs never saved anyone.

"Regardless, I'm not dancing with Rafn," I said, more loudly now.

"Care to wager on that, Master of the Scowl? Because all that glaring you two do can only mean one thing."

I tugged at my cloak's tie. It was suddenly way too tight.

"Ulla," Liv said, shaking her head. The crunch of her footsteps faded as she made her way down the path that led to her house, just beyond mine.

"I'll bet anything," I spat. "Name it."

"If you dance with Rafn, you give up those bronze hair beads."

"What do you want with beads?"

"If I melt them down, I can make a snowflake for the center of my shield."

"But that's my family's sigil."

"And I'd like to be your shield-maiden, Bryn."

Her eyes were calm, no jokes glinting from their light blue depths.

"Those are serious words."

"I mean them. You're stubborn and wild and mean as winter. That's what I want in the one who leads me."

"But I'm nobody." The truth of it cut like rusty blade, like there would be complications even if the wound healed.

"For now." Her eyebrows lifted, then drew together. "Not forever. Not if you humble a half-god."

Not knowing what to say to that, I nodded and started back toward my house, walking backwards to look at Ulla. "And the rest of the wager?"

She laughed, all the somberness gone from her shadowed face. "If you can keep your greedy self away from our increasingly handsome Raven—who, if I might add, used to make mud-cakes and actually eat them and I can't believe you are so hot under the cloak for him—I'll lose to you on the sparring field. In front of Jakob."

A laugh popped out of me. I extended a hand. "It's on."

"Agreed." Ulla grabbed my forearm to seal our wager.

"If you're so in shock that I supposedly long for him—which I don't—why did you stare at his backside not two hours ago in the cemetery?"

"Anything to rile the Starling. I am an eagle after all." Ulla grinned.

I punched her arm and sped off to join Liv. "It's the Starling that annoys the Eagle," I said, jogging backwards. "Read a book once in a while, brute!"

"Witch!"

In the cold dark of my house, the fun of being with my friends slipped away.

It was all right. I didn't want to be happy right now. It made Fellriki's looming threat too easy to forget. That was part of his power, the way we, in Snowfallen, simply went along with traditions and tried to forget how he toyed with us, how he took our blood and pretended he needed it.

And I refused to forget.

CHAPTER SEVEN

R afn ran a hand over the shaved sides of his head, the short hairs pricking his palm. His father hadn't stopped berating him since the door shut on the girls.

"I don't understand. After everything with your mother—"

An unseen weight settled on Rafn's chest. "Father. Please. Can't you just give me a thrashing and be done with it?"

It was the wrong thing to say. A vein in Benedikt's forehead pulsed and he unbuckled his belt.

The thrashing hurt, but not nearly as much as Rafn's guilt. His father was right. He shouldn't have let Bryn talk him into going through the Deadbook like it was one of the jarl's pleasant collections of stories. The Deadbook was holy. Valued. Priceless to Snowfallen.

The saga about the first settlers of the isle sailed through his thoughts. They'd been from the mainland, a place where the hills stayed green all year long. On the way north, they'd met up with a boat sailed by people with *silver running in their veins and a tale of a fog that could give or take.* The seithr. Bryn's forebears.

Together the mainlanders and the silver-haired folk built a small kingdom, set a man to rule it, and created dances and rituals *to bind the souls to the isle's heart.*

It was a beautiful saga. One of Rafn's favorite to sing. He couldn't imagine life without the Weavers' Dance or singing at the old tree. Without the festival sparring and the nights when seithr told everyone what the dead showed them in their dreams.

Snowfallen had to be the most magical place in the world. Sure, the southern empire had trees heavy with yellow fruit and a capitol city strewn with striped tents. Maybe the northern areas on the mainland had rolling hills and fighters whose voices gave them strength and speed. The far-off country of Kurakia probably had more spices than anyone could ever taste in a lifetime.

But it was nothing compared to Snowfallen's icy peaks and steaming geysers. The isle's crystal, glacier streams and crashing black waters. Snowfallen's seas weren't cursed like those to the south. They were pure here, cold and clean and wild. Not even Fellriki could influence them.

Rafn smiled and rolled over on his bed. Wincing at the pain of the thrashing, he flipped to his stomach. No, there wouldn't be any more midnight showing off with the Deadbook or casual talk about the isle's most sacred rituals.

This was home and Rafn would do what he had to do to protect it.

But Bryn didn't really mean to insult their way of life. She loved the isle as much as he did. She was just...well, Bryn. He'd talk her back onto the right path. She wasn't beyond saving yet. He hadn't been able to save the last person in danger, but this time, this time he vowed to succeed.

CHAPTER EIGHT

Ith the scent of woodsmoke and herbs twirling around me, I shut the lair's door and greeted Ulla and Liv, who raised a fist, then went back to rummaging through a trunk of dresses.

While their backs were turned, I grabbed a ribbon hanging down from the shelf nearest the door. Two earrings hung from the tattered length of linen. Liv's father, a stout fellow with not a single hair on his big head, had given her the bobbles years ago and they'd earned their way into our life here at the lair. Not for their prettiness, but for their absolute hideousness. Each earring hook held one lemming tooth. Yup. Lemming. Tooth. And to beat all, some off-the-path artist had carved tiny faces into the teeth. We moved the earrings around the lair, always in secret, and never mentioned them. It was some silly unspoken rule.

I tied the ribbon holding the earrings onto the

handle of a nearby basket of river rocks and trudged past the firebed to see what Ulla had put on for the feast.

"That actually looks pretty good." I watched Ulla tie the front of a borrowed dress. It looked like one of her cousin's.

She buckled on a wide leather belt that cinched the deep green wool above her hips.

"Yeah. I like it. Especially the bronze bits." She tapped the belt's metal decoration. "They remind me of the beads you'll be handing over tomorrow."

"Beads?" Liv parted her brown and silver locks into three and ran a braid around her head.

"I have to give up my bronze beads if I dance with the Raven," I said.

Liv tied a bright sash around her middle. "You're definitely going to."

"No. I won't." He probably wanted nothing to do with me, with us, after last night.

"Is it too strange thinking of him like...like that?" Liv smiled. With that sash, she looked like a southern trader. "I mean, we've heard him talk in his sleep." A laugh bubbled out of her.

Ulla slapped her leg. "Remember when he mumbled *sex* in five different languages?"

Liv's cheeks were bright pink and tears gathered at the corners of her eyes. "I had to translate!"

"Gods, shut it. Please." I turned away as she and Ulla collapsed in a heap of dresses and laughter. In the water bowl, my reflection wavered. My braids looked straight enough. I smoothed a hand over my pale blue dress, my fingers catching on the white patterns embroidered around the trim.

"Let's go," I said, but Liv jumped up and grabbed my arm. "No, no. Please. I have a dress that will be perfect on you."

"Yes, listen to her, Starling. I want to ensure my victory."

"I already look as nice as I ever look. Why don't we go try to find the Graybook again?"

Liv chewed her lip. "We can't go traipsing into the Lows now. We'll be missed at the meeting house."

"Until everyone is drunk anyway." Ulla gave me a half smile.

"Fine. Fine. Dress me," I mumbled.

Liv and Ulla decorated me in a dress that went from deep blue to purple, hem to collar. Amber beads made lines down from the shoulders and across my chest.

Liv clasped her hands. "It's gorgeous."

"It's blue like the other one," Ulla said.

"It's the color of the sea during a winter sunset," Liv said. "And those beads..."

Ulla and I rolled our eyes as she sorted my hair into a messy, long braid and added another braid to hang forward over my shoulder.

"You have so much hair," Liv said.

"Um. Thanks?"

"Yes, thanks," Ulla said. "The boys love the hair."

"They do?"

"Please. You know you get stares almost as often as our Liv here."

"No, I don't."

"Oh yes you do."

"Ulla is right," Liv said. "Your scowl contrasts nicely with your round face and rosebud lips."

"This is getting seriously ridiculous. Let's leave already."

Arm in arm, we left the banked fire of the lair and walked away from the sea cliffs, heading for the jarl's stead. The wind's bite lessened as we made our way inland, and voices carried from the windows of the meeting house.

Inside, Mother saw me and sighed dramatically. "Finally," she said, handing her empty horn cup to the butcher's son, who looked at it, probably wondering why he'd been chosen to take it off her hands.

Mother touched my hair near my temple, then my sleeve. She smiled at Ulla and Liv. "Well done, girls. Well done. We will get her married sooner than anyone would wager."

"Mother!"

They all laughed.

"Only joking, Daughter." Winking, Mother turned back to the festivities and headed toward Father, who stood under the giant's shield—a huge circle of painted wood with amber inlay. It had supposedly belonged to the man who founded Snowfallen.

Atli was beside the firebed braying to a group of girls about the peak owl he'd trapped and was training to hunt rabbits. Poor bird. Poor girls.

Jakob appeared next to Ulla. His blond hair stuck up at the front and sides, framing his flushed face. His longshirt clung a little to his broad chest. He gave the Eagle a lopsided grin. "You look nice."

"That'll work," Ulla said.

She grabbed his arm and dragged him into the bustle of people raising cups of flowery-scented mead and twisting to the drums. After throwing a wolf pelt over her head and his, they began dancing around the firebed, Ulla's smile wide beneath the muzzle of her costume.

"Jakob seems happy for someone who might die," I snapped.

"He understands the sacrifice," Liv said quietly.

"And I don't."

"No, I don't think you do."

"I'm the *only* one who does understand."

"Please, Starling. Let's just have a good time with everyone. I'll get us a drink, yes?" Liv blinked like a doe.

"Fine. Perfect."

She started toward the back where the jarl's wife doled out horn cups of mead and watered wine.

They'd save the ice wine for the final feast in the glacier cave. Tonight, it was a baser celebration. Dancing, sweating, drinking cheaper beer and mead, and throwing someone you longed for into a shadowed corner.

In the far left of the room, Rafn helped three of the jarl's youngest children through the steps of the Weavers' Dance. He smiled at them, showing white teeth and that dimple in his cheek I hadn't seen in a long while.

My heart stuttered.

One of the little boys said something and he laughed, taking the child's chubby hand, linking it with the tiniest girl's fingers, and urging them to pass under one another's arms.

Liv stopped beside them on her way back to me, set the drinks down, and began gesturing with her arms. She was acting out that crazy five person dance she'd read about in her book on the western regions. Rafn's eyes brightened, then a darkness crawled over him and he said something that made Liv frown. Oblivious, Liv's parents pulled her into the adult version of the dance Rafn had been teaching the children.

Behind me, cold air whispered the promise of quiet through the crack between the partly open doors. I turned toward the chill and headed outside to plot.

The winter air nipped at my eyes and chin and threw me into a memory of the evening before Grandfather lost his life.

Grandfather had rolled dice beside the fire. "I'm glad it's me for the sacrifice and not Widow Pallsdottir. It would be a tragedy to see the end of her fiskibollur." He'd smacked his lips. "Don't tell your mother I prefer the widow's cooking."

But I hadn't laughed. Grandfather was a pillar of the community and was the only one, besides Mother, who could get my father to really smile.

At my frown, Grandfather had set the dice at my knee. "My Starling, this is a good thing. A blessing for the family. If he had chosen another, like the widow, well, that son of hers can't handle those twins alone yet." I hadn't wanted to see that serious look on him anymore, so I'd dropped my questions and rolled the dice.

If I had that evening back, I'd throw one thousand

questions, two thousand, anything to make him see there might be another way to live.

Now, I dragged my carver over the snow-dusted, flat stones in front of the meeting house, shaping a Warming lykill. But the candles inside were too far away, and the late day chill crept over my dress's neckline and under my hem. I shivered and felt—for just a second—very, very small.

"Isn't it perfect?"

I jumped at the sound of Rafn's voice. "And cold," I added.

A small laugh ghosted over his lips. A little too much drink had given his eyes an extra sheen. "Yes."

"Why do we love it here?" I said. "The South is so much warmer, easier."

He waved a hand. "Pfft. Who wants easy? Easy is boring. Look at those mountains. Listen to those icy waves. Difficult is the best."

His gaze pressed against my cheek and I turned to meet his eyes.

A gust of wind lashed through the space between us.

"Dance with me," he said in a hush.

His clog bumped the toe of my boot, but neither of us stepped back. In the distance, thunder knocked lightly on the sky's door. Or maybe that was only in my head. I set my carver against the wall, nearly dropping it onto the stones.

"I thought you'd be angry after...I'm sorry we caused trouble between you and your father."

"As long as I keep from sitting, I'm fine."

"He really did thrash you? But you're bigger than he is. In height anyway."

He shrugged, his eyes cold but pulling at me in that way he had. His lips were a pale red, and I wondered what type of mead he'd been drinking, what it tasted like.

What *he* would taste like.

"It wasn't what I'd planned for my day," he said, looking away. "But it's not like I haven't been in trouble before."

I shook my head. The thought of him submitting to a thrashing made my stomach flip.

My mouth didn't seem to want to work. "We used to get into all kinds of trouble."

A sad smile poured over his face. "I know. It's... different now." He turned quickly. "Can we dance?"

"I...I guess..."

The meeting house door was mostly shut. Golden light and the scent of wine and honey poured from the small opening. No Ulla though. No Liv either. Or anybody else. I didn't care about bronze beads, but I hated losing. At anything.

His face was unreadable, but he took my hand gently enough.

"I never really know what you're thinking anymore, Raven."

A smile glinted through his eyes, but his mouth was a line, his head cocked a bit. "I'm glad. I need at least a dose of power in this thing we have."

My heart crashed through an extra beat. "Thing?"

The freezing air dissolved in our closeness. He nodded. The drums and the *langspil*'s eerie-sounding strings poured song into the dying day and soaked into my ears, my head, my body.

I raised my chin. His lips were so close.

"Wh, what dance should we do?" I asked.

"Ice in Spring."

"But it's winter."

He raised an eyebrow, but his lips held most of my attention. His breath was honey and sage.

"Fine." I jerked one hip forward, back, then the other.

He smiled and lowered his chin. Staying close, he stomped a foot and moved his hips. My stomach brushed his, and his smile changed into something sharp and teasing and daring. His eyes closed a fraction, and in a rush, he drew himself against me. A delicious burn spread through my skin, and he tipped his chin down—

"Ah ha!" Ulla pointed a big finger. "You so, so lost, and I so, so knew you would, you little fiends!"

Rafn might've growled a little.

"Ulla, fine," I said. "All right. You won." She hugged me, and she smelled like goat or mead or both. Yes, both. "Ugh. Get off." I gave her a little shove.

Ulla's laugh made the early night seem too quiet.

"Where's Liv?"

Thunder roared through the darkness.

"Whoa." Ulla's eyes widened. "Hey, the jarl is about to begin the seithr ceremony. Come on." She held the meeting house door open.

Swallowing, I grabbed my carver and we hurried inside.

The jarl ignored another rumble of thunder and

raised his hands as I tried to stop glancing at Rafn's flushed cheeks and how he was breathing as fast as me.

What had just happened? Where had our arguments gone out there?

"Tonight," the jarl said, "one of our respected seithr families invites a new member into the magic."

The farmer that managed the jarl's rye fields stepped forward with his son at his side. A shock of bright silver hair sprouted from the boy's skull like an exotic, southern coral. He was four years younger than me, but already taller. I crossed my arms, tucking my carver into the bend of my elbow.

Across the crowd, I saw Father frown. He didn't like that some seithr chose to leave the ice wine profession. I agreed wholeheartedly.

The farmer clapped a hand on his son's back. "Yes, jarl. And we thank you. My boy's magic manifested just as we stored up the last of the grain. He drew a Protection lykill across the first barn and not a rat has wiggled in yet."

Father, Mother, and I rolled our eyes in unison. Really rare. Chasing rats off.

The rye farmer's plain-faced wife handed him a carver and he took it with careful hands. His boy shifted his weight, staring at the length of yew and wiping his hands on his longshirt. The weapon wasn't nearly as lovely or as large as mine. The runes were roughly carved. The blade was fine, though; the rye farmer was close with the blacksmith. From what I heard, they played dice twice a moon and drove their wives to shouting with their wagers.

Mother would've fussed about that, but she probably didn't know. She never lowered herself to gossip. I smiled, watching her watch them with calm, open eyes.

The rye farmer kissed the blade of the carver and held it out to his son. The boy took it in both hands and waited, his chest moving up and down quickly. If the carver didn't accept him as master soon, he'd be doomed to life as a failed seithr, nothing better than a regular human.

His mother made a sad little noise behind her husband. I actually felt bad for the boy. He was their only child, and if he didn't have all the skills he needed to keep the farm going, his parents would have to hire out their work, barter for help. It was no good. Their old age wouldn't be pleasant, that was certain. And it would be all the boy's fault.

Hold it still, you little goof. Hold it firm. He was fidgeting too much to master it. His thoughts had to be clear, direct, and unmistakable.

"Think it'll take him as its master?" Ulla whispered.

I shrugged. "He has to be sure."

"And don't think I won't be asking for details later," she said with a nod toward Rafn. "That wasn't just some innocent dancing going on out there."

A hum—not really audible, but more of a vibration—spun around the room's thick timbers and over our heads. The lykill on the carver blazed and the boy's mouth dropped open. His parents whooped and grabbed him, hugging and smiling.

Before anyone could shout their well wishes, the thunder growled again and shook the wide floor planks.

Lightning shot rays of white through the two long windows that ran the length of the room, just under the roofing.

Women and men hurried to shut the windows' slats. The wind whistled through the spaces until the jarl's wife and several others stuffed the cracks with wool scraps. I went to help as a beating sounded on the roof. Children cried, hugging their elders' legs.

"What is that?" I looked up, hoping the thatched roof would hold against whatever that was.

"Hail." Rafn touched my back, then dropped his hand.

I wondered why, until I noticed his father staring at us, jaw clenched. Gods, he hated me now.

The sound of the hail increased, and water gushed through a hole in the thatch and doused half the flames in the firebed.

The jarl huffed, threw off his heavy bluehare cloak, and grabbed a ladder, shouting and pointing with ringed fingers. Men and women hustled to get buckets as children ducked into corners to escape the balls of ice tearing through the opening. I couldn't tell what was louder, the people positing theories, the little ones crying, or the storm's angry cracking against the meeting house.

Jakob peered out one of the windows, his shirt pulled tight across his broad back. A stain of charcoal marred the fine wool. He looked over his shoulder at the room, his eyes huge. "Fellriki stands on the cliffs."

Anger simmered under my fear. *How dare he threaten my mother's life?*

We hurried to look, tugging out the fabric scraps

to see.

"There," Jakob shouted above the din of hail and wind. "He's there."

Lightning whitened the view of wattle fences, huddled cows, and the snowy incline leading to the cliffs. A figure in a long, sweeping cloak raised arms and carver against the storm.

Chills raged down my arms.

Thunder roared again, and Fellriki's carver flipped in the air. He caught it and turned what I guessed was the blade's tip down.

He was drawing a lykill.

The sleeves of his dramatic cloak, so much more than anyone else's simple stretch of wool, fur, and tie, flew in the wind like wings behind him. The storm flashed and showed thick braids piled on top of his head.

In the next white blink, I saw myself there.

My braids whipping around my head.

My arms lifted and power surging from my movements.

And I would truly protect our people, not ask for lives. I would do it without blood. I could already feel the buzz of strength, the storm's wind tearing over my face, and the tug of the grin I'd wear as I carved my will on the world.

The hail lessened, and everyone eyed the ceiling and the swinging metal bowls of fire hung from chains to light the room.

"Fellriki, Father of the Weather, Protector of the People, we thank you," the jarl said aloud, putting a fist against his forehead in reverence.

Everyone but me copied the gesture.

Rafn elbowed me. I gritted my teeth and followed suit. It wouldn't do any good to be caught and punished. I had my plans.

"I hope I am the sacrifice he chooses," a man from the chosen group said. It was the slim farmer who had more sheep than grass on the hill nearest the lair.

My heart twisted. How could they be so stupid?

Jakob stepped away from the window and raised a fist. "No, I hope he chooses me. I will die for Snowfallen, for Fellriki."

"They are not one and the same," I whispered, earning a sharp look from Rafn.

"Let's offer him gifts." The jarl's wife looked a little green around the mouth, but she smiled and removed a few of her silver rings.

The jarl found a chest of blankets and emptied it onto a bench. "Yes, wife. Very good." He removed his necklace —the one with its emerald stone the size of Atli's pride— and threw it in.

Then everyone was moving at once as the hail ceased and only the slight patter of thick snowflakes smacked the roof. Women, men, and children crowded around the chest, all holding up family heirlooms and glittering baubles and simple sticks that had been favored toys not a second ago.

Even the rest of the hatchlings let the crowd carry them to the jarl and the mindless giving of gifts, so I slipped out the door and into the wet, cold night.

No one was at Linden Lows now. It was the perfect time to find a dead man.

CHAPTER NINE

With the cloud-covered moon glowing overhead, I ran, carver in hand, past the wattle fences, through the tiny, new rivers and piles of ice beads. Up the hill and down, and I was at the crossroads marker faster than ever. For luck, I touched the stone the size of a fat man and hurried into the shadowed walls of the cemetery.

Aside from the water dripping from the lone tree in the boneyard—the gnarled singing tree—the place was silent. I pulled my cloak tighter around myself and headed for a section past the one we'd searched last night.

The first grave was sunken snow like a tiny mountain valley covering the dead. I didn't want to think about why the ground had shifted so markedly. It was old. And old was what I needed.

I held out my hand, my carver, and closed my eyes, breathing in the frigid air that blew up from the sea.

Waves crashed beyond the far walls and for a second I was stuck in a memory.

During the trip to Silvania, a juggler at the king's court shared a story told by those southern traders—Calev, Oron, and Kinneret. It was about those lost at sea and fated to roam the skies with nothing but hatred and vengeance to make them. Sea Wraiths, they'd called them. We didn't see those in the seas around our isle. It had to be something in their cursed water that faded as it flowed north.

The sea breathed on me again and salted my lungs with the thought of wandering to distant lands of lemons and sunshine and tainted with vicious ghosts.

I had to focus.

Morbid thoughts of wraiths and death wouldn't help me now. This was simply a quest for a grimoire and for justice. I would see Fellriki exposed. I would show everyone in Snowfallen that I could become just as powerful as him and display what I already knew for a fact: every seithr could gain his power if they only had an arsenal of runes and a backbone.

Breathing out through my nose, I moved past the sunken area. There was no magic sleeping there. The next area was housed in a curved stone wall. The stones cupped the fog that had descended after the storm. A dipped line ran through the fifteen or so graves, maybe the pathway in less snowy seasons.

I cursed myself for not coming here more often, for not bothering to pay any attention to who was buried here besides my grandparents.

I stopped at the largest of the mounds of snow. Spaces

between the white-covered rocks showed slips of poor leather, where people had written prayers in homemade berry and root ink.

I'd done the same at Grandfather's cairn once, one section over. I'd written *Visit me, if you are able* on my piece of leather. Thankfully, it was custom to keep these prayers private, so neither Mother nor Father had read mine and been permitted the chance to lecture me about inviting ghosts into the house. *He may come to you in your dreams, Bryn, as is proper,* Mother would have said.

Sometimes I did feel him near, his big presence smiling at my back.

I pulled a prayer from the cairn I stood near now. A faded ridgrasil circle showed at the top, warning all to keep back from this grave for this person had been a sacrifice, like Grandfather had. It was the worst of crimes to disturb a sacrificed's resting place. One of the old men from the docks near the town's boundary had lost an eye for the offense. At least, that's what Ulla had told me.

Gods, give me your kind of courage, the note said.

I squeezed it tightly and shoved it back where it'd slept for who knew how long.

Courage.

I shook my head. Giving in wasn't courage. It was wasting your potential, all the possibilities in your life, for a foul seithr's lie. If Fellriki needed blood for his magic—which I seriously doubted because no other lykill demanded it—he could use his own, or an animal's. No, sacrificing oneself wasn't courageous. It was weak-minded.

After walking around all the graves in that section, I

was jumping at every sound. Every shuffle in the walls. Each sweep of glacier bats above. Dripping water made my heart stutter.

Mother and Father—and the hatchlings, too—they would notice my absence soon if they hadn't already. Ulla and Liv would cover for me, guessing where I'd gone.

But this was taking much too long.

I had to get the Deadbook and find the master's page and the little black spot that showed the location or I'd never succeed. I couldn't just keep wandering through the graves. Rafn's home sat quiet and still. I would be in an out with no one to see me. No harm done.

The cottage's dark windows stared as I cracked the heavy door open. Inside, not a sliver of moonlight or starlight or anything pierced the black. I felt inside the pocket of my cloak for a flint and cottongrass, then fumbled around for a candle with only the soft pewter glow of the lykill on my carver to guide me. My knee banged sharply into the corner of the table, and a cup tumbled to the wide wooden planks of the floor. Dull pain spread up my leg.

Replacing the cup, I braced my carver between my legs and against the table, and drew the flint across the blade to throw a spark onto the cottongrass. Finally, enough of a heat bloomed so I was able to light the nearby beeswax candle. Breathing slow and sure, I set my carver down and took the Deadbook from its perch.

The tome was nearly as heavy as a basket of frozen grapes and smelled strongly of the ink Benedikt had brewed up for it yesterday. The worn leather cover was unadorned except for the edges, which showed the imprints of fingers and palms, the occasional scratch from a quill. One row of prints ran along the top, where Rafn tended to grip the book when he was writing or singing the stories. I touched the tiny lines and swirls, wondering for the thousandth time why he cared so much for tradition. I tried to appreciate his job. I really did. But why would the dead care if we sang their deeds or not? They were either gone or existing in a state that I rather thought would be above such concerns. I wanted to see Rafn's duties as important. I longed to see past what I thought was yet another waste of effort, but I just couldn't. I'd never tell Rafn, of course, but there it was.

Nonetheless, Rafn's singing was beautiful and the Deadbook was too, in its own dark way.

I carefully flipped pages, skipping writing and images and focusing on only the ones that were marked with the ridgrasil.

It was strange to be in Rafn's homeplace by myself. The house creaked, like they always did in wild cold and rough heat, and I forced my heart to slow. I scoured each page, but I didn't see a ridgrasil anywhere.

No, nope, no.

Not there.

"Ah."

The three-colored circle showed at the top of the next page.

I grabbed the candle and held it over the saga. Three lines made up the entire thing. Surely this couldn't be the master of the grimoire's page. A sketched man with closed eyes and a cloak stood beside ancient writing that I couldn't read.

On the other side, a frostdeer leaped over a mountain surrounded in curling clouds. I ran a finger over the deer's antlers. The cemetery singer who'd written this had added starbursts to the tips, giving the illusion that the antlers sparkled and shone. The beast's flanks were thick, too, unlike a tiny frostdeer's. I tapped a thumb against the table, thinking.

In the page's top corner, a speck of ink marked the man's burial spot in Linden Lows. He lay beside the cliff wall somewhere. It was worth a look.

But I had to hurry. Mother would notice my absence at the meeting house. She might not know where to look for me, but if she blabbed near Benedikt, he'd have a good guess after last night.

After one last look, I closed the Deadbook and set it back in its place. The extinguished candle's smoke swirled as I left the cottage and headed into the night. Din's lights shimmered green and pink in the sky, over the snow-topped mountains.

"Starling!"

I jumped, but it was just Ulla, waving and hurrying through the Lows' entrance with exaggerated, high steps. She carried a huge sack, and a small shadow flittered behind her. Liv.

"You scared a year off my life, you know," I said.

Ulla laughed, her breath like a brewer's house, then covered her own mouth. "Sorry, friend. I knew you'd sneak out here. Liv and I want to help. If you find the master's grave, won't you need help digging?" She opened the sack to show three medium sized shovels.

"I don't think she'll need them, Eagle," Liv said. "I mean, it's really kind of you to think of it and haul them out here, but she'll use magic to get the book if we find it."

Ulla waved her off. "Fine. Fine." She squinted past me at the cottage. "Is the light out?"

"Of course it is. Rafn and Benedikt are still at the meeting house." My pulse sped up. "Aren't they? If they aren't, we need to get out of here."

Liv touched my arm and the sky's green and pink glimmerings shone off her face. "They are still at the meeting house. It's all right."

I exhaled and started toward the back of the Lows. "Thank the gods. Come on. I have a guess on where the book is."

Around the singing post, past the dark windows of the cottage, beyond a horseshoe-shaped curve of wind-bitten walls, and into the very back of the cemetery, we worked our way closer and closer to the old master's resting place. The snow was pristine here, unbroken by foot, paw, or hoof. The cairns looked like wrapped corpses, and it wasn't going to be easy to find the old master.

Ulla tugged her patchy fur collar higher. "So have you two learned how to raise the dead? Is that like a seithr family thing to do? While my family is playing dice," she sagged as she said the word, "you are huddled into your magic corners, getting all the gossip from the netherworld."

Liv and I scowled.

"Right," I said. "The gossip is great if you can get past the decomposing flesh."

Liv shuddered. "Is there going to be decomposing flesh?"

I rolled my eyes. "Grow a spine, Liv. You're a seithr, not a mouse. To answer your question, Ulla, we learn it through dreams."

"Seriously?"

"Where do you think we get the prophecies?" About once a moon, seithr families revealed information the dead gave us. The prophecies were usually vague warnings about strangers approaching over the sea and diseases the cattle might experience.

"Oh."

"Yeah, oh."

"Do you choose to talk to ghosts when you sleep?"

"Nope. They choose to talk to us. They're not very well behaved usually."

Liv closed her eyes. "No, they're not."

It was hard to explain how to have a give and take with the dead. "When they are around, you get this... feeling that helps you commune with them."

"It's like knowing a language," Liv added. "And there's a chant, part of a song seithr mothers sing to their babies."

"That's just strange," Ulla said.

I nodded. "It seems like all lullabies are scary as the netherworld. But yeah, the chant. Supposedly it works."

Ulla snorted. "I'll just wave my knife around, all right?"

"That'll be a big help, threatening the dead with death."

"Better than nothing."

"Not really," I said.

"Might distract it while you nab the book."

"Hm."

"Didn't think of that, did you?"

"Because it's a dumb idea," I said.

She gasped. "My plans are the plans of gods."

"Maybe the gods nobody ever hears about anymore. Because none of their plans work."

Ulla's face soured. Then she stuck her tongue out and made a noise like passing gas.

I raised an eyebrow. "Clever."

She fluttered her eyelashes while Liv laughed.

"All right. Enough messing around. Let's get to work."

Liv and I moved slowly around the snowy cairns, our hands extended to feel any magical presence.

I was about to scream in frustration when a small sun of heat rose in my palms. Magic.

"Here," I said. "It's here."

We cleared the snow and ice away. The stones covering the dead seithr were painted a color like old blood. Maybe it was blood. The hue flaked in places, the weather doing its best to clean the rocks that somehow held onto their decorative red. Prayers and promises— written on smooth, seashore rocks—dotted the crevices where the wind tried to whistle. I held out my carver.

"Wait," Liv whispered. I looked back. Dark and fog shrouded her eyes and the side of her face. "Will he be willing to give up the book or…"

"Or will he fight us?" Ulla grinned.

"He was probably the most powerful seithr in history." If this was indeed the man I was looking for. "Or at least a close second. You don't get that kind of influence without some steel in your bones."

"Ooo," Ulla said. "My kind of fellow."

I began to sing the lullaby Mother had taught me.

"Wake, sleeper, wake. Hear the seithr wynd in my mouth, listen to the seithr of my blood. Like calls to like. Wake, sleeper, wake."

A tingle sparked in my palms and in the power place between my thin and fringed seithr eyebrows. The feeling ran, cold and clean, down my forearms, my chest.

Then a blast of heat, like the lava's proud strength in the mountains, flashed against my back.

Evil. And not from me.

"Bryn." Liv's warning was hardly more than a breath.

Errant evil spirits wandered Snowfallen. Usually they kept to themselves, unless you were an idiot and you called for them—a game that ended in missing eyes and muddled memories.

I swallowed and closed my own eyes, keeping my hands firmly against the glowing lykill on my carver. The heat smacked the crown of my head.

"Three and three and three," I chanted. Liv echoed me.

The evil spirit hit the crown of my head again, but then dissolved like salt in water against the three stars braided into my hair.

Legs shaking, I continued on, calling, singing, willing.

The stones covering the grave began to tremble. The

ground vibrated like a herd of horses ready to show up any second. A hissing sound stung my ears. Green-gray wisps of smoke curled out from between the grave's rocks. The plumes drew together to form a dusky old man with a beard that reached to his toes. His cloak was drawn loosely around his ephemeral frame.

There was no evidence of any grimoire.

My heart dipped, and I stopped singing, my tongue gone dry. Maybe he held it under his robes. I looked into his face.

My bones iced.

The earth had long ago eaten away his eyes. In their place, a mess of shadows teemed, forming pictures, scenes. I leaned forward, my shaking hands nearly dropping my carver. The shifting shapes showed horrors I'd only heard around the fire.

Men slowly spitting other men on long spears. Fair-haired women like my mother with their noses cut off to the bone. Children bled dry in front of their weeping parents.

Knowledge of these events pricked at my head like needles. Some of these were seithr families, tortured in a human's misguided attempts to glean power. Others terrors resulted from seithr battling for the power of the books.

A voice echoed through me.

What is it you long for, Brynja Seithrsdottir? What is this fire I see in your face?

"Please, seithr, give me your grimoire so its secrets do not die with you," I said quietly.

There was a noise coming from the cemetery entrance. Had Benedikt and Rafn returned?

The spirit reached into the layers of materials hanging from his wispy form and withdrew an object. But it wasn't a book. His skeletal fingers gripped a small carver and as he raised it up, the lykill carved into it shone like the moon, and a pain poured into my head. As though he pressed a torch against my forehead, my skin seemed to catch fire and my brain bubbled.

Liv gasped. She must've felt it too.

Gritting my teeth to keep from releasing a scream that would bring Rafn for sure if he were around, I peeked at Liv and Ulla. Liv had Ulla's sleeve in a white-knuckled grip and her body shook. Ulla's nostrils flared once as she held the pain like a true shield-maiden.

My hand shaking, I held up my carver and began tracing the Protection lykill into the air, but Liv pushed me to the ground. She'd jerked Ulla down too. The moment my forehead hit the snowy ground, the pain ceased.

The ghost spoke over our heads, his voice like smoke in the night. "I give the Graybook to the humble."

The Graybook.

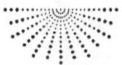

CHAPTER TEN

R afn walked away from the pile of coins, rings, and furs Snowfallen had gathered for Fellriki in thanks for turning the hailstorm back to the sea. It was a fine collection for our Protector, he thought. It should urge Fellriki to keep those kinds of storms from moving inland where they'd destroy homes, flatten crops come spring, and kill goats, sheep, and cows.

"Rafn!" The jarl gestured with a ringed hand. So he hadn't given all of his jewels up yet. Rafn pressed a hand to his forehead. That was something Bryn would've said.

Benedikt stood by the jarl. Rafn's father smiled wide and said something to make the jarl nod enthusiastically.

Rafn dipped his head respectfully. "How can I help, Jarl?"

The jarl looked to Benedikt. "See? This is what I love about your son. How can I help?" He turned to Jakob, who had a horn tipped all the way up. "You should spend more time with Rafn Benediktsson, Jakob. This is a boy who will grow into a man we can all admire."

Jakob gave Rafn a murderous look as he wiped his mouth with the back of his hand. "Of course, Father."

"I was hoping," the jarl said, tugging at his braided beard. "you had another idea for me concerning our trade with the southern ships."

"Did the large tally board work?"

"Yes. Our captain said the southerners were very pleased with the system."

Jakob edged a shoulder into the circle of conversation. "What difference did it make?"

Rafn sighed, thinking. Jakob would have accomplished his goal of pushing Rafn out a lot sooner with smart additions to the jarl's ideas instead of attacking everything head on.

"All parties involved in the trading could easily view the tallies of what had been sold and for what price. It kept everyone honest," Rafn said.

Jakob sneered. "They better be honest all the time or we'll burn their ships next time they come."

Biting his tongue, Rafn mumbled, "Of course."

The jarl's mouth bunched and he laughed lamely through his nose. "I'm sure you're joking, Son. The silver they pay for our amber and whale oil, well, it pays for the lumber we buy from the eastern isles. If we had no southern trade, we'd not only be out olive oil and those lemons, but we'd have no ships of our own."

Benedikt managed a polite laugh. Rafn was ready to escape and see where the other hatchlings had gone. They were all missing and that only meant one thing.

Mischief. He really had to protect them from themselves. Bryn had been so keyed up since her mother Rakel was selected for the chosen group, it wouldn't be surprising if she'd gone to dip into her father Agust's not-so-secret stash of stronger wine, hidden behind a rock in the press house.

Why couldn't Bryn go along with tradition? It was a good system, Fellriki and the sacrifice. One life, once a year, wasn't too much to ask for this beautiful world. The Protector probably wouldn't choose Rakel anyway. He usually took diseased people or the elderly.

"What else bothers you about our trade, Jarl?" Rafn asked.

The jarl straightened the silver circlet at his forehead. "I would like to buy some slaves from the south."

A sour taste touched the back of Rafn's tongue. "You already have slaves. From war."

"I want more." The jarl smiled. "Just a few, of course. And they'd be treated kindly. As they always are here."

Rafn snorted, and Benedikt's eyes flashed in warning. But the jarl didn't notice. He was too busy ogling one of the slaves he supposedly treated kindly.

"The southerners have a different view of slavery..." Rafn had to be careful. Surely the jarl knew this. He didn't want to talk down to the jarl. That would be a big mistake. Rafn enjoyed having his ideas put to use. Sometimes they were good ones that helped good people.

"I know," the jarl said, frowning into a freshly filled cup of mead. "Just think on it, will you, Rafn? I like to find a way to get a few of their people here. It would make for fascinating conversation, don't you agree?"

"It would. Maybe they could squeeze a little more out of our farmland."

Benedikt's eyebrows drew together. "But don't you worry, Jarl, that exotic tales from another place might make our people want to, I don't know, leave?"

Invisible fingers pressed painfully against Rafn's temples and he felt suddenly like he'd had too much to drink and might be sick. "No. Snowfallen is the most perfect place in the world. No one in their right mind would leave these mountains, or our way of life."

"Rafn, Rafn." The jarl patted his back. "Calm yourself. Your father makes a good point, although I think he worries for nothing. You are right. A few southern slaves wouldn't do any harm."

Rafn just wanted out of the stuffy room and away from everyone. Jakob had given up on the conversation and was jabbering loudly right behind them. Children at their mothers' sides whined with sleepiness and the drunken men singing beside the firebed were like broken bells in Rafn's brain.

"You'll have to forgive me, Jarl, Father. My head…I need to get to bed."

The jarl gave him a nod, and as Rafn turned, Benedikt grabbed his arm. "You all right, Son?"

"Yes. Just tired."

With another pat to the back, Rafn was out the door to the blessed quiet.

The night was murky, heaps of ice like beacons in the weak moonlight.

A tall, dark figure rounded the cordwainer's and the chandler's shop.

It was the Protector.

Rafn halted and took a knee. His heart hammered.

"You are the Deadsinger." Fellriki's voice was cutting and fast despite his age. "The one the jarl listens to."

"Yes, Protector."

"And do you think I acted quickly enough tonight?"

"What do I know about storms and magic?"

"True enough." Fellriki took four slow steps, but was still a good stone's throw away.

Rafn stood. His lips were numb. "May I ask a question? I mean no disrespect."

Fellriki nodded, honestly looking a little bored. The runes on his light-colored carver flickered, highlighting the dark blood stains running down its length.

A shiver dusted over Rafn's shoulders. "Why does this year's group of chosen include so many ages and both sexes?"

"Because that is what I need. Do you have a complaint, Deadsinger?"

"No-no. I was just curious."

Rafn wanted to ask how the choosing went, how Fellriki knew who must die and if there was any way to lessen the emotional toll it took on Snowfallen. He couldn't get the image of Bryn's face out of his mind, her eyes when she realized Rakel was in the group. But the Protector's gaze bit at his reluctance and Rafn bled into the ground, going to one knee again and thinking of how betrayal knocked the breath out of good and steady things.

When Rafn looked up, the night air teasing his hair, Fellriki was gone. Well, not truly gone. That was the good thing about the Protector. He retreated to the mountains, but always returned for festivals, harvests, in times of disease or wild weather. Fellriki could be a horror, but he consistently did as he was meant to do. He was a true Protector.

Rafn stood and wiped mud from his trousers. The other hatchlings had been gone too long. But it made no sense to wander around in the dark, looking for them. Bed called and maybe tomorrow he could talk sense into Bryn.

She was small but strong. Almost fearless. The same confused feelings flushed his cheeks. He always felt that way about her. She gave him a terrible headache, but somehow also made his stomach flip pleasantly. She'd have to let go of her arrogance if they were going to make something of their friendship.

The Lows' stone walls ran in a tumbled line at the end of the road. A prickling sensation crawled up Rafn's back and he put a hand on his short sword.

"Who's there?"

A gust draped the scent of mildew and magic's sweet, dark perfume over him. Was it coming from the cemetery? Unsheathing his blade, Rafn began to run.

CHAPTER ELEVEN

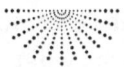

"**B**ryn." Ulla's voice shook. Her voice never wavered. Even when she lost a toe during sparring last year.

I looked up to see that the old seithr's carver had disappeared. Now he held a grimoire with tattered edges, its foggy color more solid than the spirit's fingers.

Dark drawings of antlers, wings, teeth and claws shimmered over the book. It had to be the grimoire from the writing. I'd never seen anything like it. Considering its shady hue, it had to be the Graybook.

Now the big question was, what did its lykill actually do?

When Liv lifted her chin, he leaned down and held the grimoire toward her.

"I-I can't," she said.

"Liv!" I hissed. "Take the thing!"

If he disappeared, we might not be able to raise him

again. Gods, why was he giving it to her? She was humble yes, but capable? Sadly, no.

"Finch. Take it," I said, controlling my irritation. It wasn't Liv's fault she lacked courage. "It'll be fine."

Swallowing, she whispered, "Bryn, please. You accept it."

I wanted to snatch it right out of the ghost's skeletal fingers, but if humility was what he wanted, fine.

I bowed my head again, reaching my hand out. "I would be honored to accept your grimoire, master."

The weight of the book found my palm, and I pulled it to me. The cover was so cold, the coldest thing I'd ever touched, like water right before it freezes.

Breathing deeply, I pressed my palm into the book and each fingertip sunk slightly. It was sealskin, an odd texture that was pliant and a little off-putting. I took a breath and moved my fingers, gripping the cover.

Liv's face grew solemn, reverent. Ulla smiled, her one crooked tooth showing.

The book warmed under my hand, and I tilted my head, listening for any whispers. A subtle beat touched at my fingertips like the grimoire had its own heart and pulse. The gentle drumming grew stronger and thudded against my palm, rising in tempo. The grimoire's heartbeat grew frantic, faster and faster, and I was breathing along with it, my own pulse rising, worrying Rafn would appear, worrying the ghost hovering beside us would twist into something dark, worrying Benedikt would find us, worrying this book wouldn't let me in.

My fingers drew themselves up, grasping at the cover like a starjelly on a boat's hull. I could open it. Anyone could. Even humans. But if a carver had to *accept* a seithr, it made sense that a grimoire would too. If I had the book's approval, maybe the magic would work with me and would be much stronger, just like the carver and runes made by the carver.

A click like a lock's mechanism vibrated lightly through my hand, and I looked down. A pale, forked... shape grew from my first finger, where a ring would rest. It didn't hurt even though—I flipped my hand to look— my flesh covered the bottom of the magical ring.

Ulla reached out to touch the off-white growth. "A whale's tail."

Black ash, or something that appeared to be ash, marked the recessed details, the scales and ribs of the tail on the top of the ring.

"Made of her bone." Liv kept her hands tight against herself. "Made of your bone, Starling. The book has claimed you."

Before I could say anything, power slid over my shoulders like a second cloak, heavy, smelling of poisonous herbs.

I smiled.

The book flipped open. I gripped the edges to keep from dropping it. Pages the color of ash fluttered like birds.

The lykill were so different from the ones I knew, the ones all the seithrs knew.

Their lines were more flourishing. There were no simple lengths. Each marking had a decorative detail to it: an eastern-facing slant, dots like snowflakes falling at two different speeds, a rounding curve toward the middle of basic symbols with which I was familiar—those for man, woman, and even for connection.

It was as if the old seithr, this grimoire's master and his associates, had viewed things and made associations in an entirely foreign manner to today's seithrs.

Liv touched my arm. "We should go. We'll get caught. How do we put the seithr to rest?" Her tilted eyes found the ghost.

I stood and raised my carver. "I'm not sure."

"Any more creepy lullabies at hand?" Ulla grimaced as the ghost shimmered in and out of view, his face blurring and distorted.

Nodding, I tried one.

"Rest, dear soul, the sun is gone.
Rest, dear soul, the moon is dark.
Rest, dear soul, your heart's gone black.
Rest, rest, dear soul."

Ulla eyed me. "Uh. Not working. And is it me or does he look less than *dear* at this moment?"

Liv huddled beside me.

"It's all right. Maybe this one." I held out my carver and pretended I wasn't covered in nervous sweat.

"Here me, ancient seithr.
We thank you for your gift.
Please return to your dark abode
And leave us to our bright one."

"Where did you learn that?" Liv asked in a rush, her words shaky.

"I had some rough dreams when I was little. Mother taught me a—"

The ghost's hand flashed and his carver appeared,

blazing with runes I didn't recognize. With a whirring sound, he began to increase in size.

Ulla unsheathed her knife again and stood on the balls of her feet. I put a hand on her arm.

"You may rest now, old practitioner," I whispered to the ghost.

Words raked over my consciousness like ragged nails. *I want no rest.*

I tried to ignore Liv's fingers digging into my shoulder. "Now," I said with more authority than I felt. My palms were slick, and my heart rabbited around my chest. "Return to the netherworld," I said too loudly. "You do not belong with the living."

The ghost rose until he shimmered far above the crumbling walls. He was larger than Rafn's cottage now and still growing.

My throat tightened. My carver slipped from my hand, but Liv caught it and put it back into my grasp.

The Finch and I had heard the stories, the tales of ghosts that rose and drowned seithr in their darkness, their regrets. There was more than one drawing in our books that showed seithr with wild eyes and gaping mouths, seithr gone mad and drooling until finally they wasted away.

Ulla hadn't heard these tales. But from the look on her face, she could feel the danger.

"Liv," Ulla hissed. "Do you have any fantastic ideas?"

I looked down at the grimoire. "Don't worry. I'll figure this out. Finch. Eagle. You should just leave. I'll be fine."

"Ha," Ulla said. "We're not leaving. No matter how

much you squawk."

My mind shuffled ideas, searching for a solution. There were similarities between the book's version of the tree symbol and the one we used for community. They each had wispy strands coming from their bases. The regular symbol for sight—a circle with one curved line inside—was instead an oval enclosing the full silhouette of a flame, whose light extended beyond the shape to touch the rest of the lykill. Despite my growing panic, I had to grin as I searched the pages for some help. It was as if we seithrs had a language, but we were only toddlers lisping and bumbling our words. These runes were written by fully realized practitioners, people who saw every layer of meaning in the lines, shapes, thickness, slant, and curve.

Ulla poked me with the end of her axe. "That smile is not making me feel better."

The Graybook's pages pulled away from my fingers and flipped frantically, then settled on a lykill surrounded by archaic writing. The lykill was made up of two sides of a triangle embellished with braids of thick slashes, a sweep of ridges like fangs, and a half-lidded oval much like an eye.

"What does it say?" I asked Liv.

"Good thing we didn't leave, hm?" Ulla nudged me with her boot.

I hit her. "Quiet."

Liv, shaking with arms folded in a self-hug, squinted at the lettering. "It's something to do with death. And a creature that eats bones? I'm not sure."

The ghost made a noise like a pack of wolves. We

stepped back.

I set the grimoire on the ground. "No point in waiting. Let's try it."

With my boot, I cleared the snow away. Tipping my carver's blade into the wet earth, I began to draw. My carver rolled in my hands easily as I switched my hold and leaned the sharp edge this way and that. When I finished, I flipped the carver right side up and held my breath. Surety weighted my shoulders. Something was going to happen. I just wasn't sure what that thing would be.

The ghost poured toward us, slow and growling.

The ground inside the lykill mounded. A scent like the incense Benedikt and Rafn burned wafted through the air.

A muzzle nudged out of the earth.

"Gods on the mountain," Ulla said.

The nose was followed by a large body furred in skeletal white and patches of void-like black. The creature shook dirt from its thick coat. Two eyes, one green and one silver, stared at me. It was a lion. No, a large fox. No...

"What are you?" I said, not sounding even a little bit like myself. The wind could've knocked me down.

Words, meanings, coated my thoughts like syrup. One name was bright. *Skoffin.*

"You are...the skoffin," I said.

The animal twitched its fox ears and dipped its wide head.

Liv held her carver with both hands. "Is it a fox? But it's so large," she whispered.

"Part mountain lion," Ulla added.

"It's neither. It..." My mind shifted through the words the creature was sending out and finally found more that made sense when strung together. "Speaks to the dead. It can send the ghost back."

The dead seithr shivered in the sky, but didn't give up its size.

The skoffin sat by my feet and looked at me expectantly, its eyes too wise. It wanted something.

"A trade then?" I asked.

It nodded its head and gave a small snarl. White teeth showed against black gums.

I looked at my friends, then at the far side of the cemetery. A shadow moved. I was almost certain of it.

Words and images bled into my head. The skoffin wanted a secret.

From a true friend.

I ran a finger over my carver.

"What is it?" Ulla pushed her hair out of her face.

Liv swallowed and eyed the creature warily.

I didn't want to tell their secrets. Ulla had one. One I didn't even care to think about. It hadn't been her fault, but still. And Liv, did she even have a secret I could trade?

"Liv Seithrsdottir wishes she wasn't a seithr. She'd rather be a cemetery singer."

Liv sucked a breath. "But I..."

Ulla's lips parted and guilt bit at me.

The ghost turned toward a noise. Ulla and Liv looked at me in question. Rafn or Benedikt was coming.

The skoffin touched its black nose to my thigh and I

placed a hand on its soft head. It smelled like burial herbs, musky and dark.

Facing the ghost, the skoffin made a keening sound from deep in its throat.

Chills ripped down my arms.

The ghost wavered, then struck out at the beast. It looked like lightning made of cobwebs. The fox-lion creature leaped at the spirit, meeting its force with an energy I could feel from my toes to the crown of head. My temples and forehead and skull were hot with warning as they met above the pile of grave rocks.

The skoffin seemed to fly, running and leaping, around the ancient seithr until the ghost's color had disappeared and all I could see was a blur of white and black fur.

The ghost was gone.

"Who's there?" It was Rafn.

My chills gave way to a sweat as he strode toward us, a black shadow against the blacker grounds.

"What are you doing?" he shouted.

"Nothing," I said loudly, before I could think.

I had the Graybook in my bag before Rafn was ten steps along. His face was all sharp corners and harsh angles, his hair so dark, and for a second, I forgot he was my friend, our Raven, and that I was so much more powerful than him, a mere human. He seemed dangerous, like something I could cut myself on and never be the same.

I turned back to the skoffin, but he was gone. Nothing was left from the struggle with the ghost but a slight distortion in the view of the sea beyond the stone walls of the cemetery and the slice of heavy clouds above the horizon.

Stopping beside me and eyeing the place where the spirit had been, Rafn put a fist to his forehead. "Bryn." His voice was breathy. "What did you do?"

A tremor buzzed through me. I held the Graybook. A book any seithr would want to read. One many would be afraid to open. I wasn't scared. This bestiary, this book full of runes to call up magical beasts, it was the answer to all my problems.

Fellriki was about to be very, very sorry he'd humiliated us for so long. He would regret my grandfather's death. I'd make sure of that. And he'd give up his plan to take my mother, or whoever he wanted.

This was the first day of a whole new world in Snowfallen.

"You need to leave. Now." Rafn stared right at me, ignoring the others.

I crossed my arms. "We have a right to be here."

"Not to do what you're doing. Go now, and I'll keep it to myself." He glanced at the uncovered grave. A gust of wind picked up some of the snow we'd loosened and spread it like ash. "You didn't actually..."

Ulla yanked my arm and Liv's, and jerked her chin at the cemetery entrance.

I touched my bag and tucked my cloak around it. "We're finished anyway."

Before he could say anything else, I hurried toward the opening in the lichen-covered wall, holding the braided edges of my cloak so they covered my bag. Ulla and Liv closed in around me like warm walls.

Just outside the arch leading to the road, something struck my ankle. Hard.

Ulla and Liv shouted as I was lifted into the air by my foot.

A loop of rope held my ankle as I swung from the branch of a pine.

Rafn stepped out of the cemetery behind Ulla and Liv, who spun around. The Raven leaned against the archway's crumbling stones and made a tsking noise with his tongue.

"You did this, didn't you?" I hissed and gripped my sack, hoping to all and everything the tie would hold and the Graybook wouldn't fall to the snow. Anger eclipsed worry. "You might have broken my leg. Or my neck. Then who would've been in trouble? Murder is a crime if you're not an overzealous half-god, you know."

Rafn scratched his temples like I was giving him a headache and walked over with his dagger extended. Ulla and Liv were not nearly as upset about all of this as they should've been.

Was Ulla laughing?

The Raven set his blade against the rope at my ankle. I threw glares at Ulla and Liv who were definitely snickering. Rafn tapped my nose with a cold finger. His eyes were the gray-blue of thick ice.

"Maybe I should hold off on helping until you agree to quit ruining your life," he said. Our breath mingled. My stupid body didn't get the message that I was angry.

Ulla was on her way over with her axe.

I flipped my carver and slashed the blade across the rope. The Protection lykill on the wood flashed against my palm and I landed in a sudden drift of snow. It still hurt.

Everyone tried to help me up, but I shook them, and the snow, off.

"As long as there is someone pushing others around, I'm going to be out there pushing back," I said.

With Ulla and Liv behind me, I raged away from the Lows and Rafn. Fear, guilt, attraction, humiliation, and a sense of victory battled inside me.

Rounding the crossroad's stone, I looked over my shoulder.

"He didn't follow," Ulla said.

But then I saw him. Beyond the arch and the first low wall. He leaned on the singing tree. A thread of his low and complicated humming reached my ears. It wasn't a happy tune. I shook my head to get the notes out. They were like a crowd of skinnippers, biting at me.

"Hurry," I hissed.

I sped down the snowy road and stopped at the thick ferns and tall pines that led home.

Liv held a tentative hand toward my back, toward the bag that held the book. "May I see it?"

I held it out, and her hand hovered over the cover with its animal shapes and bronze closure. The hook and latch looked like an extinct sea creature with a mouth made for devouring large things. Like humans. I started to open it, but held back.

"Let's go to the pressing house. We have to get the ice wine to present at the altar anyway. It'll work out perfectly. Just watch."

CHAPTER TWELVE

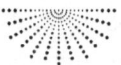

The room, quiet but full with the ghosts of triumphs and fears, greeted us with its familiar scent of wet stone, acidic grape, and ceremonial oil. The ice wine sat in green bottles on the racks, their Fermenting lykill dull now, showing the drink was ready for us to take to Altar Mount. It was the perfect set up. Mother and Father wouldn't wonder what we were doing.

We sat in a circle on the floor. The wooden boards were cold against my body. Liv took a candle from her cloak's inner pocket and lit it.

It was impossible, but somehow Rafn's humming turned in my ears long after I shut the oaken door. Would he tell someone about us? But what had he really seen? Not the ghost. Not the bestiary. Not the skoffin. I'd been fast hiding the grimoire. Not even his quick eyes would've caught it.

No matter what, now was time for more magic.

I held my hand against the bestiary, then moved back, allowing it to open for me. Liv and Ulla scoured the pages with hungry eyes. Now they believed what this could do.

The symbol the grimoire flipped to showed an eye, a flame, a sweeping and gently sloping twist, as well as four lines that made me think of fingers bunched in the motion of picking something up. Maybe a wing?

Liv tapped her knee. "It is a lykill that...it's difficult to translate."

"Why would the book claim you as its master, Bryn, and not give you the ability to read the words?" Ulla asked.

"It's a great question," I mumbled.

Liv blinked her wide eyes. "So she'd have to rely on friends."

Frustration sparked through me. "Doubt it. The language was commonplace when the bestiary was written."

Liv ignored me, and it itched at me more than it should have. "There is a reason the old seithr would only give this to you when you bowed your head." She melted under my glare. "Okay. Okay. I think this rune can raise some sort of bird," she said, "and it has the power to—"

"Of illusion." I was sure that's what the eye and the twist in the symbol meant. "Maybe it can help us with the food," I mumbled to myself.

Ulla leaned in. "Finally going to get your mother's root veg stew down by magicking yourself to believe it's roasted lamb?"

I glared. "I want to curse our food offerings to

Fellriki. I want everyone to see him humbled at the Presentation."

"But he'll—" Liv started.

Ulla cut her off. "Bryn knows what she's doing. Fellriki is already punishing us. For nothing. Let's do it."

"But the angry mountain..." Liv tapped her thumb knuckle on her carver.

"It will or will not erupt. No seithr can control that," I said. "Besides, we've seen no sign that the mountain is changing or unsettled. He's using our fear to control us. It's all a lie." My pulse jumped against my fingertips as if to prove the point.

"So," she said, pointing at the lykill. "How do you think it works?"

"No idea, but we are going to find out." I gathered the two best bottles of ice wine for the offering. "We will twist a gift into a show of disrespect. He'll find out some of us don't quake at the very mention of his name. He'll look like a fool in front of everyone."

"Do you have your knife?" Ulla asked, already unsheathing hers.

"I do," I said, and led them into the night.

CHAPTER THIRTEEN

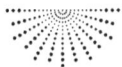

Rafn edged the door latch open, wincing at the click.

Benedikt's curtain remained closed across his bedding area. He hated sneaking out, but it had to be done. There was no way Rafn could get his father to understand why he was so bent on staying friends with Bryn. Benedikt only thought the seithr was trouble.

She *was* trouble. Rafn fought a smile.

He shouldn't be smiling. It was a problem, the way she talked about Fellriki and their rituals. But she was bright when everyone else was bland. A bolt of lightning in the dark rain. And Rafn couldn't leave it alone. He pursed his lips. There wouldn't be any more crazy jumping off cliffs or breaking into the jarl's mead stores, but they could still be friends.

If only Rafn could keep her from doing something truly terrible.

He slid out the door and eased it closed. Night air stroked his cheek, cold but comforting, as he moved through the Lows.

His gut told him Bryn might just be up to that *something truly terrible* right now. The scent of foul magic hung in the air as he passed under the archway and walked along the road. Liv had never looked as worried and guilty as she had tonight. He should've kept Bryn tied up. His jaw ached from gritting his teeth. His hands fisted.

Bryn was just so frustrating. And brave. And idiotic. And beautiful.

Rafn's steps swallowed the ground. If he could find them before anyone else did, before they threw themselves past the line of what was forgivable, he might save them from themselves. Gods, Liv knew better. He wished she would speak her mind a little louder to Bryn and wild Ulla. Of the three, Liv was the only one with any sense in her head.

Unbidden images crowded Rafn's mind. He saw himself beneath Bryn on the forest floor, her grin wicked and sweet at the same time. Her hands smoothed their way down his chest as he struggled to control himself and keep from rolling her over and kissing that mouth of hers until his lips were raw.

But Bryn was his friend. He should never have thought of her that way. It could damage their friendship even more than it already was. If only he could tell her everything that bothered him and know she would understand.

But wishing wouldn't do anything tonight. He had to simply find Bryn for now.

Where would he go if he wanted to shake up their Protector? There was only one answer.

Altar Mount.

CHAPTER FOURTEEN

A perfectly round crabapple sat on the top of Altar Bowl's bounty. The scent of smoked salmon and rye bread made my stomach growl. Snowfallen folk had been depositing their best offerings over the last several hours. Tomorrow everyone would watch as Fellriki formally accepted our offerings.

Ulla let out a loud breath. "What is the plan?"

Liv's gaze darted toward the path around the side of the mountain. "Should we...experiment?"

"Yes," I said. "Exactly that. I'll carve the rune and figure out how to use whatever it produces against him."

I flipped my carver so the bladed tip bit into the snow and mud. The familiar feeling of magic surged through the spot between my eyebrows as I carved the lykill the book had shown me. A heat tugged at my heart and the bone ring on my finger.

Of course, because this lykill came from the darker

face of magic, power beyond simple farming and basic fighting, the crown of my head warmed warningly.

I set my blade on its side and drew it down again, crafting lines that arched like feathers. Finished, I flipped my carver and breathed slowly as the magic surged inside me. I felt like I could fly.

Liv looked at the lykill, her carver back in her hands.

"Do you want to carve one too?" I tucked the Graybook into my pack gingerly. When my bone ring brushed the cover it let out a cloudy spark. It was like holding the origin of lightning in my hand.

Liv took a step back, eyeing the magical symbol I'd dug into the earth. "I...I guess I can."

Ulla extended her arms to stop us moving. "I heard something." She pulled her axe from her belt.

Liv and I gripped our carvers in both hands, readying for strikes and blocks.

"If Fellriki comes now, it'll ruin everything," I hissed.

Ulla scowled at the darkness covering our path. "I don't think it's him. Someone is climbing up here. From the path to town."

"We'll be punished if we're found at the altar," Liv said.

"We'll be killed if we're found," I corrected.

"Won't Fellriki be able to tell the food's been magicked?" Ulla kept an eye on the path. "Don't you all *feel* things like that? Like you did at the grave?"

"Yes. But with the seithr blood the jarl always rubs along the rim..." Liv said.

I nodded. "He'll feel that magic. It'll blend."

A shape emerged from the black. I froze.

"So are you going to tell me your plan now, or throw me into the fjord?" Rafn's eyebrows slanted. He wore dark clothes, and the shaved, inked sides of his head showed bright under the moon.

My body let go of a breath I didn't know I was holding. I stepped over the lykill I'd drawn in the ground.

"That's for you to decide, really." I walked over and peered up into his face.

His cheekbones looked like they were made of stone, so smooth and unmarked. Did he never get a blemish? I wondered if there was a rune for that. It might do his pride some good to suffer a red bump like the rest of the world.

"In that case," he said, tilting his head, "I choose *not* to be tossed off the big cliff, thanks."

"Then you should turn around and go back the way you came."

"And forget everything you saw," Ulla added.

Rafn scrunched his lips up and made a clicking noise. "That will be very difficult."

"You like a challenge," I said.

He looked genuinely puzzled. "I do?"

"Why else would you go after giant Jakob in the sparring?"

The corners of his mouth dropped. "Enough. I know for sure you raised someone at the Lows."

"So? I mean, why would you think that?" I stammered.

"Nice," Ulla mumbled.

"Because the dead are my responsibility. I'm no stranger to the scent of ghosts and magic. Bryn, you need permission to raise ghosts. No one's done it in a generation. And now you're up here, with the food sacrifice. You're planning some kind of dangerous mischief. I know that, not just because you are who you are, but because of what I've seen with my own eyes. No punishment ever thwarted you from doing what you want."

"And I know you're not going to tell anyone."

"What makes you say that?"

"If you were going to tell, why come up here? Why not just report us to the jarl?"

His throat moved in a swallow.

"See?" I pointed at him and stepped closer. "You don't want to ruin what I'm doing. Not really. What are you after?"

"I'm not after anything." His cheeks darkened a shade.

What was his game? He'd made it clear enough that he held with tradition and didn't share my hatred of Fellriki's bullying. He had to want something from me, or us.

"Do you want me to sneak you some of the ice wine set aside for the jarl? Is that it? Are you that eager to please your father?"

His mouth tightened at the edges.

My stomach twisted. He was better than that. "I'm sorry, Raven. You took a thrashing because of us. I shouldn't poke at you."

He looked at Ulla and Liv. "Who is going to tell me what you all are doing?"

Ulla held up a hand. "Hold on. I'm still trying to absorb the fact that Bryn apologized."

Liv raised her pointed chin. "We are cursing Fellriki's food. We think." She paled at her own statement, but I grinned with pride.

Rafn's face had gone ashen.

"All of us," I said, "not only me, are tired of him pretending to care for Snowfallen and having us murder our own for no reason other than ridiculous superstition. I'm not going to sit around and let him take my mother from me."

"The jarl said this year's sacrifice has to be done just right to hold off an eruption."

The peaks around us, the scraggy tops of pines, the ice and rocks of the ground—all was as it's always been. I held out my hands at all of it.

"And what tells you the mountain is ready to erupt? There aren't any signs at all. History tells us there are hints of coming eruptions. Shaking ground. Clouds rising from water and earth. Foul smells."

All four of us turned toward the angry mountain. It eyed us above a ring of ragged snow clouds. The sliver of moon and the green haze of Din's lights glowed down on the peak's shard-like rim.

"You truly think Fellriki isn't who he seems to be," Rafn said very quietly. Why did he seem so sad about it?

"He isn't." The Wisdom lykill shone weakly on my carver. The top curve of the symbol was the most difficult to carve of all the runes. "He takes food, wine, and blood from us just because we allow him to."

Rafn's light eyes stared into mine. His were genuine and sincere. "Don't you fear him? Even if he is simply another seithr, he is very powerful."

An odd heat sizzled under my flesh. "I'm not afraid. Wary, of course. But now I have something that makes us equals."

Liv whispered my name, but I pulled the bestiary from my pack anyway.

Rafn's arms dropped to his sides. "I knew it. You took that from one of the dead."

I ran a hand over the cover. "Isn't it amazing?"

"It is. But…"

"But nothing. This will break his hold on us."

The wind shuffled the trees lording over us and the scent of animal and birch pinched at my nose. The hair on my arms prickled.

Ulla pointed to the path. "Hide. Now."

Rafn and I rushed behind a clutch of dense evergreen bushes, the fjord a cold echo below us. Ulla and Liv climbed into the big, low branches of a shaggy pine.

There was a snap and a crunch near the altar.

Rafn edged closer so we'd both be hidden. "It's him."

No. The timing was all wrong. No one would be here to see him humbled. If the lykill even worked. I still didn't know what the rune was supposed to do! Gritting my teeth, I gripped my carver.

Rafn took my sleeve in his fingers and put his mouth on my ear. A rush of heat filled my veins. "Still feel like an equal? Hiding while that lykill you scratched into the earth fails to work?"

I jerked my arm away. "I will be his equal," I whispered, keeping my eyes on the direction Ulla had pointed. "Just wait."

Why hadn't the bestiary's symbol done anything? I'd felt the magic. Was it me?

"What about Liv?" Rafn looked toward the Pea Finch and the Eagle. His hand was shaking a little against my arm. Or, it might've been me. "Will she take on this book's power and be his equal too?"

"I wish, but she's brave as a kitten."

"What makes you so sure I'm not going to tell?" he whispered.

Something occurred to me. Rafn had come here, to the mountain, and not told anyone about what he thought I was doing, about the rules I'd already broken. He risked not only the jarl's judgment and the prescribed punishments of losing limbs or being put to death, but also Fellriki's wrath, which could be far more torturous.

So why was he risking this? I thought about our dance, our almost kiss, and I knew.

Rafn liked me. A lot.

"Because I'd take revenge," I said.

Ulla hissed from her hiding place. "I think I was wrong."

"Let's wait another minute," Liv whispered beside her.

I faced Rafn.

"Revenge worse than Fellriki's?" he asked.

"More personal in nature."

"What makes you think you could affect me so personally?" His stare held me like a snare, lashes like black iron spikes, the blue-gray of his irises, a beautiful temptation. His ink-stained fingers curled and uncurled at his sides, and I wondered what it would feel like if he wrote a line of one of his death songs along the skin of my neck and shoulders.

I dragged my gaze from his hands, up the sides of his woolen breeches, his wide belt, slid a glance over the wrinkle in his shirt right above his lean chest, watched his throat move, and finally looked him in the eye.

His cheeks colored slightly, a deepening of the sun-touched hue of his face. He was breathing a bit more quickly, though his stare hadn't wavered.

This was another type of magic. And it seemed I was good at it, too.

"All right," he said, his words like uncombed wool. "You've made your point."

Wait. I could tempt him with my body obviously, with a look, but what did that mean? That I could tease him and never give in and torture him that way? But what if he did keep the secret? Would he expect me to...

"Don't think you can trade—" I started.

He gave me a withering look. "Really? You think I'd make some sort of deal? I keep quiet if you do A and B to me?"

I wondered what A and B stood for exactly and felt very, very warm.

"Yeah," he went on. "I hope you know me enough to realize that would ruin it for me."

It was my turn to be affected. "Sorry." But wait. Ruin it for him? That meant there was something there to ruin. Something more than just attraction. Snowflakes danced in my stomach.

"Be careful with the power you have, seithr." His voice

was deep, dark. "Cities have fallen because of such games."

I blushed, but hid it with an extra spark to my tone of voice. "Now you really do sound like a cemetery singer. *Such games.*"

In a sort of crouch-walk, Ulla came over to us. "I haven't heard anything else. Think it's safe to try again?"

Rafn stared at the shadows near the base of the wide ledge. "I thought for sure that was him."

I moved out of our hiding place and studied the rune in the ground. Bits of ice stuck to the muddy shape.

Beside me, Ulla poked Rafn's flat stomach. "Hey, Raven, are you with child now?"

"Is all the iced *struva* I've been horking beginning to show?" He pinched his sides, looking for fat that he wasn't going to find.

"No, no," Ulla said to Rafn. "You're as fine as always. But that look Bryn gave you, that could probably plant a babe even in your manly body."

Liv gasped. "Ulla!"

"How can you all joke right now? Shut up, please." I rubbed my face.

All the humor left Rafn's face and he put his hands on my shoulders. "Please, Bryn. Let's go. Whatever you did, it didn't work. It's for the best. Right?"

The snowy ground trembled.

And a viciously sharp beak pushed out of the rune.

CHAPTER FIFTEEN

"Whoa. It's bigger than that last beast," Ulla said.

Rafn looked around wildly. "What last beast?"

An eagle, its head frighteningly large, emerged from the snow and dirt, releasing a screech that burned my ears.

My temples pounded as we ran for cover.

Peering between the thick, resin-scented needles of the shrubs, we watched the thing shake out its black-brown wings.

With a sound like ten heavy blankets being snapped for cleaning, the wings extended, reaching from one side of the Altar Bowl all the way to the other. The sharp edge of its golden beak caught the moonlight like a sickle made for the gods.

I couldn't hide here like a mere farmer. The bone ring growing out of my forefinger was warm and I touched the shape, marveling again at the perfect form of a whale's tail. My hands slick, I stepped into the open and raised my carver.

"Welcome, eagle. I called you, and I ask that you devour this food offering. I ask you to devise some show of ill will toward the one to which it was intended."

The bird screamed. I ducked, then straightened. Flapping its wings, the eagle blew my cloak away from my body and threw the sound of Liv's shriek off the cliffs. She was still there, huddling beside Ulla and Rafn.

The eagle alighted onto the side of the Altar Bowl and tore into the food, gnashing and gulping.

Gathering around me, the others stared. Rafn hummed a tune in his throat, his eyes steady. He grasped the necklace he always wore. It was the key to the keeper cottage. Only a spindly piece of metal, but he stroked it like it was made of the most precious silver.

The wind rose and lifted my hair off my shoulders.

The scent of a magic I knew only too well crept up my nose and leeched into me like a disease. It was the magic of the man who'd killed Grandfather. The magic that wanted to take another piece of my heart, maybe Rafn, Ulla, Liv, or even me some day. The magic that wanted to subdue me.

Fellriki.

In the now empty and shining stone bowl, the eagle nestled down and his brown feathers went gray.

"Is the eagle dying?" Liv asked. A fallen braid skittered over her delicate features.

My chest tightened. "No, Pea Finch. I think he's...disappearing."

Fellriki was arriving too early and this wasn't going to help me convince Snowfallen that he wasn't worth our worship.

The feathers dissolved into nothing. The creature's beak shimmered once before taking on the color and shape of the other side of the bowl and the pines beyond it. The last to go invisible were its black eyes. They held my gaze for a breath, then faded away.

A cloaked figure swept around the corner of the mountain path, and the moonlight snagged on red embroidery, a deep blue cloak, muddied boots, and a birch carver. Heavy-lidded eyes glittered as Fellriki smiled to himself, no doubt at something that would make the rest of the world shiver. He would've been strikingly good-looking if he wasn't a horrible creature.

Almost within sight of the Altar Bowl, he lifted his nose to the air. His face was unreadable as five of his tiny hanging dragons flapped around him.

He saw the empty vessel. His lips parted.

His eyebrows flew together, and he hurried to the edge, whispering something and holding his pale carver at his side.

With a squawk, the eagle reappeared.

Its yellow beak cracked open. Moving faster than my eyes could follow, the bird struck out at the tall seithr's head. Fellriki shouted, leaped back. His hand-sized dragons screeched and blew small bursts of flame. The eagle ate one whole. Fellriki ripped something from his cloak, threw it to the ground, then lifted his carver, flipped it, and drew a lykill in the snow, his cloak snapping in the sudden wind.

The eagle found its feet and spread its wings as Rafn, Ulla, and Liv started down the path. I gulped mouthfuls of freezing air as Rafn pulled at me, urging me on, faster, faster. He tugged at my dress, my belt. My sheathed eating knife dug into my side as I held my ground for a moment, slightly hidden by the brushy evergreens.

Fellriki hadn't noticed us yet, and I had to see what he was doing.

He had to lose. We had to win.

Orange and red tongues flamed from the ancient seithr's lykill and gathered into a man-sized storm of fire. Fellriki turned and extended his carver and threw the fire at the eagle.

I sucked a breath.

The seithr turned, his diminutive dragons above him like an ash-colored halo.

Dropping out of sight, I rushed down the cliff path with Rafn ahead of me. He looked over his shoulder to make sure I followed and jerked a hand at me, face white with fear. Ulla and Liv weren't too far past us.

"What was that creature?" Ulla asked in a hush as we caught up and picked our way like mountain goats over the ice and snow and rock.

"An eagle? I don't know," I snapped, giving Liv a hand as we poured over the pathway and past a thick clutch of boulders. "I can't believe Fellriki came early. It's all ruined."

A scream erupted behind us.

Rafn skidded to round a curve. "Man or beast?"

I was on his heels, my boots slipping precariously near the cliff's lip. Ulla and Liv passed me, then a heavy swoop of air pushed down at us, bending the pines and the bare upper branches of the oaks, maples, and birches. The eagle—long feathers shivering in the winter wind and mouth parted in a screech—was flying away, its one wing singed and trailing smoke like incense.

"Fellriki defeated it," Liv said, panting. Her hair had fled its woven crown. Strands slapped against her cheeks as she hurried on.

"Not necessarily," I said, hope lighting up my heart. "Fellriki might be dead up there."

Rafn grabbed a low oak branch and hefted himself over an icy patch on the side of the pathway as we ran along the middle section. "What will we do now when a winter storm comes blowing over the sea?"

"The same thing we do when they fall on us every other time. We will deal with it."

"You honestly think Fellriki doesn't stop any storms? What about the hail?" Rafn said. "We've never had a storm like they write about in the old stories. That's because of him."

"Maybe. Maybe not. Doesn't matter. I'll take storms over willing submission any day."

Rafn blinked and looked away, his lips pressing into a thin line.

A howl of rage reverberated from Altar Mount and gooseflesh spilled over my arms.

"I don't think he's dead," Ulla said.

Liv ran faster. "He sounds angry."

"Gods, Bryn. I can't believe you did...whatever it is you did," Rafn hissed, as we all scrambled down the mountain.

I grinned, my whole body trembling. "Me either."

Fellriki had to be right behind us. The tales said he lived in the highest of mountains. This measly path would be easy for him to manage. Or would he even follow? He had more creative ways to strike than using his hands.

Rafn's face grew even stormier. "You tried to murder the most powerful seithr in history."

Sticking the end of my carver into a rock crevice, I launched myself over a dip in the path and landed in a run. Rafn wasn't wrong. Fellriki had shown he could call and control fire. "Are you upset or impressed?"

"Both. And I'm a fool for admitting it. You are like no other, Starling. That I can say truthfully."

My heart swelled. He'd called me Starling.

"And you're going to keep her secret?" Ulla asked Rafn.

"What secret?" Rafn said. "Everyone will learn of this."

"They won't know I have the grimoire." The weight of the Graybook in my bag was a comfort.

"You think Fellriki will let this slide, hm?"

"You don't sound as reverent when you say his name now."

Rafn made a grumbling noise. "I admit he didn't look very god-like when he was about to lose his head."

He must've missed the fire. Fellriki definitely looked like a god when he called up that spinning flame.

Rafn grabbed a sapling and used it to hurry around a bend in the path.

"He is one of us and no more," I said.

"Then why are we fleeing from him like cod from the shark?"

"Because I need time to look over the bestiary, to become proficient. He does have runes we don't have. I'm not an idiot. I do know he is dangerous. But I'm going to be more dangerous."

"Ugh, Bryn. You can't be serious."

"Don't *ugh Bryn* me. You can back out of this any moment you lack the stones to keep up."

We made it to the road and the path behind us was, oddly, still and quiet.

Ulla jerked her boot off and shook a rock out. "Whose stones are we discussing?"

"Rafn's."

His mouth quirked up. "I am the only one here with that particular body part, if you hadn't noticed."

"I was being metaphorical," I said, hurrying toward home.

Fatigue tugged at my arms and legs, asking me to lie down, not even worried I would freeze to death or be captured by a crazed, powerful seithr if I did. My eyelids slipped closed and I forced them open again.

"Our wild Starling is too tired to laugh, hatchlings." Ulla took my arm.

Rafn, frowning, grabbed the other. "Let's get her home."

I couldn't keep what I witnessed from them. Risking what they did, they deserved to know. "I saw Fellriki call fire and use it to strike the eagle."

Ulla's hold on me loosened. Rafn touched the key tied around his neck.

"Will he strike out at us now?" Liv asked.

"He never saw us." I looked at the snaking path that ran up the mountain side and the black trees guarding Altar Mount. "He would've already attacked if he had, right?"

"I'd say so," Ulla agreed.

Rafn raised his head and set his serious eyes on me. "So now you'll leave this alone, right, Bryn? Because I rather like you—unroasted." He worked toward a light tone, but the heavy look in his eyes weighted the words.

I glanced at Ulla, who shrugged. *It's up to you*, she seemed to say.

"Bryn..." Rafn wasn't going to let this go. "You could destroy Snowfallen if you trouble him too much. He could ruin all of us. Keep the grimoire or whatever it is—"

"It's a bestiary with lykill that—"

He held up a hand. "I don't want to know. Tomorrow, Fellriki will come back to Altar Mount, and the Presentation will go as planned, and he'll count the eagle as something we—Snowfallen—could never have dreamed up. Everything will be fine. I'm going to pretend you, Bryn, didn't break nine sacred traditions in getting a book you shouldn't have." He squeezed his eyes shut. "Just tell me you will stay out of the mountains and will follow our rituals from now on."

I stared at his clogs and the footprints he'd left in the scanty snow of the road.

"Please?" he whispered, his voice pained. The sound reminded me of the day he lost his mother, his sadness, the set of his shoulders. My chest tightened, and I wanted to reach out and take his hand, to feel his warmth against me.

I just couldn't seem to utter what I wanted to happen tomorrow. That Fellriki would be so jarred by the eagle's appearance that he wouldn't show for the Presentation and everyone would begin to question him. I hoped it was the beginning of the end for him. But Rafn was probably right. I hadn't changed anything yet, except for maybe shaking Fellriki up a little.

"I will think about it, Raven." The lie burned my tongue.

Rafn nodded once, doubt wafting over his features, before starting toward Linden Lows.

With quiet words, we wished one another good night, Ulla and I trading a look that clearly meant *We will talk tomorrow.*

CHAPTER SIXTEEN

The jarl's gravelly voice woke Rafn. Heart beating, he sat up, rubbed his stubbled chin and touched the cottage key at his chest. He had a bad feeling that he knew exactly what this was about. He rubbed his sweating palms together, his heart warring with his soul.

Benedikt and the jarl were face to face, both flushed. Rafn's father had one hand on the Deadbook like it was his talisman. The jarl kept glancing at the window. They seemed to be arguing, but really they were both whispering about the same thing and the same worries.

"Rafn," the jarl said, holding out a hand and waving Rafn toward them. "Just the fresh young mind we need."

Benedikt gave Rafn a good nod with a half grim smile.

The jarl squeezed Rafn's shoulder. "There has been an incident."

That was one way to put it, Rafn thought. He inclined

his head, listening, though he pretty much knew what the man would say. The two big questions were: *How much did the jarl know?* and *What was Rafn going to say?*

"Well, I hate to speak of it," the jarl said. "I wish we could simply...well..." His gaze snapped to the window, the door. "Something, or someone, has fouled the Altar Bowl."

Both men stared at Rafn and a drop of sweat dragged down his back. His mouth worked but nothing wanted to come out. He took a breath, closed and opened his eyes.

"What do you mean *fouled?*" Rafn began talking to himself, running through self-berating questions like *So, that's how you've decided to handle this? By acting like you don't know? You're not a good liar, Rafn. How do you propose to keep up this sham? You are no Bryn. You don't exactly excel at deception. Especially when your motivation doesn't lie in the act.*

"The food is half eaten. The area is...disturbed. Disrupted."

Rafn tried to swallow, then coughed. "Could it have been animals?"

Benedikt's eyes narrowed.

The jarl's face smoothed a little. "Ah. Maybe. Maybe." He tugged at his braided beard.

"You think that's truly a possibility?" Benedikt turned, his scowl aimed at the jarl.

Rafn took a heavy breath. He had to ask it. His ruse would be obvious if he didn't. "If it wasn't animals, who do you think did it? And why?" Another bead of sweat ran down to the small of his back. He wished the flames weren't so high in the firebed.

The jarl's gaze sharpened. "At first, I thought it had to be a seithr."

"Why?" Rafn asked.

Benedikt snorted, frowning. "Who else would have the stones to defy our Protector?"

"But, but Fellriki is one of them," Rafn said. "Why would a seithr want to shame one of their own?"

"He is not one of their own," Benedikt said quietly. "Son. He is half god. Surely you don't suggest—"

"No. No, of course not. I only meant that they have magic as he does. The silver in their blood, like he does."

The jarl paced a small circle. His silver circlet had pressed a mark into his forehead. "Are you certain you don't know anything about this, Rafn?"

"Why would I know? Jarl, you must know that I am faithful. I would never do anything against our Protector."

The man held up a hand. "That's not what I meant. I only...you spend time with Brynja Seithrsdottir and lately she has seemed...discontent. Though her parents are upstanding folk. Has she said anything to you? Have you seen her do anything I should know about? Or perhaps that friend of hers Ulla Andersdottir? That family is known for their wild, stubborn nature."

"I don't think...I don't know anything." He took a slow breath. He was starting to talk like the jarl, pausing in all the wrong places. "I'm sorry I couldn't be more help."

Benedikt poured the jarl a steaming cup of pine needle tea. "What will you do about the situation, Jarl?"

"Animals. We will think it is animals for now. And I

don't believe we should mention it at all. I won't tell the council about it even. Keep this between us three." He took a sip of the tea, then pressed a ringed hand against Benedikt's chest. "I do appreciate...you both. It is a good thing to have counsel with those committed to Snowfallen. The council members often have their own personal motives...separate and sometimes discordant to my, to our, purposes."

"Of course, Jarl," Benedikt said, taking his empty cup.

"Anything to help," Rafn croaked.

The jarl started for the door. "If you hear any word, any whisper, let me know."

Rafn and Benedikt nodded, Rafn's stomach twisting. He'd just lied to his father and to the jarl. He'd just betrayed their Protector.

CHAPTER SEVENTEEN

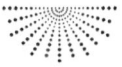

At Altar Mount, the wind lifted my braids and tossed my cloak.

Sometimes I dreamed of flying and if I stopped concentrating for even a breath, I would plummet to the pines and their limbs would rip mine, shredding my happy dream and pounding it into the realm of nightmare.

So now, awake and bursting with magic, I concentrated.

I had the Graybook in my bag. Not that I needed to see the runes. I closed my eyes and saw them all. Sharp lines like blades, beating curves like hearts, curls like breath in brittle air. But the book, humming through my bag and my clothing like a second heart, flooded my arms and legs with strength—though I wasn't sure whether that was something real or imagined.

Keeping my face clear, unreadable, I watched as Fellriki walked out of the mountains' shadows and regarded our gathered kingdom, his eyes shielded by his heavy hood. Only his lush mouth showed under the embroidery and darkness. Everyone bowed their head, their worried comments about the broken crockery and chewed ends of salmon and scattered coins around the bowl flitting around like a school of frightened minnows.

I smiled.

The jarl was talking. I didn't hear what he said. My ears hummed in time with the Graybook.

It was Fellriki and me. Nothing else mattered.

Then he spoke, his voice loud and mellow. It was only one of two days we heard his voice. My own tone would sound higher, but no less loud and strong when I decided to speak today.

"This," he started, as he held a hand toward the bowl, where his Presentation foods and goods remained ravaged, broken by the eagle, "is no accident." A black-red bone ring made his first finger majestic.

I swallowed. Would he deny that an empowered eagle had debased his Presentation and nearly taken his life too?

"I invited our good animals of Snowfallen to partake of the Presentation this year," Fellriki said. "The gods told me this was right."

My blood curdled. "Lies," I whispered. Well, he could deny what happened all he wanted. He wouldn't be able to deny what I was about to do.

My cloak blew back as I flipped my carver, the Graybook's heart drumming in my ears. Boots scuffled, pulling away from me.

"Daughter?" Father's voice was so quiet, almost not even there.

The first sweep of my lykill—a shape throwing the hint of paw, claw, and mountain peak—made me think it would raise a snow leopard. The next curve spoke of truth, something to do with the creature's growl. Truth was exactly what we needed.

I looked up to see Fellriki's lips turn down. I was doing this. I couldn't believe I was really doing this. He stepped forward. I kept carving.

The jarl spoke in a gasp, a cough. "Is this an offering? Seithr, what are you—"

Everyone began speaking at once, crying out, shouting, praying. Some fell to their knees and covered their heads at Fellriki's feet.

Before I could finish the last of three circles—spots— Father and Mother grabbed me.

"What are you doing?" Father hissed.

I jerked away, trying to finish. Almost. Almost.

Rafn's words cut through the chaos. "Bryn. Don't do it."

Fellriki raised his blood-stained carver, a sick grin crawling over his shadowed mouth. He drove a symbol into the air, his movements like lightning.

Heat exploded from my back and all over my hand.

Liv screamed.

Mother pulled my flaming bag off my shoulders and threw it down.

Ulla dove at my burning fingers, where the bone ring sang pain into my blood. She blanketed my hand with her cloak, suffocating the flames.

Bright red fire ate at my bag, a reaching beast, already devouring the hidden Graybook. I lurched, grasping for the flames, then the jarl had me by the hair.

He forced me to the ground. Fellriki's boots were there, in front of my nose, then they weren't.

The place where Fellriki had been was nothing but a haze of oily heat.

The jarl shoved my face into the mud and someone grabbed at my carver. I gripped it, fighting them, digging my fingers in, and pushed up from the ground as I won my carver back.

The blacksmith, the rye farming seithr and his family, the jarl's children and wife—everyone—rose their fists or carvers and rushed at me like a sudden wave.

I scrambled back and began to carve the eagle rune into the ground.

"Starling! Think!" Ulla shouted over Atli's head. She pushed him to the side, but Jakob held her back, his eyes slitted like a snake's. Ulla grunted and Jakob bent. She must've hit him.

She didn't need to worry. I *was* thinking. My mind had never been so clear. The eagle would be more than enough to scare everyone off me, to let me do what I needed to do.

Rafn broke through the madness, his eyes wild and his mouth set into a line. He ran at me and kicked my carver out of my hand. Pain rocketed up my arm.

I leaped for my weapon. "What are you doing, Raven?"

His hands struck my collarbone, driving me back. "Keeping you from killing everyone you love."

I opened my mouth to scream at him, but the jarl snagged my braids again and dragged me toward the Altar.

"Brynja Seithrsdottir," he rasped. "You have disgraced us. Because you are not of age, you will only lose a finger."

"More!" the rye farmer shouted, spittle flying.

The jarl's wife nodded, her hair slipping from its metal circlet. "Take her hand!"

The jarl nodded. With one hand, it would be nearly impossible to carve properly. My legs gave way, and I caught myself against the Altar, the scent of old blood in my head.

Mother shivered hard and closed her eyes, her feathered, silver eyebrows bunched. Father held her, glaring at me.

"Two fingers," the jarl said. "If you try foul magic again, if you disgrace us before Fellriki again, you will lose your hand and an eye."

My stomach lurched. I spat at his feet. "Take what you want. I'm not the problem here. It's you that should lose your eyes. You can't see the truth in front of you. I found the Graybook, a book of lykill, a bestiary, and I'm just as powerful as Fellriki. I should be your Man in the Hill. Your Protector. I love Snowfallen. I wouldn't ask for a human sacrifice, for heartblood. I would be just."

The jarl's wrinkled eyes squinted. "Bestiary? Where?"

I jerked my chin toward the ash covered bag near Mother's feet. Hopefully, the fire had been smothered before it completely consumed the grimoire. "Fellriki, in his fear, burned it."

"There is no Graybook," Benedikt called above the crowd, his cheeks flushed above his beard.

The Raven's gaze snapped to his father, his teeth showing.

"What would you know? You're no seithr," I said to Benedikt.

The jarl pressed my hand, the unburnt one, against the rough Altar's stone surface and a breath shuddered out of me.

"But he's right, Jarl," Father said. "There is no book. She has been under stress...this harvest came late and—"

"Tell them Liv." I tried to tug my hand away from the jarl's iron grip. "Grow a spine, Finch! Tell them!"

Liv paled, the pathetic little thing, but Ulla stepped forward. "Bryn did find a book. In the Lows."

The jarl held up his free hand. "Quiet. I'll not have any more of these children's ignorant tales. We will not tolerate this blasphemy. Fellriki has shown his displeasure, and we will be lucky to harvest a single plant come spring because of you, Brynja Seithrsdottir."

He took his axe from his belt. "Hold her, Jakob."

I struggled against the jarl's grip. "If you let me carve one of the new lykill, I can show you all," I said. "This isn't some story. Just listen! Let me show you!"

Jakob picked up my carver and handed it to my parents. Father blinked tears away and Mother raised her chin, her eyes cold.

"Let Ulla hold me." A terrible calm shrouded my trembling heart.

The jarl shook his head. "She has shown where she stands in this. Rafn Benediktsson, as a boy of her birth month—your faith shows in your demeanor—you may have the honor of helping in the proper retribution for this blasphemy."

I cleared my throat of the acid stinging its way toward my tongue. "No. I don't need anyone to hold me." I slammed my hand onto the stone, breaking the jarl's grip.

I would survive this. I would go on to prove to everyone they didn't need Fellriki. I would prove they needed me.

The crowd deadened as the jarl raised his axe.

The scorched flesh around my bone ring screamed as if it knew the pain my other hand would feel.

My stomach twisted, but I raised my chin and met Mother's gaze, her steely eyes giving more strength than reprimand.

Did she believe me?

The blade knocked through skin and bone.

A cold heat rushed through my hand and arm. Then, the strange feeling slipped away and left behind a pain that painted the world in the blacks and reds of Fellriki's ring.

Time swallowed me whole.

CHAPTER EIGHTEEN

I woke on the icy ground, to muddied leather boots and rumbling voices. Shutting out the world, I closed my eyes again and let Father carry me home, a blur of pine needles, my heart beating in my hands, his warm chest, and a light touch on my cheek—Mother's calloused fingers.

My mouth wouldn't open. Stuck, my tongue wouldn't work. I'd eaten burning glass, foreign desert sands, and swallowed fire that fought to escape through my hands.

Mother wrapped my butchered hand in cloth that smelled like honey and some bright herb. My lips parted to say something, but it came out in a rasp.

Her eyes met mine. She tucked my hand gently by my side and stood. "I'll get you water."

The cool liquid made my mouth work again. "Why is the room so...why is the firelight...broken?" My thoughts swirled and drowned like fallen leaves in a flooded river.

"It's the poppy. For the pain. It will pass. Sleep."

But I didn't want to sleep. "Where is the Graybook? Where is my carver?"

Mother paused in coating my burned hand in a bitter-smelling salve. "You're done with all that."

"But you can see my bone ring. You know I'm not lying. You at least know there is something to my story. Just tell me if the Graybook survived."

Her eyes pinched as she studied the whale's tail on my first finger. "We will not speak of it. Never."

Then I remembered the Announcement. Had I missed it? Who had been chosen to die for Fellriki?

I tried to sit up and dizziness forced me back onto my pillows.

Mother touched my shoulder "You haven't missed anything. We still don't know who will be honored as the sacrifice."

"And you're still going to go if it's you? You won't at least let me show you what I might do to stop all this?"

She stood. "Quiet, Brynja. Another word about any of it, and I'll lock you in here for the rest of your days."

"You won't be able to if you die."

Her breath came out in a gust.

"I'm right and you know it."

She jerked my bed curtain closed and her footsteps knocked along the wooden floor beyond.

I heard the door creak open.

"Rakel?" It was Rafn's voice.

I sat up so fast that my head nearly came off. I blinked to stop the curtain twirling around me.

"May I see her?" he asked.

Mother must've nodded, because the curtain moved

and his face appeared. He knelt beside me, his eyes clouded, his lips tight.

"I don't know why I'm here, really," he said quietly as Mother banged a pot near the firebed.

I leaned close, breathing in his incense scent. "Because you are sorry for taking his side. Because you know I'm right."

He put a hand to his forehead and let it slide down his face. A vein pulsed under the raven inking above his ear. He'd shaved the sides again since I'd seen him and his skin bled on a spot near the short braids and tangles that crowned him.

"You have to help me find my carver. They hid it. Maybe with the Graybook. Tell me they didn't break my carver. If they broke it—" My throat closed up and the Raven handed me my cup of water. If they had destroyed my carver, that would be it for me as a seithr. I'd just be a common human at that point, with no chance to use the traces of silver blood inside me.

"They didn't break it. I don't think so anyway," he whispered, setting my cup on the floor. "But I don't know where it is. That, or the book. I wouldn't tell you if I did."

I sat back and closed my eyes. I couldn't take the spinning. Nothing he said surprised me. "Then sing to me. I need your voice." Somehow I felt it would feed me, heal me, bring my solution.

Rafn was silent. His breathing was soft and steady.

"What?" I swallowed around the imagined glass in my mouth and throat. "Am I not allowed that either? Am I too evil to enjoy music?"

Mother's noises stopped beyond the curtain. "Bryn." Her voice was a warning.

I went back to whispering. "Please, Raven. Forget your stupidity for a minute and—"

"Starling, I—"

My eyes flew open. I found something in Rafn's gaze. "You called me Starling."

"I always do."

"Not since summer."

He looked away, the man's knot in his throat moving.

I lay back again. "Just sing. Please."

And so he did.

The words were from some ancient language no one spoke anymore. Or maybe from a land I hadn't learned about from Mother's lessons. The sounds tripped around his mouth in mellow, short notes and blurred together like a grape skin's stain spreading into ivory wool. His voice rose light, but strong, straightening my spine and taking the haze from my head.

I breathed deep. "That was escape turned into sound."

His eyes darted right and left. "Escape? No."

"Yes." My smile cracked my dry lips, but the pain was nothing to the growing thrum of my injured hands.

He got his feet under him and stood. "I should go."

I tried to take his fingers, but my hand didn't want to do anything but shake and hum like a dying calf. "Raven?"

"Yes?"

"Come back later?"

His clogs ground against the grit on the floor. He sighed. "Okay."

The darkness claimed me before he left my bedside.

I woke a few more times to Mother and Father drawing Healing lykill in the air over my head. Time flowed around me and I let it go, pain and herbs crushing my mind under an immovable weight.

Afternoon sun peered through the cracks around the window and nudged me awake. Someone had pulled my bedding curtain back. Liv and Ulla stood beside Mother at the firebed. The scents of hazelnuts, pork, and green soup with spinach, eggs, and nutmeg soaked the room. Announcement foods. It was time to find out who Fellriki had chosen. Something flickered to life inside me.

Strange. I was excited about the Announcement.

Though the jarl would act as Fellriki's mouthpiece tonight—the Protector wouldn't be there in person—I wanted to know Fellriki's choice.

I wanted a fight. This time, I was determined not to lose.

I had to get my carver back.

Liv clasped her hands. "She's awake!"

An odd emotion washed over Ulla's fair features. "So she is." She smiled. "Feel good enough to walk outside the house with us?"

Surprisingly, I did.

Winter showed its growing strength in the gray snow clouds above the far mountains and the ice inching farther and farther from shore and into the fjord. We marched through the white, past the goat pen, and started down the worn path into the pines behind the house. It was as good a place as any to start searching for my carver.

Her carver tucked under one arm, Liv braided her hair, pulled it loose, and braided it again. "What are you going to do?"

"Is the Graybook completely burned or is it simply hidden like my carver?"

Ulla sighed. "It's hidden. I think. Not that I know where. Your parents and the jarl took everything."

"Bryn." Liv tugged at my sleeve. "What are you going to do?"

"I'm going to find what's been stolen from me, and the real question should be *What am I not going to do?*"

There was nothing in the trees, the snow, or hiding beneath rocks. Maybe they'd hidden my weapon in the press house.

The Eagle and the Finch were too quiet as we hurried to the stone building and peeked inside. The place was empty, so I pushed the door open and we slipped into the dank room.

Ulla sat near the window as I pushed baskets tall as me over and bent to look under the shelving behind the press.

"Why aren't you helping me look?"

Ulla rubbed her knee and started at the floor. "Starling, about what happened..."

I put a hand on her leg. "Thank you for speaking for me." I shot Liv a look.

She paled and pathetically began rifling through baskets that were too small to bother with.

Ulla stood. "You can't expect Liv to risk her life when you were being...wild. You were like—"

I faced her. "I was like what?"

She swallowed. "Like him."

A dangerous heat pricked at my heart. "I'm nothing like Fellriki."

Her eyebrows drew together. "Not Fellriki. The jarl. You were acting for yourself. Like the jarl would."

I stepped back. What did she mean?

Her cheeks reddened a shade. "When you tried to call up the eagle to save yourself from everyone, it was something he would do. He doesn't care about the effects his actions have on others."

She didn't sound like herself. Where was my Eagle, my powerful friend, my shield-maiden now? I started to speak, but she stopped me with a hand up.

"I wanted to follow you, to be your fighter, Starling, because you aren't like him. You keep me from teasing Liv too harshly. You lecture her to move her forward because you want her to be her best self. You are honest with me like I'm your equal even though I know, deep down, you think yourself higher because you're a seithr. And you want life to be bright around you, not stuck in tradition just for self-preservation like the jarl."

I'd never thought of the jarl like that, but now that she mentioned it...but who cared? The jarlship was one thing, taking Fellriki down was the first thing.

Waving a bandaged hand, I said, "Fellriki will do anything and everything to win this. I must be ready to do the same."

Ulla's mouth tightened and she looked away, out the window.

I planted my feet. "Are you two with me or not? We can argue over little things after all this is over. I—we—are so close. I could've taken Fellriki down at Altar Mount if it weren't for everyone being a bag of fools. I could've been the Protector. I will be." I squeezed my stiff right hand—the one that Fellriki had burned. My bones ached for my carver and my bone ring hummed with power.

Liv breathed slow, in and out. "I'm with you."

Ulla shook her head, but she nodded.

The heat inside me rose again. It didn't necessarily feel great, but it was strong, whatever it was. And strong was what I needed.

Now, I had to find my weapon. No way I was living this life, bending and scraping to Fellriki and the jarl. Gods, without my magic, I was worse than a perfectly respectable human. I would be a stripped seithr, disgraced, pathetic.

"Please help me find my carver." My voice echoed off the stone walls. I didn't care at all if Liv's parents or mine heard me. Fear tried to leak into me, but frustration's itching, pinching acid filled me to the brim. Like I'd downed a bucket of spirit of salt. No, it wasn't merely frustration. It was the acid of desiring something so much that death was no deterrent. I longed for power over Fellriki, and the feeling sizzled in my blood.

Atli burst through the door, laughing. "Bad mood, Bryn?"

I went for his throat.

He grunted and brought a knee up, hitting my stomach and driving the air out of my chest. I fell back into Liv's perfumed arms.

Ulla's hands latched onto me as Atli rubbed at the red marks on his neck. "Starling," Ulla said. "Stop. Stop."

Thrashing, I broke away from them and ran.

The Raven found me at Linden Lows. I was staring at the Graybook master's grave.

"Come," he said and took my bandaged hand.

CHAPTER NINETEEN

We climbed the hill to the lair as the wind picked up again. As I lifted the door's iron latch, a quick gust pushed Rafn's hair around, the short, loose locks stirring and the braided bits snapping. The air bent his long, black eyelashes at the sides. He didn't say a word, and it had to be killing him not to say *I told you so.*

A shout built inside me, and I fought it down, not wanting to make Rafn think I was losing my mind.

Before we opened the door to go inside, my question exploded from my mouth.

"Do you know where they hid the book and my carver?"

"No. But if you are worthy—"

"Don't. Just. Don't."

When a seithr's carver was taken, their family was required to hide it. The belief was that if the seithr deserved to have magic returned to them, they would find it. But this wasn't some reprimand to a child. This was my insurrection. Everyone who wasn't with me, was against me.

The lair's beaten dirt floor was familiar, comforting, under my feet. A little of the imaginary spirit of salt inside me calmed, allowing me to take a fuller breath, to blink more regularly.

Past wall hooks holding fishing poles, coils of thin rope, and that ridiculously huge pot, I ducked under the clothesline that stretched across the room. Nothing hung from it but one sad pair of long, woolen socks, a truly intimate remnant of the house's former tenant.

Another soul given to Fellriki. Another one given to a lie.

"Talk to me." Rafn's words were soft as lambs' wool. "I'll just listen."

My heart clenched. I took a breath of the sweet ilmreyr grass Liv had strewn on the floor near the pile of furs. The place smelled like fresh hay, vanilla, and woodsmoke. Rafn woke the smoored fire, moving coals, blowing gently, and shifting peat to burn. We settled on some woolsacks and I took up his offer to talk.

"Fellriki is not a god. He is not so special. He only has lykill the rest of us don't." To his credit, he didn't argue. "Remember when I told you there were more of these grimoires?" He nodded. "I think one holds runes that control the elements. Including storms."

I took the largest of the flatrocks around the fire and set it between us. Grabbing a slip of charcoal the fire hadn't bit in a while, I started to draw.

Light fell through the one window, joined the threads of illumination from around the door and from the fire, and lit my crude sketchings of the Graybook. A snarling bear. A leaping fish. The broad feathers of the great eagle. From the rock near my foot, I fished the old piece of vellum Liv had found and held it out to Rafn, who took it with steady fingers. He ran a thumb over the ridgrasil, his arms tucked close to his sides. He was cold. I scooted closer.

"There were three books. Silver for simple magic. Gray for beasts. Red for the elements."

"You think Fellriki has the Red. That it is why we call him a half god."

"He simply has the grimoire with the lykill to control water, wind, earth, and fire."

"So anyone could hold back the volcano if they had the Redbook's lykill."

"Well, not anyone. The Redbook would have to accept the seithr as master." I held out my bone ring. "Like the Gray did with me." I drew antlers and sparks on the flat rock. "The volcano isn't going to erupt. Fellriki uses the fear of it to control us."

"He enjoys killing. That's what you think."

"He doesn't need blood to work the runes." Setting the rock aside, I stood up and started pacing. "We don't need it for growing things. I didn't use any blood to raise the eagle. The elements can't be more complicated than that."

"They could."

I glared.

Rafn glared right back. "Just because I'm not a seithr

doesn't mean I'm not entitled to my own thoughts on the matter."

I rolled my eyes even though a part of me was proud of him for arguing against me.

"But even if he isn't half god," the Raven said, "and he simply has a powerful book that shows elemental lykill, he has shown he can still hurt you."

I stopped, my throat catching. "That's why I'm going to bring him to his knees."

"Bryn." A world lived in the tone of his voice. Pain. Fear. Loss. "You'll destroy us all doing this."

"Not if I strip him of his power first."

"What if it's the lykill and their strength that made him the way he is? What if it's too much for a person?"

"I'm not a regular person. I'm a seithr."

He pointed to the three-colored circle. "So were those who gave this warning."

I breathed out in a rush. Then I held out my finger, the one with the whale tail bone ring. "I am the Graybook's master—"

"Master of a book that lies in ashes."

"No. I don't think it's destroyed. I think they hid it. But it doesn't matter. I have the lykill here." I tapped my head with a finger and his black eyebrows lifted. "And I will master the Redbook too. Fellriki has it. I can feel it." I pushed a fist into my gut.

Rafn looked at his hands.

The acid in me rose. "Why don't you just leave if you're so against everything I'm trying to do?"

His fingers alighted on my wrist, just above my bandage. A shiver spread out from the point of contact.

His blue-gray eyes softened and pulled me down gently, to kneel beside him. The scent of incense and old stone laced his presence with the illusion of wisdom. Or maybe it wasn't an illusion.

"I know you're only trying to protect us—Liv, Ulla, our parents," he said. "I know you're trying to do what you see as right."

"It's not just *right*. It's what we have to do. What I have to do. None of the elders will listen if I try to explain all of this. They're too stuck in their ways. You saw what they did to me. And even if I could convince them, it'd be too late. In three days, someone will die."

"Isn't the sacrifice worth it? You love Snowfallen the way I do. Its black cliffs and clouds. The fjords that speak back if you listen hard enough." He was nearly singing and I felt every word like a heart's beat. "Nowhere else can you live among other seithr with carvers and stories and your dreams where the dead talk to you. There are places where a woman can't be a warrior like Ulla. I've seen the awe on your face when you look up at the mountains and when you smile through the fire at celebrations and meetings. You'd give your life to keep Snowfallen safe." His eyes flashed. "Why won't you allow others to give theirs? Why talk Ulla and Liv and me into destroying this tradition of offering blood to Fellriki when it so far has kept Snowfallen protected?"

In a blink, my fingers were curled into the front of his longshirt, my skin burning as I gripped hard and harder. "Because this tradition is a falsity. It mocks us. He mocks us. If we peel away this hold Fellriki has, we will be stronger. We will live through the storms, the weather, or we will learn to control it on our own terms. Not his. Not that liar's."

His hands cupped mine, his skin cold and solid as ice on my exposed fingertips. "But you don't know for sure that Fellriki is a liar. This is your stubborn arrogance talking. You could ruin all of this—our mountains, our homeplaces, our dances and songs, our smiles, our fights —with your blind, iron will. It's one of the thousand reasons I long for you, Bryn. Your iron, stubborn love of our home. But it is also the reason I will argue this to my last breath."

We were both shaking and grabbing one another, our forearms braced wool to wool and skin to skin.

"Listen to the part of you that longs for my iron will, then," I said. "I'm right. I'll show you that everything I do, I do for Snowfallen."

"I can't let you do this."

"It's not your decision to make. Don't act like this is your thing. It is very much my thing."

"I don't care whose thing this is. I'm keeping you from getting yourself killed. He won't choose your mother. I know it. You don't have to take over all of Snowfallen just to keep her alive."

"You don't know he won't. Besides, I don't want to take over..." Not really. That was the wrong phrasing. Though I would definitely take care of our isle better than anyone else. I had the spine no one else seemed to have, save Fellriki, who obviously hated us. How could I get Rafn out of my way? He was just so stubborn.

There was something I could use to push back at him. He adored tradition, our history, our isle. But not that long ago, he whispered to me, and only me, about how much he longed to wander, to travel to other places and see other cultures. Since the summer, and whatever had happened then, he'd acted like he never once wanted to leave Snowfallen. I didn't know what was going on with him, but there was something to this. And if I edged his secret desire to wander into the thought that he might leave us...maybe then he'd back off.

"I may be willing to risk everything to have the free Snowfallen I want," I said. "But at least I'd never abandon it."

His hands fell to his sides.

My mind said it was right to say it. He needed to get off his high seat. But my gut told a different story. A heaviness swamped me and mired me in guilt.

"Rafn. Look. I'm sorry. I shouldn't have...I know you—"

He stood and started toward the door. I grabbed his sleeve, but he jerked away.

"You don't know anything." He choked on the last word. I hated myself. "I can't believe you'd throw that at me."

Throw what at him exactly? Why was his wish to wander now a thing he wanted to keep hidden, a thing to deny? I couldn't breathe.

"I had to," I said. "You made me." The collar of my dress felt like a noose. My cloak's tie was a vice grip. "I can't just let this go." My pulse hammered in my throat, and the acid, the frustration burned into my cheeks and temples. "I won't lose my magic because of him. My place in Snowfallen. I won't lose myself. I won't lose my mother."

And then I was crying like a child and cramming my face into my tender and butchered hands. I turned toward one of the lair's sloped, earthen walls.

Rafn's hand settled onto my back. His touch was gentle, but when he spoke, his words were not. "I should leave and never speak to you again. You know that, right? That was a secret I told you. About my desire to wander. You can be a really terrible person."

I looked at him. "Seithr."

He spun. His clog scraped the edge of the firebed's stones and he hit the door with a fist, raising dust like ghosts.

I licked the salt of tears from my upper lip. "At least I don't lie to you, Raven. I tell you what's in me, no matter what."

He pressed the heels of his hands into his eyebrows and groaned. "Gods, why do I..." Then he stepped forward and cupped my face with those angry hands, but his touch had gone gentle again. "You and my wanderlust. My two greatest challenges."

"Neither of which you should be ashamed of." I raised an eyebrow, the feathered edges catching at my hair.

A pained smile tripped over his mouth. "I'm not ashamed of you. I'm scared for you."

"What I said...about you leaving...I was being stupid. Just because you long to wander doesn't mean you'd leave us for good."

He swallowed. His silence made me want to start crying again.

"Rafn, what aren't you telling me?"

"It's about my mother."

She'd died so long ago. What could she have to do with this?

"She is alive," he said.

I forgot about everything for a breath. "What?"

Closing his eyes, he raised his chin and sighed. "You know she wasn't from these isles."

"She was from the easterns, right?"

Blinking, his face fell into cold lines. "Never mind. I'll...I'll tell you some other time. I can't..."

"It's okay. You don't have to tell me. Even though I can most likely fix everything for you."

"Bryn."

"You mean Starling."

He almost smiled. "Starling." His gaze was hot.

A warmth slid over my chest and down my stomach, below my navel. I shook it off to focus. "All right. For now, let's agree to disagree." I forced every ounce of my *wanting more* and *longing for control* into my eyes.

A muscle in the side of Rafn's jaw tensed. He took a heavy breath. "For now."

"Believe me, I'm scared enough for all of us. But I can handle this. We are doing this."

His eyes flicked to mine. "Maybe."

I raised an eyebrow. "Definitely."

"I'll stick around for now."

"You better."

"Or?"

"Or I'll sic Ulla on you."

His lips turned down and his eyes went wide. "Not that."

"I'll tell her you made yet another pair of clogs."

Rafn came close, his warm mouth at my ear. "Thank you, Starling, for not pushing me to talk."

"You're welcome." My voice went hoarse. I felt gutted.

"But I'm still going to do my best to thwart this mad plan of yours."

I faced him, our noses brushing. "I'm very focused."

"We'll see." His gaze slid over my cheek and down my neck like fingers. "We will see."

To hide the delicious shiver running through me, I walked back to the woolsacks. I liked him better tortured by me rather than the other way around.

He trailed me. I hid my smirk as I began to sketch again, filling the antlers in.

"If you find your carver, what would you do?" Rafn's gaze strayed from the sketch to my legs.

"I want to find the cave."

His eyes sparked. "Fellriki's cave? But no one—"

"Because no one has had the courage to look."

Runes leaped through my mind like a herd fleeing a pack of wolves.

"If we find him, what then?" Rafn asked.

"I'll figure it out."

Rafn held up his hands. A vein in his head pulsed under the inking of the Raven's talons. "You'll *figure it out*. Okay. Of course. Years of a seithr holding all the power and you'll take him down by *figuring it out*."

"Why are you repeating everything? Yes. I'll make a way."

The skin around my bone ring shivered, and I imagined thick, furred antlers, a white and sloping back, and markings that glowed green like the winter night's lights.

I wrote an ancient word on the rock. "Do you know what this is?"

"The frost-limned *hreinin*. I've seen it in the Deadsongs book."

The lykill in my mind came through my fingers and I drew it—keeping the lines broken so it wouldn't take. I didn't want the magic to work yet. Two diverging lines made valleys in the calfskin, deep and shadowed. "This part is the symbol for Want."

"You use that in your Growing lykill, don't you?"

"You noticed?"

"I saw you carving when I came to get the dead's wine last year—the portion we pour on the cairns before we sing at winter's height."

I nodded. I knew the tradition, though I wasn't a part of it. It was much like our ceremony to the mother vine at the vineyard's core. A prayer, a pouring, and a circle walked three times by the three eldest in the group, the ones closest to returning to the earth.

"Why didn't you talk to me when you came by?" I asked. "I didn't see you watching, but you must've been close to notice the lykill."

"You...seemed busy. I didn't want to interrupt."

That wasn't it. It was him pulling away. "From now on, always interrupt me."

A grin tugged at his full lips. "All right then."

"What is the old tale of the frost-limned stag, the

hreinin?" I asked. In my mind, green and blue lines waved behind the lykill like the winter night's lights. "Isn't the creature sometimes known as the Winter Seer?"

"My grandmother mentioned it once before her death."

"I need Liv," I said. "Only she can read all of this. And she might know the story. There are more than extravagant braids on that mind of hers."

The door blasted open. Mother and Father stood side by side.

I froze.

"What exactly do you think you're doing, Daughter?" Father's face was red.

I stumbled to my feet, Rafn beside me.

"Atli said you'd left the vineyard, and I told him you'd never leave your family after such an event," Mother said. "That you were surely in your Place praying." Mother let out a breath. "I am so disappointed."

An invisible hand fisted around my stomach. The afternoon before the Announcement, everyone in Snowfallen crawled into small places designated for prayer and solitude. But it wasn't time for that yet.

"You don't understand," I said.

But what could I tell them? I couldn't explain.

With a boot, I nudged the stone I'd drawn on under the woolsack.

Father stepped inside and took in the messy shelves stacked with bottles and crockery, the hanging dried herbs, more rare than what we kept at home. He frowned at the bedding at the back of the lair and his gaze snapped to Rafn.

"Benedikt and I had a heated talk about you two," Father said. "He doesn't seem to think my daughter is good enough for you. After everything, he might be right."

It felt like he'd hit me.

"You should go home, Rafn," Mother said. "Bryn, you'll be doing the same since you seem to be well enough now. And you'll stay there, in your Place until it's time for the Announcement."

Chills dropped over me like the ice that had fallen from the sky.

Rafn gathered his things, taking up my cloak too. He glanced my way.

"Mother. Father. Just what are we in trouble for? We didn't do anything wrong."

Father erupted. "After what you did at the Presentation, I should take your tongue, Daughter!"

Mother hushed him and motioned for Rafn and me to go out the door.

Father grabbed my arm and near dragged me down the hill. Rafn raised a quick fist in farewell and took the path down the other side of the rise.

CHAPTER TWENTY

Another storm brewed off the sea coast, sending a strange fog over the vineyard.

To indicate it was time for the reflection and prayer of Solitude, the jarl's slaves blew the horns, a jarring sound that echoed in my bones. I fisted the hand with the Graybook's ring—my skin was nearly healed from the burns—and took a breath to remember the power I now had at my fingertips.

Years and years ago, when I was old enough to require a Solitude Place of my own, Father had simply dug out a fox den behind the house, near the rainwater barrel, widening it and protecting the entrance with a few pine boughs. I leaned against the earthen wall and closed my eyes, imagining every rune I could remember from the Graybook.

"Bryn." Liv poked her head inside. "What happened?"

It showed some guts that she was here. She'd be punished if caught out of her Place during Solitude.

"Any new ideas on where they might've hidden my carver?"

"Ulla said she had a guess. She's going to try to sneak over too before the Announcement. But—"

"But what?"

"She wants you to promise you're not going to hurt anyone."

"Of course I'm not going to hurt anyone." Unless they deserved it.

I filled Liv in on Mother and Father catching Rafn and me and the subsequent lectures and demand that I talk to no one until tonight's Announcement.

"But I need to ask you something. Rafn and I found an interesting lykill."

"Is he with you on all this now?"

"We...suspended our arguments. So the Graybook's ring, it showed something about a hreinin. About the Winter Seer, maybe?"

Liv eyed the mounds and hills surrounding our houses and the vineyard beyond. "You can see the runes without the book? Because of the ring?"

"Yes. Do you know anything about the Winter Seer?"

"This is a long story."

"Cut what I don't need to know."

"How do I know what you don't need to know?"

"Good point."

"The stag's tale begins with fire." Liv settled into the cadence of a storyteller at the firebed even though it was just us two and no fire to warm us. "Once, there were thousands of them. Pale white and blue hreinin—a far lighter blue than a bluehare—with thick antlers. Young ones with spots like snowflakes. Herds of their sinuous bodies rushing up mountains and through the valleys during the worst of storms and the sweetest of springtimes. They nested in one certain inland forest. Leaves served as their bedding in the spring and twigs in winter."

"Bedding isn't something I need to know." I looked past her at a shadow crossing the side of the house. A vulture maybe.

She jerked around. "Did you see someone?"

"No. Go on."

"A boy tried to catch a hreinin. He set traps, but the hreinin evaded them. Desperate, eager, he lit five fat-soaked torches and threw them into the hreinin's homeplace. They say the peak owl learned its song that night. Its shrill scream is a perfect echo of the hreinin's misery. In the fire, the dry twigs of their bedding and the trees surrounding that part of the forest went up like great bonfires. Does fell, their fur singed and smoking. Stags and young ones died too, their bodies clogged with smoke, their sides heaving as they fought to breathe."

When Liv told stories, she was like another person. She spoke more in one breath than she usually did in an entire moon cycle.

"A buck bleated for his mate, but the black plumes blocked his sight. Taller than any of his kind, he stretched his head through the miasma and saw the night's lights shimmering in the sky. He called out to them and their magic, asking for the ability to see more, to find, and to survive. The lights answered him. His body glowed green and blue with powerful symbols. His muscles and tendons and bone became immutable, immortal.

"Desperate for fresh air, he dashed from the fire with the speed of a falcon. His ears, withers, and mane—tipped with an eternal frost—glittered like silver as he ran the boy down and drove his body into the earth."

"Whoa."

"Yes, but the story doesn't end there. The gift of power demanded a trade, and the stag, though he wanted nothing more than to find his mate, was destined to forever find things for others, but never for himself. He bides, always lonely and bitter, and at the command of those who have the strength to call him."

"How would he be able to help us find Fellriki?"

"I don't know exactly."

A voice called out from beyond the fallow garden between our houses.

Pea Finch reached out and squeezed my arm. "I'll see you tonight."

"I'm impressed you risked coming over here. Thank you."

"I'm trying to be brave, Starling."

"That's all I ask."

With Liv safely away, I sat back to wait on Ulla.

The jarl's face flitted through my mind. His look of disgust and dismissal. The acid in me burned inside my heart and slithered down my arms to my aching hands. Everyone had looked me up and down, not believing I had the power I claimed. I would show them. I would show them all. And the jarl would feast on his mistake to turn on me.

Ulla crouch-walked to my Place and nodded her head in greeting. Her eyes were bright.

"Did you find my carver? Do you have it?" I crawled out of my hole, past her.

"I need a promise from you."

I swallowed. "The Finch mentioned it."

"Don't look at me like that. You nearly killed everyone, trying to raise that eagle at the Presentation. You have to be careful."

"A warning to be careful? Who are you and what have you done with my Ulla?"

She huffed and kicked her toe against the side of the hill. "There are times when it'd be good to use that great brain of yours, seithr."

"I swear not to hurt anyone, except in situations where survival is in question. Does that satisfy you?"

Nodding, she turned and waved a hand for me to follow. "Fine. Now, hurry. I know where your carver is." She glanced at me, her mouth pinched and her eyes wary.

Relief thrilling through me, I linked my arm in hers and we hurried through the fog, toward the pine forest behind the houses. "You are my savior."

"You remember that."

Mother and Father had hidden my carver in a mound of snow and moss behind the vineyard's first altar to Fellriki. Ulla helped me dig it free while I whispered the gist of my hreinin talk with Rafn and Liv.

Even through the linen bindings around my injured

hands, my carver flooded power into me. I took the first full breath since Rafn had kicked it away.

"How do you feel?" Ulla asked, stepping back.

"Wonderful."

Now that I had my magic back, the Graybook's lykill became clearer in my mind.

Ulla looked about ready to be sick. "What is the next step, Starling?"

We kept to the clearing in the pines. I just hoped no one came out of their Place and spotted us. But if they did, I had my carver, and I was ready for anything.

A slight figure jogged around the side of the house and Ulla stood between me and whoever it was.

"Gods, it's Liv," she said, breathing a cloud of white.

Liv panted as she made her way to us. "I told Atli I had to make water. I don't know why Mother made our Places so close together." She wrinkled her pretty nose.

They turned to look at me, their eyes wide, ready to see what I could do.

I needed to make a lykill that could help me convince them these Graybook runes were good. Something simple to get my friends firmly back on my side. Maybe a creature that could help the vineyard?

Taking a breath of the earthy, damp air, I closed my eyes and clarified my intent.

I ask for a creature who makes the soil fertile.

I really, really hoped I didn't raise an enormous goat whose contribution was a giant pile of—

In my mind, three shapes lined up in a neat row like fingertips and an array of starbursts flickered above them. With the shape of the magic firmly in my head, I drew the lykill in the cold mud that tried to soak through my boots. My blade scratched over a rough patch of icy ground and a small rock, making the curved lines of the symbol uneven, but the magic felt strong in my ring and in my forehead, so I held my mind on what I wanted.

With the rune complete and shining silver in the earth, I leaned back to wait.

"What is it?" Liv whispered, eyeing the house for signs of movement.

Hopefully, everyone else was praying and meditating.

A scraping noise sounded from the lykill. Countless little mounds of earth appeared.

Ulla's lips opened and Liv gasped.

I gripped my carver, my heart in my fingertips and the space between my eyebrows. If this went bad, I had to try something to stop whatever creature I'd called up.

A buzz vibrated through the ground, humming through my boots and in my legs. Maybe I could carve an adjusted Protection lykill, not that I'd ever changed a symbol—except for Memory; it had to be personalized. If I added a symbol to represent the house and vineyard to the Protection lykill maybe—

All the buzzing mounds exploded into fist-sized bronze…somethings.

Holding my breath, we trailed them as they raced over the ground toward the dormant mess of rosemary, thyme, and lavender at the back of the house.

"This is too close," Liv hissed. "They'll hear us."

Ulla unsheathed her axe like that might somehow help.

Each creature had a sloped back, a smooth surface, and six legs. I'd called up beetles. Bronze, shiny, horrible beetles.

I stopped in my tracks, flicking my thumb rapidly over the lykill on my carver.

Beetles were not good for farms. The ones we had—Greenbiters, we called them—did as their name implied. They bit, ate, chewed everything within reach.

Flipping my carver so the blade touched the earth, where the insects swarmed around its tip, I scored the first two vertical lines of the Protection lykill. Maybe I could shape a vine around the lines in place of the usual starbursts.

My heart raced, and my mind didn't want to work. Somehow the beetles, who now climbed under the sleeping herbs, were more frightening than the skoffin or the eagle. This was home and I was directly ruining it.

As I began the vine shape, a heat soaked through the bottom of my boots and the icy mud turned soft.

I looked up to see the herb garden's ground greening, snow melting at its edges.

Ulla stepped forward. "Starling..."

My hand went to my mouth, and I checked to make sure my parents weren't barreling down on us.

The rosemary's withered stems gave way to new shoots of ashy green. Flowers popped up along fresh lavender sprigs like it was spring. The scent of growing things wafted through the sharp air and tiny emerald leaves sprouted inside the thyme's dead crown.

The beetles weren't only warming the ground, they

were somehow giving the plants what the sun did, but from the ground up.

Impossible. But why did I think that after all I'd seen so far?

The new rosemary snapped neatly under my fingers. I gave Liv a piece to marvel over. She sniffed it and smiled.

"See? I'm not the problem. The Graybook isn't the problem. The ridgrasil was there to warn us about bent seithr like Fellriki, who would only use lykill to submit others. I am meant to do this." Ulla and Liv watched as I began shaping another lykill in the ground. "I can't let the jarl get away with humiliating me. He needs to see the truth. I have just the beast to make that happen."

My friends stepped back.

"Is this the one you tried to carve first at the Presentation?" Liv asked.

Ulla kept her axe at the ready. "You sure this is a good idea?"

"Positive." I finished the snow leopard lykill with a deep scour. Power surged through me, rocking me a little. I took a step to steady myself.

The ground shuddered and a muzzle pushed from the dirt.

An enormous, spotted leopard maneuvered its way into being, its thick tail swishing and its glowing gray eyes on me. Its chest was entirely transparent, showing the guts of the beast and its beating heart.

Ulla, ever the Eagle, grinned and reached out to touch it. "What'll it do?"

The beast snarled and snapped at her hand. She jumped back and raised her axe.

"Somehow, it'll make the jarl see the truth. About everything."

Circling us, the leopard made a noise in its throat. A humming, invisible connection ran between the creature and my carver. I felt like a fisherman with an unwieldy catch on the line.

Atli appeared and yelped, his face going from smug to struck in a breath. "What—"

The leopard sprang at him. Liv screamed.

Atli grabbed a fallen branch and tried to swipe at the beast, but the furred body drove him back and leaped onto his chest with two massive paws.

"Bryn!" Tears tore down Liv's face. "Stop it!"

I smiled at Atli. "What will you give me?" The donkey had earned this and more.

"You're sick," he spat. "Get this thing off me!"

The leopard eyed me, and I moved my carver a fraction forward in the air. The creature set its teeth against Atli's brow.

"Brynja!" Atli had gone gray, and his eyes iced over.

I walked around him. "What do you see, donkey?"

"Starling, please," Liv said.

I whipped around. "Stop whimpering. You are a seithr and a hatchling. We share the same moon. Start acting like it."

"Bryn." Ulla's voice was low with warning.

"Atli, tell me what you see and I'll let you go."

His glassy eyes blinked and moved like he was dreaming. "Everything. Everything I've done." His head twisted toward me though I knew somehow that he couldn't see me. "Everything you've done."

A shiver rode over my chest. "Beast, give him something to remember this truth he sees."

"No, please." Liv was crying and it was pathetic.

"Shut up, Pea Finch. I'm not going to kill him."

Atli wailed. The leopard sank ghostly teeth into his shoulder.

Ulla's hand snaked around me and snatched my carver before I could do a thing.

I spun as the connection between the beast and me snapped. The leopard disappeared. "What are you doing?"

"Just think for a minute. Think about what you're doing."

"It's Atli. He gropes me any chance he gets. Don't tell me you're standing up for him?"

"Definitely not," Ulla said. "But if you send this thing to the meeting house—"

The Finch's fist pressed against her lips as she knelt by a shuddering Atli and drew a Healing lykill over his head. "What if it kills the jarl? Or one of his children?"

"Give me my carver, Eagle."

The horns blared, marking the end of Solitude. It was time for the Announcement, time to learn who would die.

Everyone on the vineyard came out of their Places, ready to head to the meeting house.

Whatever I was going to do would have to wait. I didn't need a repeat of the Presentation chaos. The moment of my revelation had to be perfect. Before I showed off what the beetles had done for our herbs and how I could finally end Fellriki's reign of blood, I needed the hatchlings' full support.

"Please, Ulla. My carver."

"I can't. We need to talk first."

There was no time for me to argue with her. We had to meet the adults at the gate.

"Hide it then," I hissed.

Ulla tossed my carver lightly into the snowy ferns beneath the pines while I pushed snow over the greenery the beetles had produced.

"And Atli," I said, "you better lie."

He nodded mutely beside the five points of blood on his shoulder. Liv moved his cloak to hide the injury.

I WALKED beside Mother and Father, listening to Atli tell a fine story about falling against the side of the press house and into the bracken. Good donkey.

"Remember," Father said quietly to me, "if you do anything to shame us tonight, Fellriki will likely destroy everything we've built."

"But he is angry with me," I said. "Not you. Not Mother. You've been perfect, dutiful seithr."

"Brynja. Watch your tone," Mother said.

Father kept his eyes trained on Ulla, listening to her make excuses as to how she got to the vineyard so quickly after the horns. He whispered, "I want you acting like a proper seithr, too. I don't want to lose you, Daughter. Or our vineyard."

"Oh, I know exactly how to act like a proper seithr."

Mother smiled. "Good. I look forward to seeing that knowledge in action."

I squeezed my tender hands into fists, feeling her simple ring and my bone ring cool against my skin. My maimed left hand couldn't grip like it used to. My heart beat in the ghosts of my fingers. Weak. Weak. Weak.

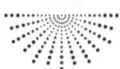

CHAPTER TWENTY-ONE

Outside the meeting house, the sun crept into the mountains, trailing its purple robes. Beyond Snowfallen, the fjord's waters were still as a stone slab. Inside the meeting house, humanity in all its glory reigned.

Inside, the air was a woolen sweater and I coughed, trying to take a full breath. I remained by my parents as Liv and Ulla went to theirs. Beside Benedikt, Rafn eyed me over the rim of his horn cup.

You all right? he mouthed, lowering his wine and glancing at Atli.

I nodded once. Why was he looking at the donkey? Had word spread already? Until I had my carver, I couldn't afford anyone squawking. Rafn locked eyes with me and cocked his head like he was trying to figure me out. There was nothing to ponder on until I got my carver back.

Jakob was doing some squawking, but not about the

leopard. He blabbered on about the warmer weather, the storms, and about how all of it was testament to the angry mountain's imminent explosion. Like he remembered any volcanic eruptions. He wasn't even close to being born the last time one happened.

The Eagle bent toward her mother and said something. Her mother shook her head vigorously and Ulla put a hand on her back.

We sat on benches surrounding the jarl's long table. Two tall slaves handed each of us a cup of last year's ice wine. The pop and snap of the fire and the clang of plates and cups was a little too much and I almost longed for the quiet of my Place again.

The jarl stood, raised his bronze cup, and struck a ringed finger against it twice. Everyone went silent.

"In light of the warning signs coming from the mountain. And the...trouble"—his gaze snapped to me —"we've had of late, our cemetery singers should give us the saga of the only man who lived through the mountain's destruction."

All heads turned toward Benedikt, then Rafn, and back again. Benedikt noticed Rafn behind me and his jaw clenched.

"Of course, Jarl," started Rafn, keeping a humble tone though I could tell he, for once, wasn't in the mood for singing.

Benedikt elbowed him. "My son will be happy to sing it, Jarl. He knows the story well."

Rafn opened his mouth to sing.

Everything else disappeared.

He hitched one foot up on the bench where he sat and

his fingers lay loosely on his knee. Closing his eyes, he wove deep dark notes with occasional high ones like flying birds. Chills flew up and down my arms.

His words soared in and out of our modern language. Those exotic phrases, lilting in his haunting voice, made my toes curl inside my boots. As his throat moved and his song carried through the smoky room, my chest ached and my blood buzzed at the mournful beauty of him and his song.

The saga sang of moving fire, and smoke like shrouds thrown over the land and sea. It spoke of a people much like us. They danced, they loved, and they had their traditions. They had loved the isle like we did now.

I wondered how different the land was before that happened. Had there been more trees? Had the soil been more fertile or less?

Rafn sang of tears, of screaming babies dropped, and families ripped apart in the crush to sail off the isle and into the far off waves untouched by the land's anger.

The saga said only a handful of small boats made it when the mountain erupted. Those aboard those boats watched their people drown, watched their loved ones burn to ash. The final notes of Rafn's song pooled out of his mouth like dark liquid. It was suddenly very, very difficult not to cry.

What a tragedy. I could not fully imagine it. Mother and Father had seen it, though they'd been too young to remember. Fires leaping from the mountain top and eating the Lows' beautiful blue grass and the sloping hills and the pines. The very stones themselves flaming to life like wild red beasts gnawing, devouring our homeplaces, our livestock, and our limbs until it was all nothing but black rock and plumes of smoke.

Rafn closed his song by looking up at me through his black lashes. I shivered. He was such a beautiful thing inside and out, and his saga, the antithesis.

The jarl smiled widely and raised his cup. We echoed the gesture and drank to the dead.

A slave walked in through the front doors, his skin a little paler than normal above his brown longshirt. He handed a small roll of parchment to the jarl.

My heart spasmed, reached out, waited.

The Announcement.

The flesh on the faces of everyone in Snowfallen alternated between a flickering orange—from the fire— and the darkness of shadow. I knew almost every face as well as my own. Snowfallen was no southern port city or king's retreat. Nearly everyone here had a hand in my upbringing. A jug of goat's milk traded to Mother when she was too sick to nurse me one winter. Grandfather had told me that story. My first pair of boots formed with skilled hands by the jarl's own personal slave. That mouth had praised my first win on the sparring field. The one next to her taught me a curse that didn't work, but had made us hatchlings laugh for days. Snowfallen was home, and they were each a part of it in deed, word, appearance, or intent. And every year Snowfallen was less because we were less one of these people. Hatred for Fellriki gnashed inside me.

The jarl set his cup down and put a hand on his wife's bony shoulder. She gave him a grim smile of support as he blinked and cleared his throat.

"I am so proud of our stead. Our sacrifices always go willingly under the blade. I'm certain the man or woman chosen this year will be selected for their purity, or perhaps their strength, their presence of mind."

The jarl's wife took her son Jakob's hand. Tears welled in her eyes, but oddly she didn't seem sad. She raised her chin and gave him a smile.

"The mountain grows foul again and we have heard its tale." The jarl's cool gaze found me. "We cannot make the mistake of listening to those who would disrespect the wisest, most faithful choice." A few eyes strayed to look at me, but most kept their focus on the jarl. *This is bigger than one seithr's pathetic rebellion,* I thought callously. "We must give up this individual and celebrate this one with the same awe and pride."

The jarl's chest rose and fell slowly.

I dug my fingers into the table's rough grain.

Across the spread, Rafn pinched his lips and stared at a spot in front of him.

"The chosen sacrifice, the one who will give their heart's blood to save the rest of us, is an honored member of Snowfallen. A respected member."

His throat moved in a swallow.

"Rakel Seithrsdottir."

Black waves crashed along the sides of my eyes.

I turned toward my mother.

"No," I whispered.

Mother stared at the jarl, her lips slightly parted and her chest rising and falling under her simple woolen dress. The amber and blue glass beads at her neck moved with each breath.

The room zoomed away from me and everyone seemed small, tiny, like I'd had some bad herbs or those mushrooms Atli is always talking about.

The jarl moved toward us. A wolf to its prey. Of course he was smiling. Fellriki hadn't chosen his son Jakob.

Mother's hands, flat on the table, shook. Like they weren't her own, she looked at them and Father took one, held it. The skin around her knuckles was heavy and showed her age, the hard cleaning, digging, cutting, and pressing she'd done all her life. They were veiny and splotchy and were so, so beautiful to me.

He could not take them from me.

The jarl was behind her then. He glanced at Father and drew his eyebrows together in sympathy.

I touched Mother's arm. The fire popped and a child laughed, not knowing it was a moment for silence.

The jarl cleared his throat. "Please, honored sacrifice, allow me to escort you to the meditation house."

Mother stood, leaving Father's hand alone. Not looking at me. Her eyes blank.

She'd never go home again.

No one returned home after going into that dark wood building. The place smelled like the sage smoke sticks the doomed lit to wash themselves of any discordant thoughts before the blood sacrifice.

Father seemed made of stone. He didn't blink. Didn't breathe. Didn't argue or fight or do anything worth doing.

That was not going to be me.

I pushed away from the table. My fingers brushed the

place where Mother's hands had been. The wood grain held a breath of her warmth.

Pointing a finger at the jarl, I whispered, "You are not going to do this. I saw your face. Just now. When you looked at Father." My words were low, a growl, perfect for this wolf who worked for a demon. "You showed sympathy in your face. You know this is wrong. Where is your courage to stand up to this false god?"

The jarl's eyes went red and glassy. "Where is your courage, child?"

"Sit, Daughter." Father said it like he was asking for butter at a meal.

"You sicken me. All of you." I threw a hand out at everyone in Snowfallen. "Especially my fellow seithr. Why do you settle for a quiet life on a farm when you could be as strong as that disgusting Fellriki?"

The jarl's hand cracked across my jaw and hot blood poured from my lip. He raised his hand to strike again, but Mother grabbed it, stilled it.

Leaving the jarl's side and Father's, she ran her capable fingers down my temple, my cheek. She kissed my forehead. There were no tears in my eyes. Only fury, burning, burning, burning.

"I am glad to give my life for you and your father. So you may live on, happy and safe and productive."

"Mother. You are smart. You are wise. Don't let him take you like he took your father."

She drew back like I'd hit her, though I was the one with the bloody lip.

Several in the room hissed like snakes.

"Careful," someone whispered.

"Watch," another said, gaze drawn to the roof like Fellriki was about to descend on us.

I supposed that person was right. He was descending at this very second. His will, the control he had over Snowfallen was here in this room as much as I was. His will breathed here, foul and hot and choking.

Stunned at last to stillness, I watched Mother let the jarl lead her, a heavily ringed hand at her back and pressing into the even seam at the waist of her dress. That alone should've sparked Father to movement.

I spun and faced him as Ulla and Liv found my side, raising their chins defiantly.

"Aren't you going to do anything, Father?" Tears tried to blur my vision of Father's face and the fires in the bronze bowls hanging from the ceiling. I willed the drops of salt water back inside my traitor eyes.

"I am doing something," he said. "I'm doing everything. I'm giving up my heart for our home."

There wasn't enough air in the room to breathe. I clutched at my chest and whirled as everyone made a line to follow the jarl and Mother outside to the meditation house.

"Brynja." Ulla was at my side, pulling at me. "What do you want us to do?"

Liv got behind me and whispered over my shoulder. "Can you use the new runes? What can we do?"

"Without my carver, I'm worthless," I said. "You know that."

Even Rafn made his way to me, his face grayed. He didn't say a word, but he walked beside me, stately and serene. I hated it. I loved it.

~

THE MEDITATION HOUSE'S roof spiked into the night sky like a fang turned on its end.

Dizziness swamped me, and I felt Rafn's strong hand on my arm. His incense scent wafted over me like a blessing.

Liv was crying silently and I wished she'd stop. Ulla glanced at me. Her mouth was colorless and sad, but her eyes burned.

Mother and Father had taught me well about how hardships were necessary in life. Trials and pain gave us an opportunity to show that we loved one another and to demonstrate courage. "A perfect life," Mother always said, "would be a limp thing without relief, smiles, soul-lifting surprise. Because how can you know joy if you never know pain?"

She was right. But this, this was too much. I was fine with the presence of sickness. War was inescapable in creatures who had the quick, cutting minds of humans and seithr. But Fellriki's bullying was not the healthy pain of life. It was a corruption.

The jarl removed Mother's bluehare cloak. His wife took it with gentle hands and gave it to my father with his stone face. My feet wanted to go to my father and stand next to him, but my heart wouldn't let me.

He should've been fighting this.

Mother shivered as the jarl lifted her dress from her body, leaving her in only a linen shift as the winter wind tossed strands of hair around her head. She removed her boots and woolen breeches and socks. The jarl pulled the smooth, wood stick from her hair and her silver tresses spread over her shoulders like a waterfall.

I pressed a hand to Rafn's, met Liv and Ulla's eyes briefly, and ran to my father.

"Don't let them do this," I hissed.

The jarl opened the meditation house's door and followed her inside. The door shut with a solid thud.

I knew very well what was happening in there with my mother and the jarl. He was taking a bit more of her blood, weakening her. Death circled like a vulture.

The heavy door creaked open and the jarl held up a metal bowl.

"*Blood to start the road,*" he sang.

"*Rubies of the body to pave it,*" everyone but me sang back. "*A path to blue sky and sun, to crops high as roofs, and days of peace and power.*"

Surrounded by the leaves, fish, and clouds carved into the meditation house's walls and frames, Mother's face appeared at the window. Snowfallen sang the songs over and over.

Ulla and Liv found my side, touched my arm, my back. A numbness spread over my senses like I was underwater.

The color had fled Mother's cheeks, leaving only the moon-white circle of her forehead, cheeks, and chin. She lifted a hand and splayed her fingers against the window's frame. Her dark gaze met mine. The numbness thrashed its way out of me, leaving raw pain. A sob tied a rope around my ribs and tugged hard.

Behind the gathered crowd, though a break in the

bodies gathered, Rafn threw something toward me. "Starling!"

I caught my carver and magic thrummed through my bones.

"Stop her!" someone shouted, but their words were drowned by the singing.

Ulla clapped a hand on my shoulder. "Now or never."

I gave her a quick nod, pride rising in me like a wave, and pierced the ground with my carver. The Winter Seer's lykill took shape. The ground shook. Everyone turned away from the meditation house to see what I was doing. I could almost feel the fear in my friends, but I kept my eyes on my work.

When I drew the last sweeping line of the rune, the snow and mud flattened itself, drawing away from the shape, extending it without any more work from me. The ground under the lykill drummed like thunder.

Rafn came up beside us, breathing heavy, eyes bright.

People gasped as the areas of flattened mud sunk with a heaving sigh. Father ran at me, shouting. Rafn pulled me away from the churning, dropping ground while Ulla and Liv fell back and away from the growing crater.

The dark earth that had been falling mounded. The churning dirt rose high above our heads, blocking out Father and the rest of Snowfallen.

Antlers wide as a sled reached through the soil, followed by a broad head and four legs. The creature's white fur sparkled with blindingly bright green and blue lykill.

A chill like the breath of Winter himself coursed over me, tightening my lungs.

Frost glittered from the great hreinin's body and head as if he'd come from the highest peaks. He stomped the ground. Earth fell away from him and raised the scent of sleeping roots and the eerie perfume of magic. An eardrum shaking bellow poured from his mouth as he tossed his head like he fought invisible reins.

I raised my carver, and my mother screamed from inside the meditation house like I'd killed someone right before her eyes.

The stag knelt at my feet. Though my blood shivered, I rounded his shoulder and climbed onto the animal's back.

The hreinin reared. My body shifted, my carver hitting one of his antlers.

I was slipping off.

Heart tripping, I grasped thick fur and held on, the animal's warm muscles moving under me.

Ulla and Liv wedged themselves between the people and us, shouting and pulling at their fur coats.

Rafn blasted from the group, and my heart reared along with the hreinin. He held a rope he'd looped it into a makeshift lead. The stag huffed forcefully as Rafn worked it over the animal's muzzle quickly. He hurled himself on behind me.

"Go!" I shouted.

Ulla and Liv struggled with Father and the jarl as the stag took off.

I looked back at my parents, my voice reaching, straining. "I will not let him do this to us!"

CHAPTER TWENTY-TWO

The hreinin drove fast and straight toward Grimsjökull, the icy pass that led to the highest elevations on Snowfallen. Leaping over the jarl's wattle fences, riding atop the hreinin was like flying. Wind ran fingers through my hair, tossing it at my cheeks. We could go anywhere, faster than anyone. No one could stop us. This was freedom, joy, and power all rolled up into one. And Rafn's warm strength sat right behind me. A fierce grin tore at my lips.

I would stop Fellriki.

But at what cost? my mind whispered. I soundly ignored the weaker side of me, the human side.

The stag's hooves beat the earth as he zigzagged through the first section of Grimsjökull. The towering rock on either side missed knocking me out by a breath.

Worry for Ulla and Liv itched at me. I turned and tried to lean, to see behind us.

"It's not as if what we're headed into is any better

than what they're up against," Rafn said over the wind in my ears.

I faced forward again and bent low over the hreinin's long, wide neck, breathing in his chill, his icy strength. A cracking sounded from overhead. A plate of black rock shifted from the cliff side and plummeted in rickety circles.

As the stag dodged the slam of the rock onto the ground and shifted to jump, I held my breath. Rafn shouted as we soared over the debris, seemingly suspended in mid-air with my carver to the side of us, humming and glowing in several places.

I leaned toward the hreinin's head. "Do you know what I need to find?"

He didn't use words, but images like memories came into my head that made his meaning clear. First, he showed me water, nuts and rounds of cheese, the shelter of trees—need. Then, I saw fine, smoking meat, warm fires, and pelts of bluehare that were perfect for new coats—want. *Need or want?* he seemed to ask.

"Need," I snapped as we galloped onward. The lykill on my carver glowed bright. "And you never answered my question."

"Brynja." Rafn's eyes were wide over my shoulder. "Show some respect."

I sighed. "Please, Winter Seer, do you know I'm searching for Fellriki's homeplace? The place only you can find."

He showed me an image of a tall man in a hood and dark corners. The man's face was hidden, but I knew who it was.

"And you are taking us there?"

The Winter Seer swung his head roughly from side to side, and I took that as a *yes*.

Our winding route widened slightly, and the white velvet of undisturbed snow reached from the stag's hooves to the next tight pass-through.

"That's not snow," I said quietly.

"No. It's not." Rafn let out a breath in a hiss.

I started to ask the hreinin if he thought crossing this patch of what had to be deep water iced over and blanketed in snow was a good idea or if he actually had a brain and thought we should go around, but he stepped one hoof forward before I could spew my doubts.

The animal's weight shifted onto that one hoof. I held my breath. Rafn's hand spanned my stomach and froze there. I strained to hear any snapping or deep echoes under us. Nothing.

Another step.

Sweat beaded on my chin and forehead. "Maybe we should dismount and walk. Spread out the weight."

"Good plan."

But the stag moved three more steps.

"I'd love a nice image of us on the other side of this, Winter Seer," I whispered.

Rafn's hand tensed over my ribs. "What are you talking about?"

"The stag. He showed me food and shelter as need. And bluehare as want. He showed me Fellriki. It's how I knew he knew where I wanted to go. Needed to go, I mean."

"And he isn't showing you anything at the moment?"

"No."

"Great," he said.

"Not really."

"I was being sarcastic, Bryn. It's your birth language. You should know."

"Shut up, Rafn."

"Done."

And then a sound like a plucked langspil string echoed across the white expanse. It was a twanging I was all too familiar with.

Rafn and I traded a look. The ping and knock grew louder, deeper.

"Move!" we shouted as one.

The hreinin was fast, but the ice was faster.

Veins of blue and black folded across the surface of white. The space beneath us dropped away.

Water, cold as fire is hot, rose in three sheets and seared my skin under my clothing. With every lunge of the stag's mighty weight, another wedge of ice floundered, broke. We galloped on glorified icebergs, dipping, sliding, the water's burning splashes promising a quick death.

A chunk of ice soared up, rising like a growing wall, and the water swallowed the hreinin's back legs whole.

My heart exploded against my ribs.

The stag scraped and dug and leaped from the chunk of ice to the cracking expanse beyond it.

Rafn's one hand latched around my middle and his other waved pointlessly in the air. My shrieking lacked a purpose too because no one lived out this far, not this near Grimsjökull. If we slipped beneath the cracked ice and into the black water, we were gone. Frozen corpses for the scavengers, if their teeth could manage the job.

My fingers ached as I gripped the Winter Seer's pelt and flattened myself against its back, Rafn covering me, heavy and gasping.

A snow drift marked the end of the ice. But we weren't going to make it.

"Go!" Rafn shouted near my ear.

I was made of ice and wet, a frantic pulse, and gritted teeth. My carver glowed against the hreinin's white, white fur and I wondered if that was the last thing I would see, the green runes flickering off the wet-wicking spikes of fur.

The stag bellowed as it bunched its muscles.

Rafn's grip tightened. "Hold on, Starling!"

We left the ice and soared as the stag leaped toward the drift and the end of Grimsjökull. The black walls of the pass seemed to lean in threateningly as the jump's arc reached its summit, then before I could take a breath, we were on solid earth, tumbling to the snowy ground in a pile of woman, man, and hreinin.

Snow crusted my chin, and the water had soaked me so badly that I feared my skin would ice over, then crack open.

"What are you smiling at?" I asked Rafn, as he dusted snowflakes from his hair and offered me a hand up.

"We're alive, aren't we?" He grinned again.

"Until we freeze to death."

"You have to admit that was fun."

"I have to do no such thing." But it did make me

wonder if the old Raven was coming back to me at last. The daring one, the smiling one.

The Winter Seer found his feet—hooves—and gave me a nod.

"A nod?" I stalked toward him. "You almost drown us, then you nod like our very lives are just a nice little surprise, a cute gift for your royal mythicalness? You nearly killed us, taking the Grimsjökull!"

The stag stared me down. I glared right back.

I sighed and raised my carver. With movements as large and dramatic as I could manage considering my arms were limb-shaped icicles, I drew the Warming lykill in the air. Where the magic would find heat to give us, I had no idea.

As I pretty much suspected, the rune didn't work.

The hreinin blinked at me, and an image of my carver's bladed end flashed through my mind. I lifted it.

"What's going on?" Rafn took a step closer.

"I'm not sure."

The stag nuzzled his own shoulder and jerked his muzzle at my carver.

"I think...he wants me to cut him."

"What? Why?"

Our words quaked and clipped off at odd moments because we were shivering to death.

"I don't know. But let's try it. He deserves a slice for getting us into this anyway."

I saw myself in my mind, drawing the lykill for the hreinin in the ground. The stag was telling me it was my idea to raise him in the first place.

"Fine. I have a hand in it, too, Seer," I mumbled.

"It's for the magic, isn't it?" Rafn said quietly.

I paused, my blade tipped toward the stag's flesh. "I think so."

He didn't say anything else, but I knew what was going through his head. If this worked, it meant blood did move magic. It meant Fellriki might actually use the blood sacrifice we give him for magic.

I refused to believe it. After all, it hadn't worked for me in the vineyard. "It's only because the Graybook's lykill work on submission, on humility. He is being submissive, giving up his blood. It feeds the master's magic. My magic. It's not the same as what Fellriki does."

"It's awfully close," Rafn said.

"No, it's not. Fellriki demands heartblood, death. This is just a show of humility from the Seer. It isn't the actual blood giving me power. It's the energy coming off his being during the submission."

"Ah."

"Yes, *ah.*"

I slid the sharp edge along the beast's body, deep enough to draw blood, but not damage muscle or important tissue. Red unfurled from the cut like a flag. I pulled my carver through the tiny flow, cloaking the magical weapon in the sticky fluid.

My chest tightened, and power drew nails lightly down my arms and spine. I made the shape of the Warming lykill again in the air, urging the magic toward each of us in turn. Water and ice steamed from our skin, hair, and clothing and a heady heat traveled from my heart and beat through my body.

The stag shook its head and Rafn let out a slow breath. Then he gave me a look.

"It doesn't mean much," I said. "I only took a menial amount of blood. I certainly didn't murder him." I pointed at the hreinin. "Fellriki takes lives, not just a little blood. He claims far more than he would ever need for any kind of magic."

Rafn nodded, then went to one knee before the stag. "May I?" he asked the beast.

The Winter Seer bent low, and we climbed onto his broad back. The creature's cut was already healing, but blackened blood stained the injured spot. As we sped off toward Snowfallen's highest elevations, I wondered if I'd have to bleed anyone again to accomplish my goal. I didn't want to. But I knew I would do that and more to take Fellriki down.

My mind beat a question through me as we galloped. *How much? How much? How much?*

CHAPTER TWENTY-THREE

Color slowly filled one strip of the winter landscape. Sickly green sand and eye-jarring orange rock painted the peaks. Steam twisted from cracks like ghosts, hissing and spitting water hot enough to cook with. Away from the mist and geysers, hard snow lined the ground and hid fist-sized rocks. The place smelled like foul magic, full of sulfur and forgotten, damp places. The only vegetation besides rough moss and stunted grass were the small trees as hunched as old women.

The day started its descent as the stag slowed. A towering passageway of gray-green rock walled us in on either side. The hreinin's hooves clicked and snapped against the icy ground, his feet sure. No fatigue bothered him. I, on the other hand, was about to fall right off onto the ground for a long nap.

"You all right?" Rafn put a hand on my leg, helping me

keep my seat. "You can lean back on me and rest. I'll wake you if we stop."

I didn't want to, but I did as he suggested, a yawn stuttering my words. "Aren't you tired?"

"As the oldest man in the world. But I'll make it."

I smiled, and before I could say anything clever, I was asleep.

I WOKE TO QUIET SINGING. Rafn's chest vibrated with song, and I listened, pretending to be asleep still. The words were so very, very quiet, I strained to untangle them from the deep notes drumming from his throat.

"Silvered hair, the moon's last wish
Eyes, tongue sharp as winter's fist
What dwells inside
Pulls me to bide
I wait, uncurling
Painted in her light."

Was the song about me? It had to be. Maybe *the moon's last wish* meant I was the last of the hatchlings born under Din's Feather. Sharp tongue. Yes, that was me. But there were other seithr girls born with stripes of silver seithr in their hair. Most weren't as completely silver as mine, but there were a few.

I was afraid to move, worried he would stop humming like he was now. The song echoed though his body and into mine and every bit of him pressed against me, so warm, so strong. I shuddered a little and looked up at Din's lights now shimmering pink, green, and white in the night sky.

The tight path opened into a small clearing blanketed in pure, white snow. A rock cave yawned ahead, and wind moaned lightly from its depths along with the scents of woodsmoke and something else…

"Blood," I whispered.

Rafn swallowed as we slid off the stag's back. Facing the Seer, he went to one knee again. He didn't say anything, just stayed there, head bent, submissive.

"I don't think he expects us to do that," I said.

The hreinin lifted one hoof and set his long muzzle against Rafn's tangle of black hair. The animal stepped back and Rafn's head jerked up, his mouth dropping open.

"What is it? Did he…tell you something?"

"A warning. He said, well, it was images, memories, but I think he meant, *Remember Yourself.*" Rafn scrambled to his feet.

The hreinin twisted and sprang with amazing lightness into the darkness, the white of his eyes showing as he glanced back.

A scratching sound turned the hairs on the back of my neck into tiny icicles. Din's lights and the crowd of stars overhead glistened off the ice and the small, gnarled trees that grew in this high altitude.

One spot in the snowy wood remained unlit, dark, unknowable.

Rafn stood closer to me. "What is that?" I glanced at him and watched his throat move in a slow swallow. The wind stirred the gray rabbit fur at his cloak's collar.

The black space shifted and came closer. "No idea. But I can't say I like it."

A note, maybe three, danced through the draft of wind that came through the tiny pass and out of the cave. A sigh echoed the piece of song.

Rafn took a step toward the dark shape. "It's indescribable."

"Oh I can describe it. Creepy nothing."

"That's a start."

The darkness lightened, growing lines and curves, blinking eyes, and water? No. Hair. Long, long hair.

It was a woman.

Her thick hair cloaked her body as the wind dragged through the trees and around us. A gust curled the silver, blue, and black strands around the place her feet should have been and stirred the locks lying across her cheek and mouth. Pale, pale eyes stared out at us.

I rubbed my own eyes, trying to see.

The air was too light. Even at this elevation. My lungs couldn't quite take a good breath, but I didn't care. My head and hands floated and I could only watch curiously as Rafn reached a hand toward the woman, his feet moving slowly like he was almost asleep.

The odd music repeated itself. The same three notes and the same sighing. Or was that only the wind?

The woman circled Rafn, whose eyes were glazed with lust.

A fire sparked in me, and I wanted nothing more than to throttle the singing lady. She came closer, turned a tighter ring around him, her hair catching on his clothing and hands. It partially covered his smile, then tangled over the lip that he bit shyly.

Something uncurled in my gut. I was ready to fight or bed, to do something wild and raw.

She spun faster and faster until it was as if Rafn was enveloped in a waterspout of silver and icy blue.

A black space showed for a moment on each turn. I stepped closer. The dark spot was on her back.

Rafn laughed. He sounded drunk. Not that Rafn had ever, ever been drunk.

What was hiding beneath that hair of hers?

During the next spin, the space pulled at Rafn, blurring the lines of his fingers and arm, his nose and chin. Gooseflesh poured over me, pleasure dulling my worry. I was supposed to be afraid of this, and maybe angry, but I couldn't keep a thought long enough to act on it. They slipped through my mind like quick minnows through slow fingers. The song felt good and she was lovely, more beautiful than anything in the world.

The woman met my gaze, and I heard words clear as I heard my own heartbeat.

You are next, my sweet.

Darkness welcomed me with heavy arms and one thousand fingers. I couldn't open my eyes. No sound touched my ears. I didn't think I was moving, or could move. I was a lump of nothing in the black. The only real feeling was the cold. If I had a mouth, I could laugh—an unfunny laugh—at how I'd thought Grimsjökull's icy water was cold. This dark caress held a chill that should've earned cold a new name. A freeze so consuming that I had no room for anything else.

Then another sensation flickered through me. Fear. But not for me. For someone else.

I sucked a breath.

Rafn.

I breathed again, remembering him and myself.

I had a mouth. My lips moved.

Where was he? In the black with me? I didn't want him to be here. This wasn't his kind of dark, the dark of old tales, quiet respect, of wisdom from the long dead. This wasn't good enough for him.

Where did he go?

His face came to mind, sharp chin, searching eyes, and smooth forehead crowned with an inky shock of braided and tangled hair. With the image planted in my head, my senses roared to life.

Pain like red thorns. A bright point under every one of the darkness's fingers. I tried to scream, but I couldn't move. I lay on the snowy ground and cried my pain to the night sky, my eyes and my heart the only moving bits of me.

The woman's voice echoed.

Oh. Did you wish to see, sweet?

I did and I did not.

I blinked tears away. My body lifted into the air, sucking a gasp from me. A rock the size of a room glowed silver and blue beside the cave's entrance. Inside the stone's opaque surface, two dark figures moved. One, quick and willowy. The other was Rafn.

My insides clenched.

He'd been stripped of his cloak and longshirt and he hung, suspended much like I was, his arms useless at his sides. The woman-creature, all flowing hair and eyes like ice, spread fingers over his bare chest and his muscles tensed beneath. She smoothed the contours of his stomach, and with her other hand, loosened his woolen breeches. Her fingers danced at his waistline, then dipped low, away from his navel. He winced, then groaned. Pain and pleasure both showed in his tightly closed eyes and his parting lips.

A new breed of hate for Fellriki ripped into my heart. This was his doing, this foul creature. He'd set her here as a deterrent, a lure filled with foul magic.

The woman-creature swarmed over Rafn's shoulder and twisted around him again until she stopped to press her lips against his. The tip of her tongue dragged across his lower lip, and her breasts, mostly hidden by her long lengths of silvery blue and black hair, drew up to his chest. Rafn shuddered, and his fingers flexed. He tried to move, his head and shoulders jerking forward a fraction, but he was as immobile as I was.

The voice pricked at me.

That's enough for you, sweet.

Black swallowed me. The cold tore over my skin and ravaged my bones, cracking me, breaking me. But the numbness never came. My mind and heart were painfully aware. I was forced to stillness while everything in me raged to know if she continued tormenting Rafn or if she would do more than kiss, touch, and tease. A silent scream railed inside me. I was no help to him. I was a prisoner. And all I could do was lay there imagining the worst happening to Rafn and waiting for my own coming torture.

I couldn't reach my carver, though I'd seen it against an exposed rock below my feet as I'd floated. The only thing I could move was my eyes. I wasn't even sure about that. It felt as though I could move them, but looking left or right was no different. All was void. I imagined the blinking shimmer of a rune, the light of magic. Maybe if I moved my eyes as I would move my carver or a hand, I could form a working lykill. I'd never heard of such a thing, but it was the sole idea in my little brain.

But what symbol?

The Protection lykill wouldn't do any good. Too little and very much too late. What Graybook shapes might help? A flash of tingling heat washed over my bone ring, but no fantastic revelations sprang to mind. I really couldn't remember any of them. I wanted to crumble. All I could remember was the simple magic of home.

Wait.

Remember.

The hreinin had told Rafn: *Remember Yourself.*

Blood pounding behind my eyes, I looked left and up, starting the shape of the Memory lykill. It was a lesser known symbol, but Father had taught me so I'd always recall the proper timing for planting and culling, the exact sound of him crushing a grape perfectly frozen and ready to become ice wine.

My eyes strained to follow my commands of sweep down, loop, diagonal slash. In my head, the Memory lykill was now complete and I imagined it shimmering like ice in the sun.

It was a vague magic. When done correctly, it brought forth a general flow of thought that extended what the subject pondered at that exact moment.

I focused on Rafn, me, Ulla, and Liv, though I had no clue how this might break us free.

And then I was plunged into a world of silvery blue shadows.

Her voice was everywhere.

Sweet. Sweet, feel. Just feel.

The laughing, the off-kilter song. She faced me, two eyes chilling my cheek, then my collarbone, my breasts. The fabric of my dress bore a tear from neckline to stomach, and every place she looked turned to ice. The sounds, the notes, the voice rushed like an engorged river, then came into one. She spoke from behind her swirling hair, but in a language I didn't understand. She ran a fingertip over me and I sighed in spite of my fear. Her lips tasted mine and the hint of sugar and fire crossed my tongue. The creature pressed her body against mine and I jerked in shock at the intimacy, but it was wonderful, intoxicating, like the best of mead, honey and heady.

Remember Yourself.

The Memory lykill I'd drawn in my head, with my eyes, blazed though my hazy thoughts. I saw Rafn in my mind's eye. His quill moved as he wrote a song in the Deadbook, his left forefinger extended, a quirk of his. Ulla and Liv laughed in my mind, both wearing that enormous bowl from the lair on their heads. Rafn's song, the one about the girl with hair like mine ran through my brain like clean water. In my memory, his warm, muscular body, the delicious press of strong, wise, infuriating, kind, brave Rafn pushed lightly against my back.

That was real. That was beautiful and filled me with true longing. I wanted to throw him on the earth and taste his mouth and tease his chest with mine.

I wanted reality.

I opened my eyes wide and pushed back at the feeling of cold pleasure, at the sensation that was so similar to taking too many medicinal herbs or a cup of too-strong wine.

This is not what I desire, I said with my thoughts, hoping she'd hear me somehow and it would matter. I stared into her glacier pupils. *I remember myself and Brynja Seithrsdottir does not find joy in this.*

A force knocked me back.

I landed hard on the ground, my breath leaving in a gust. No woman, no shadows or tempting hands surrounded me.

I sat up. She was gone.

And there was no sign of Rafn.

CHAPTER TWENTY-FOUR

The clearing was empty. Only snow, ice, rocks, and the cave. I grabbed for my carver, my hands sweating and my hair sticking to the back of my neck. A stone, hip-high and partially covered in blue moss, huddled under a stand of pines. It was oddly translucent and had a dark center. Had the stone been there before? I'd never seen moss that color.

The ground crunched as I walked toward the strange stone, then reached out a hand. The surface, partly the cold of rock and partly the uneven softness of growth, vibrated like a rapped drum.

"Rafn?"

A noise like a moan or a shout from miles away eked through the air. My stomach lurched.

Rafn was there.

Inside the stone.

His mouth twisted. His eyebrows drew together in pain. I grabbed at the stone, trying not to be sick and gulping great heaps of foul air. Everything smelled of sulfur. Coughing, I straightened and shook my head to clear it.

My mind whirred. He was still there, alive.

Another groan whispered from the rock. A crack echoed from inside.

The smell of blood blew from the cave.

Fellriki was nearby.

Taking up my carver, I scratched the Memory rune into the stone. The lines were like wisps of smoke, whose ends seemed to curl even as I finished etching them into the rock. My muscles burned with the effort, my knuckles white on the carver. Images floated around me as I completed the symbol's pluming strokes and the lines like reaching fingers and beating hearts.

I saw Mother smiling down at me as she lit the candle strapped to my head during the first ice wine harvest I could recall. Then Ulla and Liv appeared, missing teeth. Liv spun like a dolphin in the summer waters of the fjord. In a long ago forest, Ulla punched her in the arm and giggled as they played at fighting.

My heart clenched. They would be suffering now. A branding or fingers lost like me. What would the jarl choose? Or would their parents shelter them? I gritted my teeth. Most likely not. It wasn't considered a mercy to shelter wrongdoing. It only encouraged more of the same activity, the jarl always said, my father an echo to the sentiment.

But these memories of Ulla and Liv I was having, they weren't Rafn's. These were mine. I needed to focus the magic toward Rafn, away from me.

Sound trickled from the cave. Footsteps?

How could I adjust the lykill so it called up Rafn's memories and brought them forward in his mind?

My hands seemed to work without my direction as I lifted my carver and drew a swooping line diagonally across the Memory lykill. With three upward strokes along the line, it looked like a bird's wing. I extended the last mark up, down, and up again, thinking of Deadsongs and their lilting melodies.

The pale, colored moss that surrounded the rune shivered. It rolled like a wave. A gasp, in a woman's voice, issued from the air around me. Then, silence.

I threw my carver down and went to my knees. "Rafn," I whispered, my heart burning. "Please, remember yourself. I'm here. I'm here for you. I'm not leaving."

The rock cracked. Fissures in the stone rippled, and the surface clouded. I reached out a hand, holding my breath.

And then, suddenly, it was Rafn crouched and shivering on the ground.

I launched myself forward and wrapped my arms around him. Despite his magically restored cloak, he was too cold.

He pulled back a little and his eyes opened, the color of fog and tombstones and dark blue grasses. "You saved me," he said.

"Are you all right? Can you stand?"

A tear shone at the edge of one of his eyes and I hated Fellriki so much, so much, so much.

Standing, he took a breath. "I'm fine. She didn't...do more than...we didn't..."

I put a hand on his chest. "You don't have to talk about it."

His gaze snapped to my face. "Starling, I'm sorry."

"For what?" I slapped my hands against him. "Don't be stupid. None of this is your fault. It's that bastard Fellriki. And we are going to destroy him for this." If he doesn't kill us for trying.

He nodded and ran a hand over the back of my head. "It's not your fault either. How did you send me those memories? Because I know that was you."

I smiled. "I carved a Memory lykill into a stone. You were trapped in a stone."

His fingers gnawed at his hair and the shaved sides of his scalp. "It was like she was the most perfect woman and I wanted her very badly."

My stomach twisted, and I realized at last what that creature was. "A huldra."

"Yes. I think so. I couldn't resist her."

"It's a dark magic."

I wanted to ask if he'd seen me with the huldra too. Had he been as jealous as I had been when I watched her touch him? But the biggest part of me didn't want to talk about it anymore.

"No one has seen a huldra in...I don't know how long," he said.

I jerked my chin at the cave. "It's him. He put her here."

Rafn roughed up his hair and paced. "I just want to get out of here. Everything went so cold and I thought you'd leave and I'd be caught forever."

I shivered. "You thought I'd leave you?"

He shrugged. "You're so driven…"

"Even if I wasn't growing particularly fond of your presence, which I am, I can't go in there alone. That would be seriously stupid. I wish I had Ulla and Liv too. Gods, I wish I had an army. This isn't going to be easy."

"Particularly fond?"

"Maybe."

The corner of his mouth moved in an almost smile and my body warmed in all the right places.

I nodded and took the lead. "Come on. Before you lose that wisdom I like so much."

"So you're saying it wouldn't be wise to wash away that evil thing's kiss with one from you?"

A hint of color tinged his cheeks. My pulse decided to beat like a drum and I couldn't think of anything except his tall form just a breath from my body, the shape of his shoulders, the look in his eye.

The haunting scent of incense rolled over me as he drew me in with one hand and set his mouth on mine.

Our hands were everywhere. Pulling at collars, brushing over bone and muscle. My blood pulsed at my neck and inside my hips. Our fingers tangled together and I kissed him hard.

A bright drumming of thunder broke us apart, both of us breathing heavy.

Fellriki stood at the mouth of the cave with his carver raised.

My joy shattered, and I grabbed Rafn's sleeve for support. The cloaked seithr clicked his tongue and shook his head. He waved a hand at Rafn.

"Collect yourself, boy. You are not permitted to enjoy such dalliances on my doorstep."

Swallowing, Rafn pulled his longshirt straight. I bent, grabbed his belt and knife, and threw it to him.

I edged one foot toward my carver. Fellriki held up a finger and smiled. I wished he was ugly. It was wrong for someone so evil to hold such beauty.

"You won't need that, farmer," he said.

White heat poured over my head and shoulders. "I'm not just a farmer."

"Oh, but I believe you are. Do you not tend vines and use your kitchen magic to keep little foxes at bay?"

I spat on the ground. "You're a monster."

"A monster you need."

I snatched my carver and raised it, bringing a Graybook lykill to mind. There was a beast, something with fur and claws, raging through my mind and making my bone ring hum.

"I'm not truly here, little farmer." He waved a hand, and his finger appeared to be made of tiny flames and smoke. "I'm only an illusion. And you will not find me. Not with your life and his still shining." He turned his back to us like I was no threat at all. "Now go. Save yourself the trouble."

The gathered rolls of his cloak hissed into smoke that moved up, up, up, until all that was left of him was a dissipating column of black.

I ran toward the cave with Rafn at my heels. The faint light from the winter night's lights and the stars showed a wall immediately inside the cave that I hadn't at first noticed. "I wonder what other surprises Fellriki has for us." Bitterness ate at my words.

"I hate surprises," Rafn said.

The cave's inner wall only led to another and another. What little light we had from the outside died further with each step. Only the glowing runes on my carver helped us keep our feet.

"One of the Graybook's lykill flashed into my head while Fellriki was showing off," I said. "It was something to do with a furred beast with claws."

"Like a mountain cat."

"Not really. Bigger. Meaner. Well, maybe not meaner, but more capable of inflicting bodily damage."

"I like how you say that." Rafn stepped aside as I squeezed through a tight pass. "As if you're considering the fate of men, of seithr, like they're little ants under a child's angry heel."

"I value ants above Fellriki. I'm only telling it like it is."

"How did you steer that Memory lykill at me? I wasn't within your reach, your eyesight. That's what you need to work, right?"

I nodded. "I changed the lykill."

He tilted his head and studied me with ashen eyes.

"I gave the lykill a Raven's wing." My gaze went to his inking and he touched it briefly. "And lines that were like a Deadsong."

A smile spread over his mouth.

"I don't understand all of it."

"I know. That's all right."

The corridor of smoothed stone opened up, four smaller passageways marring its length. I traced a finger over the lykill on my carver that stood for light. Silver luminescence flickered more strongly from the entire length of carved up yew wood, even into the iron tip. I eased some of the energy away from the carver, leeching it out slow and easy, with gentle but firm intent—like us hatchlings used to suck the sap from the bright Lava Cup flowers that grew on the mountains in springtime. I pulled the power back into my body. I'd need every bit of strength for humbling Fellriki. It wouldn't be like simple vineyard magic.

"Which way?" Rafn's deep voice bumped against the high ceiling and close walls.

I answered. Or, I thought I answered, but no sound came from my mouth.

I tried again.

Nothing.

A flicker of unease wrinkled Rafn's brow and made his lips pinch. He started to say something, but he couldn't even whisper. His eyes went flat, and his chest moved as he breathed faster.

So we couldn't talk. That wasn't such a big problem. We could move. This had to be magic.

I turned and looked at the floor of the cave. Past a wide puddle that reflected my carver's glow, a line of what looked like chalk marked the ground. I could just barely make out three foreign runes that had been scratched into the stone. Their shape and look was blurred, but surely they were responsible for this lack of speech.

Rafn put a hand to his dagger, then ran fingers over

his throat, his mouth. His voice was his most valued treasure. Without it, he couldn't sing the dead's deeds and give them honor. He couldn't fulfill his role in Snowfallen. And everyone knew a man without a role to play was no man at all.

I touched his arm gently and ran my hand to his, lifting it to point at the chalk line and the lykill. I hoped if he saw we'd simply crossed a silence barrier of sorts, he'd realize his voice would return as soon as we escaped this dark place.

Magic, I mouthed. *That's all.*

Then I pressed my lips together and pointed my carver at the first passageway.

He nodded—it looked forced—but steadily walked by my side and into a new tunnel within the mountain.

It was generous calling it a tunnel. The walls hulked around us like we were mice in a rock giant's hand. We maneuvered up the imaginary, massive palm's lifeline, a foul stream eking under my boots and Rafn's clogs. Working our way down the slope of what could have been the base of enormous fingers, we ducked smoothed ridges and leaped over more than one small waterfall of black water.

I stopped Rafn with an elbow to the side and counted out the number of turns we'd taken since entering this passageway on my fingers. One, two, three, four.

He nodded, flattened his hand, and gestured, indicating the direction of each of those turns. Right, left, left, right.

It was amazing having the Raven with me. He was a

smart bird. He raised the bluehare collar of my cloak so it better covered my neck.

We turned, and two new openings belched ghostly air at us. Rafn looked to me. I led him left. The tunnel's walls closed tighter and tighter until we were crawling, one behind the other, and I wondered if this was what the Graybook's former owner felt like in his cairn. I peered at Rafn over my shoulder and waved to go back. This couldn't be right. Fellriki in his finely embroidered robes and broad shoulders wouldn't crawl like a slug into his homeplace. Every drag of our knees and hands against the floor sounded loud in the tiny space.

"Let's go back." I could talk! "It's only getting smaller."

"All right." A nervous smile passed over Rafn's mouth. "I'll have to go backwards. I don't think I can turn around. But I'll try."

He twisted until his knees were in his face and one of his shoulders butted against the ceiling.

"No, no. Just go backward," I said.

The floor scraped my knuckles as I dragged my carver as carefully as I could in one hand. The air was wet and stale. It felt like an entire day had passed by the time we crawled out and made it back to where we'd been.

We went down the closest path, and it was the other pathway's complete opposite.

The tunnel opened into a space that grabbed the scrape of stones under our shoes and our clipped whispers and hurled them into the domelike ceiling and across the far-reaching walls. The path led to a ledge that overlooked a circle sliced into uneven rows, columns, and...

"What am I seeing?" I blinked and blinked again.

Rafn's hands hung useless at his sides, his mouth slightly parted. "A maze."

Then it all came clear. We were in this maze already. This was how Fellriki protected himself. First, the distant location, next, the huldra, now this.

"What do we do?" Rafn crossed his arms, eyeing the maze like a sparring partner.

One of the Graybook's lykill lit up my mind. "We fly."

CHAPTER TWENTY-FIVE

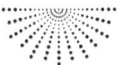

I f we could gain altitude, the maze's path would be far less daunting. The dead ends would be apparent, at the least.

Working the magic, I whispered words I'd never spoken before, phrases from the old language. I traced the lykill into the grit on the rocky ground. My bone ring buzzed like a bee on my hand, and I saw the Graybook's page. The final loop of the rune complete, I took a deep breath, drawing up my wynd—my spirit breath—and blew over the symbol and toward Rafn.

A sudden cacophony of beating wings filled the huge space.

Tiny white birds burst from the lykill. They wrapped around him, stirring his hair gently and rippling his cloak. He made a noise and his clogs pulled up from the ground.

"Starling. This is amazing." He looked around as he rose from the cave floor. The birds dissolved in bunches, gone in a breath, and he drifted back down. "What did I do wrong?"

I shook my head. "Maybe if I had some candles. The fire helps sometimes."

We took the only two we had from Rafn's bag. I breathed in the smell, drawing in their comforting herbal scent. I had a bit of cottongrass in a leather pouch. Using my flint, I lit it and put it to both wicks as Rafn shielded the tiny flames from the cave's errant breezes.

But it wasn't enough. I called up the birds, but they faded before we could get the length of five paces.

"What else gives a seithr power?" Rafn handed me a piece of dried venison, and we ate, thinking and trying not to panic.

"Light is key. I grow stronger vines faster when I stand in the sun." I held up my hands toward the cave walls. "Not going to be getting any of that."

"Do you feel any stronger now that you've eaten a little?"

"Yes. But I don't think that's enough."

"Okay. Sun and food help. Fire helps. All types of fuel, yes?"

"Not sure where you're going with this."

"What is the ultimate fuel for our bodies?"

"Water?"

"Yes, but, what is—"

And then I knew. "Blood."

"So Fellriki does need the sacrifices."

"You don't have to murder anyone for blood. He does it to frighten us, to keep us submissive."

"I hope you're right."

"Of course I'm right. If I called up the Winter Seer with no blood at all, why would I need so much to work other lykill into existence?"

Rafn unsheathed his dagger and the blade threw my carver's glow onto his sharp cheekbones and the stubble beginning to show on his pointy chin. "Take my blood."

"You've been through enough today." I turned my carver on myself and drew a burning line across my palm. Red welled up and rolled down the weapon's edge. I stood and drew the lykill in the air, but still, the birds only held us for a second or two before disappearing.

"I don't understand." I tied up my cut with a length of fabric cut from the hem of my cloak. "I guess...I guess I don't know how to use the blood properly."

The maze loomed, taunting me. Fellriki was out there somewhere, laughing at me, smirking at my pathetic attempts at being a true seithr. If I quit now, I'd go back to growing vines and harvesting wine like the sad little farmer he'd deemed me at the cave's entrance. I'd suffer punishment, embarrassment.

I dug my nails into my carver. I couldn't do it. I couldn't stop now.

Rafn touched his key necklace. "We need to do something, Bryn. We've been gone a full day."

They would give up the sacrifices at the end of the celebration.

In less than twenty-four hours, Mother would lay dead on the altar. Unless I could trap Fellriki here, stripped of his power, or better yet, dead himself.

"Come and get me!" I shouted into the maze.

Rafn grabbed my arm. "What are you doing?"

"I'd rather get the fight underway than play this game until he escapes us and Mother's blood cloaks his sick altar."

Rafn took a heavy breath and raised his head. "Fellriki!" His voice was full and gorgeous and my heart pounded for him. "We will never stop searching for you. You will never scare us enough to make us quit. You'll have to kill us. What are you waiting for?"

I raised my eyebrows. "You don't do anything in half measures, do you?"

"If it's worth doing," Rafn said, "it's worth doing in full."

A pounding like iron drums knocked from the tunnel we'd come through. I scored a Protection lykill on the floor for all the good it would do and pushed Rafn behind me, summoning courage and rummaging through my memory for a Graybook rune that might work against whatever this was going to be.

The hreinin galloped into the space. The ice particles on his fur glowed, and steam shifted from his heaving sides. His thick antlers nearly scraped the passageway's lower entrance as he stepped forward and bowed his head slightly to Rafn. Rafn looked as shocked as me.

"What is happening?" I fought the hope rising in me. If he hadn't come to help us...

"Not sure. Maybe...he's helping us again?"

The stag put his nose into Rafn's hand and Rafn stroked him gently. Then a wicked grin poured over Rafn's mouth.

"In appreciation for my earlier show of respect, he will bring us directly to Fellriki." He mounted up and held a hand down to help me join him.

I let my hope soar. "I suppose you're going to get all superior now."

"Now? I thought I've been giving off the superior tone for ages."

"A little bit. But nothing too obnoxious."

"So I have room to grow?"

"Definitely. But you know you'll have to lose the clogs."

He sighed as the hreinin took off and we dug our fingers into its thick fur. "Not you, too. Ulla must stop spreading this hatred of fine footwear. I thought you liked my clogs."

"I like you," I said, heat flaring up my neck, "in spite of your clogs."

"Right," he said wryly.

"Right."

He breathed a laugh into my hair and a shiver sledded down my shoulder blades.

"Will you keep your sword ready?" I asked.

The Winter Seer's pace increased.

Rafn released the hreinin's fur and grabbed me to keep his seat. As the stag darted down stone corridors, Rafn's blade blended with the silvery stalactites and stalagmites.

We rounded a corner. The hreinin's hooves slid through a stream. He jumped to get past the water and my stomach reached toward my throat. To the right, a small opening belched hot springs water and had stained the rock there a bright orange.

The hreinin bucked us off gently, and we turned to face another cavernous room. I almost dropped my carver as Rafn sucked a breath.

Shelves built into the rock held scores of crockery pots, each marked with astrological signs like the one bright star of Vani's Toe and the oval shape of the night sky's Spindle. Black marred the lips of each container. Dried blood. This was Fellriki's collection from the sacrifices. I fought the urge to be sick, wrestling my stomach down.

Fellriki sat on a throne of melted stone.

The back of the throne reached high above his thick pile of tied and braided hair. Rubies the size of my fist, bits of a clear rock I'd never seen, and rivers of silver colored the high seat. At Fellriki's feet, a chest sat unopened, and beside it, a gathering of swords and axes that would've made Ulla swoon. Mountains of silver coins, crowns, clasps beads, necklaces, rings, and belts. Stripped trunks of birches glowed with thousands of lykill. The light beamed and flashed from Fellriki's hoard. My eyelids shuttered against the glare.

Fellriki laughed. "A bit much?"

"You think?"

"Are you certain you don't want to do away with this Deadsinger and spend your days with me, Brynja Seithrsdottir?" He stood, his cloak shifting off his legs and swinging as he stepped from his throne. His throat moved as he dipped his head to the side to grin. He gave me a slow grin. It was like the huldra's touch. Delicious. Tempting. Unfeeling.

"You are not even close to what I want."

"You want the Deadsinger."

I grabbed Rafn's hand, no longer worried about embarrassment or rejection or anything. "Yes." I pushed the word out like a punch. "He has more magic than you and me both."

Fellriki clapped his hands together. "Ah. You talk exactly as one would expect. Like a young woman in lust." He flipped his cloak as he walked around us. His hand reached out to Rafn and he dragged one finger over Rafn's chin. "Good bones, this one. Strong face. But handsome enough for you? I don't think he is. And definitely not powerful enough, little Brynja."

"If I'm such a weak, little farmer, why do you care?"

Fellriki was standing in front of me before I could even see him move. His breath was ice and blood, fire and smoke. "Why do you think?"

Three hanging dragons flapped around his head, white fangs bright in the dim cave.

Fellriki lifted my bone ring and studied it. The skin around his fingernails was caked in something black, the wrinkles of his knuckles too. And under his nails. I shivered. It was blood. Old blood. He ran one of those blood-stained fingers down my wrist, my forearm.

His bone ring was white, turning to an ashy black, then to a bright red, like the lava people told stories about.

Fellriki followed my gaze and grinned. His finger flew up my arm and to my throat, goose flesh following along my skin. I hated the part of me that liked his touch.

Rafn stepped forward. "Get away from her."

My heart surged. "I'm fine." I pushed between him and Fellriki.

"This is adorable." Fellriki walked back to his throne and dropped into the deep seat. His small dragons returned to the darkness of the high ceiling. "I think I'll keep you two here for a while." He flicked a hand.

Fire enveloped Rafn.

The Raven screamed.

I dove toward him, lost on what I was doing but just needing it to stop. Flames lashed out at my skin, and I jumped back.

"Stop, stop, stop!" My voice cracked as I held out my carver, my mind a worthless blank in the face of Rafn's shrieking and the sound of his flesh popping. Bile raged up my throat.

The fire went silent. Rafn fell to the ground, arms limp.

I ran to him, but his skin was clear of blisters. He sat up and looked at me, panting. Sweat poured off of him.

"Please figure out what to do now," Rafn rasped. "This isn't fun anymore."

I swallowed and wiped my mouth. "Got it."

Fellriki leaned forward, elbows on his knees. "Show me something from that book you dug up."

"What book?"

"Don't be dull. I know you found a grimoire in the Lows. Entertain me, and I'll have less need to use your boy there to do the job."

My throat closed, then opened. I swallowed. "Missing your exciting friend from the Altar Bowl, are you Fellriki?"

His eyes sparked and light flashed through the cave. It blinked off the stalactites and the heaps of shining treasure. "How about a new creation, sweet?"

Sweet. That was what the huldra had called me. Further proof that he'd controlled that creature somehow.

"Something less likely to bite off your handsome head?" I bared my teeth even as my mind shifted through the Graybook's lykill.

"Deadsinger." He leaned forward and eyed the Raven. "Feeling chilly? I can remedy that."

"Wait," I hissed.

The image of a rune came to me. It was similar to the Warming lykill, but wider, stronger. The V of the first strokes was layered with finer lines that gave the illusion of movement. Fire. But there was no controlling type slash across it, nothing in the symbol that led me to believe this was an elemental lykill like the ones Fellriki had access to.

I looked at his ring and swallowed, trying to focus. He could burn us to ash with a few flips of his carver.

The lykill in my head had an undulating and thick stroke hanging from one end. It terminated in a ring of jagged dashes. Yes, whatever that beast was, it held the power of heat.

A grin tugged at my bloodied mouth. Liked playing with fire, did he?

I scored the cave floor with the first part of the lykill.

My carver's blade threw sparks as Rafn shuddered beside me. Fellriki left his throne to stalk around the growing shape, occasionally stopping and tapping his lips with a hand.

"Interesting."

As he spoke, a new curiosity swamped me. Why hadn't he tried to claim the bestiary at Altar Mount? Was it because the Gray demanded a certain level of humility, some submission?

I didn't care what his grimoire demanded. As soon as I had him busy with the beast I was about to invite to our little party, I was going to find that grimoire and take it. No matter what. It had to be here in this glorious mess somewhere.

"Do you think," Fellriki said slowly, "that whatever this is will best me?"

I didn't like how calm he was. I didn't like it one tiny bit. "I hope so."

"Because you are ignorant."

"I disagree. It's you with one grimoire, and me, with another. What is there to understand?"

"I have another seithr, though. And a warrior too, working on my side."

I looked right. Left. It was silent except for Rafn's pained breaths and the drips of water from the ceiling. Fellriki smiled, his carver tucked under an arm. I switched my grip on my own weapon and drove the final vicious slashes into the lykill. The ground trembled, but Fellriki only shrugged.

"We've had worse tremors than that of late." He

strolled to his dais. "Haven't we, Liv Seithrsdottir and Ulla Andersdottir?"

My heart stopped beating.

He moved his hand up, down, around, and my friends appeared.

I fell back as the cave's floor opened like a great mouth and released a ship-sized serpent.

CHAPTER TWENTY-SIX

R afn, pale and sweating, reached an arm out
and lifted me up.

The serpent, crowned with five red and twisting horns, reared and flicked a tongue at Fellriki.

And there, chained to his throne, stood Ulla, axe and shield in hand, and Liv with her carver extended and glowing.

A noise like a great flint being struck sounded from the serpent's belly, and I knew what would come next.

I ran in front of the serpent and raised my carver to hold off his fire.

"Behind you!" Rafn shouted.

Tears burned my eyes. I couldn't possibly protect them all. What were Ulla and Liv doing here? How had he captured them? Had they been coming after us?

After the way I'd ignored their pleas when Atli got in my way...they still risked everything and now they were here and probably going to die—

The serpent hissed. Orange and black flames shot at Fellriki. Fire ate at his cloak and singed his hair. Fellriki drove the tip of his carver into the ground, twisted it, and drew it slashing backward. Wind roared in my ears and flung my cloak over my arm. Flames rippled from the serpent's mouth.

Liv shrieked as Rafn ran to her and, with the hilt of his short sword, banged at the metal cuffs circling her wrist.

Ulla's eyes were big as boulders as I drew an Unclasp lykill in the air over her chains.

The wind lifted Fellriki above the serpent's swiveling head, out of the fire's path. Pieces of his hair whipped across his face as he shaped a lykill. A massive spike of white and sulfur-orange stone above the serpent shook until it released a cloud of debris and dust into Fellriki's windstorm.

Rafn had freed Liv. Ulla and I raced to get behind the action.

"The fire didn't hurt us," Ulla said, over the rush of wind and the roar of heat. "It only burned Fellriki."

"That tail could do us in just as easily." I pointed toward the serpent's back end.

The creature snapped toward us, sweeping the ground. We flattened ourselves against the wall, Rafn facing me and his eyes wide.

With a bellow, the serpent belched fire, the other side of Fellriki's cloak burst into tongues of flame. The seithr looked up, shouted, and waved his carver. The stone spine above the serpent broke from the ceiling.

Amid a horde of spark-spitting, hanging dragons, the

pillar of rock plummeted toward the serpent's lashing body.

The stalactite pierced the creature's scales. Blood gushed from the wound as the beast hurtled itself out of the room and into the maze, its cries following like a wake.

Fellriki's gaze fell on me.

He shaped another magical symbol.

Half of my bone ring broke from my body and clattered to the ground.

Pain crawled into my blood and poured out my mouth in a shriek.

"Do stop screaming," Fellriki said. A light rain fell on him, dousing the flames that ate at his clothing. "Your power is broken. Your friends, well…" His carver flipped and scribbled a rune at his feet.

Rafn, Ulla, and Liv grunted, shouted, and fell to the floor, an arm or a leg bent at bad angles.

I took five steps toward Fellriki, away from them, hoping to keep them out of his next attack.

He held up a hand and traced his finger, the one with the lava stone bone ring, over his palm. His gaze snapped up to meet mine as a slash of silvery white flashed near his cupped fingers. Lightning cracked in his hand.

"Lightning is fascinating. It can kill and wake. I'll make you a deal."

He opened his fingers and flicked his wrist. My friends gasped. Their veins lit inside their cheeks and eyes and necks and hands. Fellriki clasped his hands together and all three collapsed into silence, eyes unblinking.

I couldn't move.

"Are they..." I whispered with numb lips.

"Oh no. Not yet. And I won't have to if you simply agree to do as I will. For the rest of your life."

"Why did you choose my mother? What is it about my family that makes you want our blood?"

"It's not your family. This time, I could've taken Jakob." He swaggered back to his throne and put a foot on the wooden chest. He kicked it open to show the jarl's simple silver circlet, a velvet bag, and more silver coins. "But the jarl paid me well to choose otherwise."

"The jarl knows you can be bought?" Ulla shouted. She only seemed capable of moving her mouth.

I stepped forward. "He bribed you and didn't tell any of us a thing? Has he done this before?"

Fellriki leaned back in his throne and looked to the ceiling. "Will you do as I ask or do I need to kill your friends one by one first? You know you'll crumble under this pressure, little farmer. You tried to be a Protector, but you don't have the spine."

Liv coughed. "She has something you don't, Fellriki! A heart!"

I thought of when I'd put the magical beast to Atli's throat, of his pleading, and hers. Did I have a heart like she claimed? I had to prove to myself that I did. A weight settled on my back. I would never disappoint my friends again.

I threw my head back and took two more steps. "So you're content to hide out in a cave with treasure instead of living around others or having anyone who actually cares for you?"

A frown splashed over Fellriki's mouth. "The people and seithr of Snowfallen care for me. They offer prayers. I hear them on the wind. And sacrifices. Food. Blood. They love me. All of them. Well, all except you."

"And us," Rafn growled.

"They don't love you, you fool." I banged my carver on the ground. "They are afraid of you. They think you care for them."

"I do care."

I laughed as loud as I could.

"You know nothing, Brynja Seithrsdottir. I keep Snowfallen safe."

"And take all our first fruits and my father's wine and our lives, when you choose to." My broken bone ring pulsed through my finger and hand and I had to fight to breathe through the pain.

Fellriki stepped toward me until his nose was a breath from mine. "You would all be dead long ago if it weren't for me and the blood I spill."

"Lies. More lies." I ran to the jarl's chest of bribery and kicked it over. "You keep the rich alive and watch as the jarl kills the rest of us slowly, one by one, as it pleases you."

He uncurled his palm and threw lightning into my skin.

Pain lashed through me like whips made of glass and hot steel. Ulla, Liv, and Rafn screamed along with me. He was hurting them too.

Fellriki tsked as he released us. My face was hot on the cave floor, and I dragged my cheek along the grit to look at my friends. They looked back.

Fierce Eagle. Trembling Pea Finch. Smoldering Raven.

"I can't...do anything," I croaked, wincing at the heat around my broken ring.

"Try it anyway," Rafn said.

"What's to lose?" Ulla nodded. Gray circles hounded her pretty eyes.

Liv pressed her lips together and gave me a brave smile. She wasn't crying anymore and I wasn't sure whether that was good or bad.

I pulled myself to standing and faced Fellriki. "I'll do it. But let my father keep my mother."

"I can't do that, I'm afraid. But your friends are free to leave. A little battered, but they'll live. Thanks to me." He turned and reached for the jarl's silver circlet.

Now was my moment. Though it wasn't going to work, I dragged my blade over the ground, hissing old words that flew into my mind. My breath was hot and cold and strong with seithr's wynd.

The rock shattered. Fellriki whirled around as a bull raged out of the symbol.

"Go!" I shouted at the thing and pointed at Fellriki.

The great bull raised its thick, bright red head and charged. Its hooves drummed against the stone, a vibration I felt in my chest.

"Gods, that is enormous!" Ulla shouted.

I ran to them and tried to examine everyone at once.

"We're fine." Rafn struggled to stand, one arm limp.

Ulla nodded, her lips white, and her elbow pointing the wrong way.

Liv stayed on the floor, but managed a terrible smile. "It's only a broken leg for me. Fight on, Starling."

I loved them so very much.

The bull tore through Fellriki's windstorm and knocked the seithr down, throwing him behind a pile of rubble. The beast ripped a shining horn through the seithr's shoulder, and he screamed.

I lowered my carver and the bull dissipated. My ears rang in the sudden silence.

"Are you finished, Protector?" I smeared my words in bitterness. "You don't seem quite as keen to fight at the moment."

A breath shuddered out of me as I came close. Sweat covered Fellriki's high cheekbones and wet his gray and silver hair. His chest moved erratically in and out, his wound pouring blood.

"What?" I jabbed my carver at him. "No sarcastic words? No demands now?" I stalked him, enjoying the sight of him lying there like a sacrifice himself. "So. We've had our battle. I won. What now, oh great Protector? Should I be merciful and let you live out your lonely days here as a weak little seithr?" I checked on my hatchlings. They watched me with pale faces. I spoke louder for them. "Or should I give you a taste of what you could've had, if you'd been willing to be submissive for just a minute to claim the Graybook?"

"Let's just go, Starling," Rafn said quietly.

The carved tree trunks's light and the small fires around the high-ceilinged room lit his smooth forehead, strong jaw, and the dimples that tried to hide in his growing beard. He looked like a saga hero. I wondered for a moment if we could be happy here in this cave together. Just forget the world. The others. I blinked the idea away.

"I think you should listen to your friends and leave." Blood streaming from Fellriki's mouth garbled his words.

"I could harvest some heartblood before you actually die. The Redbook, I assume that's the one you have, will claim me once I have a bit and then you'll get to see what a real Protector can do before you head off into your next, shall we say, adventure?"

Rafn grabbed my arm. "Liv's leg is broken. We need to go now."

I ripped my sleeve away from him. "Don't you understand what is going on here? How important this is? I finally toppled the one who has made Snowfallen suffer under his sadistic thumb for years. No innocent folk will need to die ever again. Liv understands. A broken leg can wait."

The hatchlings' eyes widened. Rafn took a step back.

My heart broke a little. "Don't look at me like that. I'm your Protector now."

Ulla touched her bottom lip. "Bryn. We love you. We're just—"

"I'll only be a minute, Pea Finch. Then we'll leave quickly and take care of you." Fellriki reached an arm toward his carver. I kicked it away. "No, no, little seithr." Gods, it felt amazing to shove his words back at him. "You are finished with that." I put a toe under his carver, kicked it up, and caught it with my free hand. "It's the end of an era."

Tucking my own carver under my arm. I laid his over a boulder and stomped one end, snapping it in two. Fellriki wailed.

"Don't start that. You've been a wonderful adversary. Don't go weak on me now."

I drove my carver's blade into his chest, beside his heart, not through it. Red spooled from the wound like a skein of dyed wool. He coughed more blood. I bent and smeared my hand through his heartblood. He was already greying around the mouth. He'd be dead soon.

"Where's the book, weakling?"

He swore and spat blood onto my dress. I put a foot on his wound and pressed. His skin went white and he fell back.

"The throne," he gasped. "Under the throne."

"Get it please, Eagle."

Swallowing, Ulla nodded and hurried to the partially buried rock seat. She reached into the dark below it and pulled out a tattered leather book dyed the color of old blood.

Handing it to me, she said, "Don't forget who you are, Bryn."

I met her gaze, but spoke to the broken seithr on the ground. "You see, Fellriki? This is courage. This is what you should've been." I put a hand on Ulla's shoulder and squeezed it before she went back to where Rafn was standing beside Liv.

The Redbook warmed under my bloodied palm. The grimoire's heartbeat shuddered under my fingertips once, then opened. I gasped as a new bone ring grew from my left hand and glittered, black and red, beside Mother's family ring.

Fellriki stared at his own empty fingers.

I laughed. This was the best day in the history of the world. I couldn't be stopped. No one had my kind of power. Not the jarl. Not the southern salt witches or those who gained ideas from the Holy Fire. Not the western Invaders or even the Silvanian fighters who supposedly called power with their battle chanting.

No. This was so much more. I was so much more. I could command mythological beasts. I could call the storms, the land, fire, the very air everyone needed to breathe.

I was the pinnacle of power. Power incarnate.

I lifted my carver. Magic spun through my limbs like the best of our ice wines, cold and clear and intoxicating. Lykill formed and reformed in my mind's eye, giving me every chance to do everything.

I was invincible.

My carver moved in my hands like another limb, free, easy, not a second thought needed. I peeled fire from the contents of the room—air, colliding particles—and threw it at Fellriki's hoard. The jarl's silver circlet and his pile of coins—given to save Jakob and turn Mother into a sacrifice—melted under my wrath.

I walked to where Fellriki lay bleeding and put my foot on his head. His skull felt surprisingly soft. One move and—crack. A smile pulled at my mouth. One move was all it would take.

"You should apologize, Fellriki." It felt good to say his

name and not call him Protector. "Tell me how much you regret taking my grandfather from me."

"It was for the magic," he slurred, his face smashed against the ground.

I pressed the heel of my boot into his temple. "Tell me how sorry you are for taking my mother's father and trying to take my mother. Tell me how terrible you feel now for taking and taking and taking and taking and taking." My jaw ached from clenching and unclenching between words. I'd never been so angry and so perfectly triumphant.

"Maybe I need to ruin more of what belongs to you so you'll understand." A rune, lines like whips and the three eyes of intent, blinked through my thoughts. It needed young blood. My own would work.

I slit my arm just a bit, then drew the symbol in the dust. Wind coursed through the cave's lofty room and danced around me before I pointed it toward the throne. The wind rushed over the chiseled stone and smoothed it, sanded its edges, until Fellriki's perch was no more than a lump of rock.

"Starling!" Liv shouted.

I turned as Fellriki rose. Only a seithr wrapped for so long in strong magic could still be alive. He whipped a carver from behind a pile of rubble and slashed its steely end against the floor.

But it wasn't his. It wouldn't work. Would it?

Bright fear had me raising my weapon, but before I could shape a lykill, a flash of silver flew past me. The bright thing crashed into Fellriki, driving him to the ground. His new carver clattered out of reach, but not before he managed to shout a string of ancient words, the Eagle's axe protruding from his chest.

But his magic had already cracked the cave's roof.

A section careened down. Ulla disappeared.

Liv was shrieking and Fellriki lay still on the ground, Ulla's axe pinning him down.

Only Ulla's arm remained visible past the fallen rock.

I fell to the floor.

I couldn't breathe.

My friend, my Eagle…Ulla was dead.

"No." Liv collapsed, sucking a breath as her broken leg hit the ground.

Rafn raged toward Fellriki both his dagger and his sword out, but the seithr was stone dead.

Then the entire cave moaned. Cracks crawled up every surface. The mountain was falling.

CHAPTER TWENTY-SEVEN

The walls shifted. Dust and rock rained down. Rafn gathered Liv in his arms and ran for the maze. But I ran for Ulla. My Ulla.

My feet couldn't move fast enough.

"Starling!" Dirt streaked Rafn's face. The light from Fellriki's carved tree trunks flickered and lit his cheeks. "Now!"

The ground rocked as I knelt and touched Ulla's cold fingers. No blood worked through her wrist. She was truly gone. I pressed my palm into hers and choked on a sob.

"Brynja!" Under the archway leading out, Rafn stood, chest heaving. Liv clutched his shirt.

The rest of the ceiling broke free from the walls and roared down. Grit covered my eyes. Wiping my face, I looked toward the throne, then spotted it over the mountain of rock. Dust gathered in thick piles around

Fellriki's body. Ulla's axe glittered from his chest. I couldn't leave her weapon here, with him.

The tunnel's arch broke in half. Rafn dodged the orange and black stone.

The axe's handle still showed the imprint of Ulla's fingers. I pulled and the blade came free with a loud sucking sound.

The archway's rock coughed again and trembled, Rafn and Liv's pale faces just beyond, their hands reaching for me. I dropped to roll under the remaining stretch of stone before it could squeeze past the diagonal chunk that had already fallen. The arch slammed into the floor beside my head, catching a length of my hair. The Redbook fell from my hand. I grabbed my braid and ripped it.

Rafn, seeing that I'd made it through, raced on. I took up the grimoire and trailed him. His feet were fast, leaping over debris and growing puddles of water, heading right, left, right, and through the maze toward freedom.

"Where is all this water coming from?" I shouted, my face wet with tears. Ulla's axe pinged against the cave's rumbling walls and I held it closer to keep it sound.

Rafn jumped a new crevice, then nodded at the cavernous opening. "It's hot. Can you feel it?"

The crack bubbled like Mother's cauldron.

I started to jump, but stopped, not sure I'd make it. I had too much to hold and it was too far.

"The cave," Rafn shouted over the din. "It's cracking the earth open. Must go deep. To the hidden fire lakes. The ones that feed the angry mountain."

Liv pointed a shaking hand to the pale root of some mountain tree. "Throw us the book and the axe. Then grab that root."

"Too high." I looked around. The slab of stone beside me could serve as a bridge.

Water spat and gurgled from the crevice, steam rising and gathering on our faces.

I kicked the stone, but it barely budged. *My carver.* I laid the yew wood across the gap. "Hold it steady with your foot, Raven."

I couldn't believe I had to stoop to this kind of thing when I had two bone rings to my name. But I couldn't picture any lykill. None. The runes from the vineyard, the Gray, and the Red, whirled through my head, blurred and unrecognizable. The only focused point in my mind was that Ulla was gone. She was really, truly gone.

Rafn closed his eyes briefly, but did as I asked. A rumble shook us and an impossibly heavy crash of rock sounded from farther on in the maze.

"Gods, please don't let us be buried," Rafn said.

Liv pressed her head into his shoulder and stared at me, giving me a firm nod of support.

I threw the axe and the Redbook to their side, and set a foot on my carver. Heat climbed out of the black crack in the ground and curled around my legs. My feet were sweating inside my boots and the wool of my dress tightened in the hot air. I put my other foot out, toes one way, heels the other, and began bit by bit to shuffle across.

The carver jerked under my weight.

"I've got it," Rafn said, lowering Liv to her one

unbroken foot. He pressed his clog onto the bladed end. He reached out a hand to me, and our fingertips brushed.

Rafn's eyes didn't leave me.

I lost my balance for a breath. I was going to fall. My mind was so hazy, like my very brain was burning.

"You have it," Rafn said. "Keep on."

Liv leaned as far as she could and reached toward me too.

I wasn't going to make it.

After all of this, beating Fellriki, losing Ulla, the jarl would probably still sacrifice my mother, not knowing Fellriki was dead...

"You are going to do this. I know it. And you told me I'm smart," Rafn said.

I edged closer, closer. "I said you're wise. That's different." I gripped his forefinger and his family ring. His thumb pinched my fingers against his, but it wasn't enough to pull me.

"Quit being stubborn, Brynja."

"Not likely." I snagged his hand and he tugged me over. I was across the crevice.

A cloud of dust bloomed out of the throne room. We coughed and hacked, gathering Liv and my carver to take off into the dark maze.

"Where did we turn? Here?" The Raven's voice echoed off the walls.

The scratching of rubble rained down behind us.

We were lost. Very, very lost. "Where is that hreinin now?"

I turned to smirk with Ulla, then remembered, and

my chest squeezed. She was gone. Gone. Gone. I fought a sob and kept hurrying. I had to get Liv out of here. Why couldn't I get a clear rune in my head? Something, anything to help us? We had to get to the glacier cave where they would hold the celebration before they took Mother up to Altar Mount to kill her.

Running and twisting and turning, we grew more and more lost. Darkness crowded closer and closer.

"I can't carry you anymore." Rafn set Liv down at a turn in a tunnel that looked nothing at all like any we'd been through.

This broken palace of stone and ice and boiling water was going to eat us alive and even with all the magic in the world, I didn't know the first thing to do.

I crouched and handed the book and axe to Rafn. "Help her onto my back. Liv, you really might be a pea finch. You don't weigh a thing." Fighting tears and exhaustion, pretending to function normally, I squinted into the near dark and led them into another tight corridor. "Don't know why the Raven had so much trouble."

Liv's head pressed against the back of my shoulder. "I can't believe we lost her," she whispered.

Tears burned my eyes, but I didn't let them fall. Not yet. I swallowed around the fist gripping my throat. "Someone will die for her. Fellriki's death isn't enough. Not nearly enough."

Liv didn't add anything. She just held on, her breathing shallow. She could be stronger if she wanted. If she'd just feel the silver magic in her blood, she'd be so much more. I gritted my teeth, frustration and grief pulling at my limbs.

Inside the maze, the dark was another world.

A world where every noise I made was magnified in my skull and the very air tasted like dust, metal, and the sweat of fear.

We would never stop walking.

Turning right, left, crawling under, working our way over—on and on and on we trudged. Little streams made trickling sound, echoing in all directions so there was no way to follow their path in or out.

As I grew weaker, the shining lykill on my carver dulled, making this world blacker and blacker. The rumbling had stopped, and the maze became like a massive tomb, like the kinds southern kyros were buried in.

Only Liv's head on my back, Rafn's warmth behind me, and the desire to make Ulla's death mean something kept me going.

How was I going to make it back before the jarl sacrificed Mother?

I didn't know when my legs had started shaking. My stomach tremored too, and my arms, my fingers and toes. My lips were ice on my face. And the place where my maimed fingers used to be felt hot and cold and that made me shiver more.

No power bloomed from the bone rings on my fingers. Not in the lava one on my left next to my mother's ring, or the whale's tail on my right.

I'd been buried alive. Buried alive with the Raven and

the Finch. We would wander aimlessly until we ran out of energy.

Soon, the jarl would lay his blade on my mother's throat. He'd sever her flesh. I'd never see her smile again with that glint in her eye that was only for me. The vineyard, press house, our home would be so empty without her.

If we did escape this maze, how would my heart beat without Ulla and Mother?

I had truly lost the battle. Fellriki may have died, but he'd won this. He'd died quickly. And here I was, sentenced to grope through the dark while horrible things happened to the person who gave me life.

As we struggled to pass under an archway, eyes straining for light, I wondered what wrong turn I'd taken in life. Maybe I hadn't been ruthless enough. I should've gone straight for Fellriki's throat at the Presentation. But I'd hesitated, and now Ulla was dead. Mother would be dead very soon. Then Liv, Rafn, and I would follow them to the grave.

My knees quaked. I put one foot in front of the other and kept on and on and on.

"I'm proud of you, Starling." Rafn's voice echoed in the underground world.

"Don't be." My words tried to fall apart, but I lashed them together with anger. "I ruined everything."

"You didn't."

Liv's head rolled a little from side to side and her arm fell limply down my back. "Leave me alone," I whispered to the Raven. "Please."

"All right, Starling. For now."

Then a lykill whispered to me. An image of shallow swirls and a deep arrow shape flashed behind my eyes.

"The air," I said, setting Liv down with Rafn's help. "I can ask the air to guide us out."

I tipped my blade to the dark ground and its tip scraped the rock, raising ghosts of dust that further coated my tongue and nostrils. The lykill shimmered a bright silver as I said a word, a phrase I didn't understand. Somehow it was air and it was direction. The ends of my hair lifted around me and wind buffeted against my back, urging me forward, to a tunnel leading left.

"This way." I waved to Rafn and Liv, whose clothing and hair rippled like we were underwater.

The air pushed us through path after path, a mossy passage, then one with teeth of stone. The ground grumbled under our feet several times, and I fought chills, focusing on getting Rafn and Liv out of here. I may have lost one hatchling, but I refused to lose us all. A shudder ripped through my bones and my rings flashed hot and cold.

Out of the darkness and the sulfuric, thick air, came a pale light. The air teased my cheeks and lifted my cloak. Power pooled between my eyebrows and in my temples.

The tunnel opened to a moonlit clifftop clearing and a massive bowl.

"Altar Mount." It had worked. The air had led us out.

Rafn set Liv down gingerly.

"We're out," she whispered between clenched teeth. I looked at her, her raised chin, her fortitude. She did have strength. It just took a No-Other-Choices situation to get it out of her.

Rafn gripped Ulla's axe in a white-knuckled hand. "If we'd known…"

"What day is it?" Liv positioned herself on a boulder, catching her breath.

The Raven met my gaze. "I'm not sure," he said.

My heart lifted, paused, before beating again. I walked toward the altar. If the blood was fresh, Mother was dead. If not, the sacrifice was set for tomorrow. It had to be tomorrow, right?

My fingers quivered as if Fellriki's lightning spasmed inside them. The altar was cold to the touch. My heart hung in my chest, waiting. The blood was dark. And it was dry.

I took a full breath, my pulse returning to normal. "We haven't missed it. We have until tomorrow."

In near silence, a quiet that was both heavy and painful, we splinted Liv's leg and took turns either helping her walk and sometimes carrying her on our backs until we reached a sleeping Snowfallen.

Tomorrow we would bury a friend. I would rise as the new Protector if the kingdom accepted me.

And I would save my mother's life.

BEFORE WE MADE it to the healer's homeplace, the jarl met us in the road.

"Where have you been?" The wind moved through his braided hair. His eyes were dark as mud.

I held out my hands, showing him my bone rings. The Redbook's ring glistened black and red like lava rock. My other hand glowed ghostly gray with half of the bestiary's whale tail marker.

The jarl's beard moved as his lips turned down. He reached toward my hands, but seemed to decide against that and dropped his arms to his sides. His gaze slid up to meet mine. "So you took him down." The old man swayed like he might faint. "Then you must prove yourself."

The Raven left Liv to me and stepped forward. "Are you joking, Jarl? She holds two rings. Brynja Seithrsdottir is our new Protector."

"I do not accept her."

Liv winced, then looked at the jarl. "It's not something you can deny, Jarl."

I just stared. There was no room for arguing or proving anything. I needed to bury Ulla's axe and I needed quiet.

"Ulla Andersdottir is dead." If I said Fellriki killed her, they might claim she earned the death. That was a fight for another day. "From a rock fall. We will discuss the rest of this after her proper burial in the morning."

"But tomorrow is the final feast and the sacrifice."

"Yes." I moved Liv's arm to rest more securely over my shoulders. "Liv needs the healer. We will talk soon, Jarl."

He let us move on, but did nothing to help us. I looked back once, and he stared, his arms crossed, the amber beads on his bluehare cloak clicking in the wind.

The moon poured light over his broad form and lit on the sword at his belt.

The Raven swore, a shock to all of us, as we made it to the healer's door. The old woman took Liv in without question. Rafn and I clasped hands once before going our separate ways to our homeplaces.

I was walking a ledge. One wrong move, and I'd plummet into grief or be shoved into the black by someone who didn't want to hear my story, someone who still believed whole-heartedly in Fellriki. Someone like my father.

~

THE SUN HAD ALREADY STARTED its rise when I cracked the door open at home. The cauldron sat empty beside the firebed's glowing coals.

I sank to the floor.

The curtain around Mother and Father's sleeping area swung open. "Who-who is there?" Father's voice was rough.

"It's me," I whispered, putting a hand on the cold cauldron. My insides were eating me up, Mother's absence gnawing and gnashing against the lining of my stomach and heart.

Father threw question after question, then yelled, cried, and finally collapsed beside me in silence, his heavy arm around me.

We slept on the floor until the sun speared through the cracks under the door.

I sat up and slowly, slowly told Father my story.

CHAPTER TWENTY-EIGHT

The afternoon sun shone down on what was supposed to be the last day of Winterskvöld, a time for feasting and fortune-telling.

But I stood in the center of Linden Lows, surrounded by everyone in Snowfallen, watching them wrap my best friend's weapon in a shroud.

Liv stood beside me, supported on a crutch the healer had provided. She wept openly and it made me jealous. I couldn't seem to cry.

Ulla's parents touched the stones at the edge of their daughter's burial place. Pain glazed their eyes. Ulla's mother clenched her stomach like she was about to be sick.

I rubbed the burial herbs between my palms and their full scent of shaded woods and sun-soaked hillsides rose around me.

"This is not good enough for you," I whispered, as I

tucked the herbs around the steel and wood and all that I had to focus my grief on.

But Ulla didn't whisper in my ear. Of course she didn't.

Rafn began to sing.

"Out of the air,
She flies, she leaps,
Beyond our ken,
She knows, she dreams,
Brave and bright,
Woman of the Isle,
Loyal, pure,
Woman of the Isle,
Fought for her heart,
Rose to the fight,
Fight on fair Ulla,
Fair Ulla,
Fair Ulla."

"Starling." It was Liv. Her face was blotchy. "Are you all right?"

I closed my eyes. "Liv."

She followed me back to the line of mourners. "Do you want to stay with me tonight? We could go to the lair and remember her and—"

"No. I'm, I'm sorry. I just, I can't…"

"It's fine." She touched my sleeve, then pulled her hand away.

"Everyone is staring at my bone rings," I whispered, scowling.

"Do you blame them? When will you finish telling

them everything? You need to show the jarl what you are now."

"I have to go." I whirled. "Don't think I don't care. About this. About you. I just need to…leave."

Her thin lips pressed into a determined line, and her eyes softened. "Then go, my friend."

$\sim$

BEFORE ANYONE COULD STOP me or ask anything or make me feel worse than I already did, I made it to Altar Mount.

As I climbed the twisting slope, my mind raced through all I'd won, and all I'd lost.

I didn't see the craggy peak before me or the pines black and green and white. I saw Ulla's eyes as she struck out toward Fellriki. The bend in her fingers as she released the axe. Her chest lifted in a breath. In my memory, her smile beamed wide and showed her one crooked tooth.

My fingers burned into my carver and my rings sang with power.

"What good is all this?" I shouted to no one. "I can do this." I whipped my carver in a circle, then swiped it across my body like a great claw. Air and energy roared together into a flash of fire and consumed a once beautiful pine. "But I couldn't kill Fellriki on my own." My magic's flames consumed another tree and another and another. "I couldn't save Ulla. I failed. I failed. I failed!"

Like it had its own will, my carver dipped and cut

shapes in the ground. The rocks bubbled and melted into glowing liquid that even from a distance almost burned my cheeks and singed my hair. I drew another lykill, my body shaking with rage, and found my next several movements could control a focused and devastating slice of wind. With one wide arc, I cut the tip of the peak above the Altar Bowl. A slab of gray rock crumbled at the edges, shifted, groaned, then fell to the fjord's black water far below with a mighty crash.

I waved my carver at the Altar Bowl. The wind drove the bowl from its pedestal and threw it sideways to the earth where it cracked in half.

My arms, limp and worthless, fell to my sides and I dropped my carver. The damage I'd done crumbled and smoldered around me. It was nothing compared to the ruin I'd brought to my friends. I'd broken us. We could never be the hatchlings again without Ulla.

Gods, it hurt.

It hurt so, so badly.

I could hardly take a breath, the pain grabbed my chest and shook it hard. I bent at the waist and turned away from the altar.

Rafn stood beside the one pine I'd left standing.

He was dressed all in the palest blue, the color of mourning.

"The jarl announced the final feast will be held at the glacier cave. Just there." Rafn pointed to the icy dome beyond the path near the altar. If I was still a child, or still fully immersed in the myth of Fellriki, I'd think of how auspicious the position of the temporary cave of ice was. Now, I didn't care.

Rafn's gaze slid to my rings. "You are more powerful than he ever was."

"And I still couldn't save my best friend."

The loss was a deep, dangerous wound, and it brought that hot-cold pain that came when the agony-stopping poppy seed oil ran out after a battle with another northern isle. "Every time I remember she's gone, it's another death. She dies over and over in my head." My throat clenched and I fought down a sob, my face hot. "When I look for her to share a joke or tease her or to move the horrible lemming earrings at our lair and then I realize, again, she is gone."

"She would want you to—"

I held up a hand. "Do not start with that *She'd want you to live and be with your family* thing."

"I was going to say she'd want you to wear those awful lemming earrings just to let her laugh from beyond."

I smiled. A little. "Beyond. That is so stupid. How do we even know? I mean, do you truly believe the dead know about burials and sagas and all that? And if they do, why would they care?"

Rafn winced.

I picked up my carver and frowned at it. "I'm sorry. I just…"

"You are the one who hears them speak in dreams, and some instances, in my cemetery. You tell me whether or not the dead care."

I heaved a ragged breath. "Maybe they do, Raven. Maybe they do."

"Even if they don't, can't you see the purpose in

keeping a record of past deeds? Of what we've overcome and accomplished and survived? It's our courage. Our wisdom. Our fortitude in word and tune and ceremony. It is beautiful and strong. Like Ulla. Like you."

I wanted to curl into him then, but a cold wall still housed my soul and I couldn't get myself to turn. It wasn't him or saga songs or tradition I was mad at.

"I'll go," he said. "But I'll be at the final feast if you care to meet me there."

Finally, I turned. "Rafn?"

He raised his eyebrows in solemn question, and I knew. I loved him.

"Hm?" Rafn said.

"Thank you."

As soon as his form disappeared beyond the rise, I fell to my knees and cried.

CHAPTER TWENTY-NINE

On the snowy ground outside the meditation house, my tongue went numb. I didn't know what I was going to say to Mother. I had to tell her why she wasn't going to die. But she'd be like the others. She wouldn't believe it at first. Who would? Would she even let me drag her out of that awful place? Out of the dead silence and back into the world? I didn't have it in me for a fight right now. Maybe I could simply look the part and that'd be half the battle won.

I drew a lykill from the Graybook.

A bright purple beak cored through the rune, and a bird with dainty purple-gray feathers sprang to life. One wing tipped to show a brownish black underside. Ornate versus simple. Well, I needed ornate. Something to show Mother what I was now. Not just another seithr. Not just an ice wine farmer. A heat twinged my insides. Could I show her something amazing? I took a breath. I was gutted. Grief held my power in manacles.

Dipping my head respectfully to the bird, I shaped the words that went with the lykill.

The creature flew up, lightly, and circled me. A silver and lavender dress unrolled along my torso and limbs, silver embroidery shining beneath my bluehare cloak. I had to look the part of a powerful seithr so my mother would immediately believe me and wouldn't scorn me for all I'd done. The bird swept into the air again and its wing ruffled my bluehare cloak. Every fiber on the piece of warm fur stood straighter, was softer to the touch. Like new.

The animals carved into the meditation house's door warmed under my hands, the wood answering my new power.

Mother turned as I walked in, her eyes glazed from lack of sleep or from not eating enough. The scabbed cut, where they'd taken her blood, grinned, Fellriki laughing at me from beyond.

"Brynja. What has happened? What are you—" Mother waved her hands at my fine dress.

"I killed Fellriki. I hold his power now." The high ceiling tried to swallow my voice. "I am Snowfallen's Protector now." I held out my hands and my bone rings caught the weak light.

Mother dropped to her knees. "How? Why? Who died? Who did Rafn sing for?"

I shouldn't have been surprised she could hear his crooning during the burial. My mouth didn't want to say the truth. If I said it, it would keep being true. "Ulla. Fellriki, he...she is dead."

I felt like I was the one who'd been crushed under the

cave's weight. My knees wobbled and I let Mother pull me to her.

"She'll be the last to die for Fellriki and his lies. You, Mother, are going to live a long, long life."

My voice broke, and I held her, both of us crying silent, slow tears.

CHAPTER THIRTY

The cave the council had chosen was in an area of rocky plains that started east of Altar Mount and extended north to the Dark Sea. Black and charcoal-hued stone, partially moss-touched, covered the entire area. As a child, the little stones had made me feel like a giant looking down on a town bursting with turf houses.

Now, I really was a giant.

I watched from the top of the cliffs as Rafn, Liv, and all the others unloaded packs from spotted, wide-bodied horses. They were probably murmuring about Fellriki's cracked and broken bowl, but I couldn't hear it from where I stood. The jarl had at least told them all something, I was pretty certain. If he hadn't, there would've been more questions, demands, and chaos.

Women wore fine woolen dresses. Men had donned their best cloaks and some showed off extravagantly woven hats with long arms of tassels. Children wiped their red noses and scanned the mountainside with excited looks.

I eyed the glacier cave, wishing time could stop for Ulla. It was wrong that we were about to celebrate. Deeply wrong.

Water, warmed by the angry mountain, had hollowed out the glacier cave. The council, Father included, had checked for cracking and listened for grinding sounds to indicate the glacier was moving more than it should have been in the winter. It was deemed safe and so the celebration would go on despite my crumbling, burning heart.

In front of the cave, the jarl's voice rose. "We have arrived at the final feast cave. I humbly ask Brynja Seithrsdottir to accompany the council and myself as we light the first fire."

I worked my way down the pine-shadowed path, but I didn't take the jarl's extended forearm. Rafn, Liv, and I traded a look. I wasn't like them anymore. But I wasn't Fellriki either. I wasn't sure where I fit. And my best friend, my Ulla, my Eagle, wasn't here to help me figure it out.

"This is how it's done," the jarl whispered to me, lifting his arm.

Some of that acid, that heat of power and anger, stirred inside my dark grief. They should've put a ridgrasil warning on me. "Not now it isn't." I walked past him, into the glacier's blue-green hall.

Light filtered through the thick ice and glowed around us in subdued shades of ivy, deep ocean, emerald, and summer sky. The gray rock and dirt of the cave's floor hosted a small but rushing river of melted ice and the air was brisk. It smelled simply of clean water. Beside a cleft of ice like jagged glass, the jarl stacked a fine pile of wood, then stood back, smiling.

"Please, Protector, would you light the first cleansing fire with your newfound power?"

The Redbook's symbols flashed in front of my mind. Carver outstretched toward the jarl's chosen place for the sacred fire, I dashed the lykill's strokes into the air. Flames blazed from the end of my weapon and ate at the birch, oak, and beech he'd stacked for the blaze.

All of Snowfallen stood under the glacier cave's icy arched entrance. They raised fists to me and shouted approval, Rafn, Liv, and all our parents joining in. But there were no smiles. There was no feeling of triumph.

Using branches from the blaze, council members lit the rest of the nine sacred fires. Their orange-red hues colored the ice. It looked like a fiery beast thrashed inside the walls, trapped behind the frozen water.

The women set the food on flat stones along the walls and everyone began eating as well as drinking Father's ice wine. As soon as they'd downed a cask, the revelry began in earnest. The cave smelled of a thousand things. Too sweet sugar, choking woodsmoke, overpowering spiced meat, and the sweat of dancing bodies.

Sitting atop a stump, away from the crowd, I ate sparingly and watched Rafn talk with Benedikt. Rafn's father didn't glare at me but didn't exactly smile either. Liv smiled sadly at something our parents said. Atli sulked in a corner with more boys just like him, planning something, I was sure. Widow Pallsdottir bent low, her scraggly white hair waving a little in the cave's cold breezes, and handed a cookie to each of the jarl's youngest children.

Jakob stood beside his sister, his smile wistful as he looked around the room.

Acid burned around my ribs, and through my shoulders and stomach.

I found myself snaking through the crowd to stand beside him.

Jakob dipped his head to me respectfully. "I am sorry you lost your friend," he said quietly, his gaze on my bone rings.

"Did you know your father bribed Fellriki to choose my mother instead of you?"

My words were somehow louder than all the noise, the drum and langspil, the fire and the conversations. Jakob's sister drew away from me. The cave grew quiet.

Jakob swallowed. "No." He looked over my shoulder. "You know he had to have one."

"One? One of what?" I turned to see the jarl. My smile dropped him back a step. I was coming back to life. If my smile induced fear, I could only imagine what my scowl would accomplish. "How many times did you give Fellriki silver so he wouldn't choose one of your own to die?"

The jarl's brow furrowed. "That's not what happened. The mountain—"

"It is your fault my grandfather lies dead. It is your fault Ulla Andersdottir isn't here to celebrate. To live out her life."

He shut his eyes and shook his head. "That had nothing to do with this."

"Yes, it did." I stalked forward, pushing the jarl back, toward the fire I'd started. He scrambled, trying to keep his feet under him. "If you had listened to me about Fellriki and about the bestiary I'd found, Ulla wouldn't be rotting in a cave right now."

He put out his hands, wrinkles and silver rings vying for spots around his knuckles. "Now, wait, Brynja."

"Do not speak to me as if we are equals."

I took another step and he fell against the stones circling the bonfire. He made a noise of pain and tried to move away from the flames, but I trapped him, standing over the monster.

"I don't need to take anyone's life to be Snowfallen's rightful Protector," I spat. "Heartblood isn't needed. It was a lie. It was all a lie."

I whipped around. Faces stared, mouths gaped, and children hid behind their parents. I faced the jarl down again and pressed the tip of my carver into his chest. Smoke rose from his hair and his cloak, the fire grabbing at him. I pressed and pressed and pressed until a spot of blood bloomed over his heart.

"But I should take your heartblood, Jarl. For your lies to our people." I faced the crowd. "He gave Fellriki his circlet, silver coins—all to keep his son safe from the blade. He doesn't care about my mother or yours. My life or yours. Only his family, his blood. I should kill him right now." My blade dug deeper and sweat poured down the man's cheeks. The stench of burning flesh rose and I loved it. "Burn, you filthy liar. Burn and bleed. I'm going to let you live though," I said, pressing, pressing, pressing. "I am so very, very merciful. Thank me, pig."

"Thank you, Protector. We thank you."

I dug my blade a little deeper, then kicked him sideways, out of the fire's fingers. "Don't speak for Snowfallen. You are one man. Not even a seithr. I am your jarl now and your Protector. Snowfallen doesn't need liars and killers to lead it. It needs someone who cares about everyone. Not just themselves."

I strode to the center of the cave. "Now, celebrate, Snowfallen. Celebrate your new jarl and Protector." Tears burned my eyes. The acid from my core filled my limbs, my heart. I was burning to death in the middle of the ice. "Dance! Play the music!"

I threw a spark at the musicians' feet and they hurried to fill the cave with the sound of strings and drums. My hand shook as I gripped my carver tight. One group began the Weavers' Dance.

"Yes. Dance and enjoy yourselves. Enjoy what my friend and my grandfather and so many more who died for a lie cannot."

Rafn stood at the edge of the dancing, his eyes wide and trained on me. My stomach dipped down and up.

"My Raven." My voice cracked. "Raven, dance with me."

He found my side. "Starling, this isn't you. Why don't we go outside and talk? Will you come out and talk to me?"

The acid burned any kind words I would've uttered. "This is me, Raven. The new me." I pushed the corners of his mouth up with my fingers. "Don't frown. This is a celebration." Magic surged through me, mingling with the dark pain of not having Ulla. I bent double for a breath, my stomach churning.

Rafn's hand found my back. "See? You're grieving. And your power, it's probably difficult for you with all these emotions."

I stood straight and grabbed his hand. "Stop lecturing and dance." I drew myself against his side, then pulled away again, turning my feet and spinning in the Last Harvest Dance. He stiffly held my fingers and walked around me, dancing with his body, not his heart.

The whole room was dancing like that.

"Do you all think you're still at a burial? This is a celebration! I'm going to protect you all from everything now. Storms. Bad weather. All of it. Just imagine! I'm not even of age yet!"

My laughing broke into dry sobs. Rafn grabbed me and wrapped me in his arms.

Then the ground moved.

A crack snapped the ice from floor to ceiling. A wedge of the glacier crashed into the bonfire.

Screams tore through the space.

We ran to the cave's entrance, where Widow Pallsdottir pointed toward the higher elevations. She shouted something, but a sudden and deafening rumble drowned her words. The tiny specks of thousands of hanging dragons dotted the sky above the peaks, then one enormous mother dragon soared into the distance.

Thick, black smoke billowed from the mouth of the angry mountain.

CHAPTER THIRTY-ONE

T hose around us gasped and Ulla's parents fell against one another. Father and Mother came up beside Rafn and me, Liv nearby with her family.

My new bone ring flashed heat through my hand, into my forehead. The Redbook's runes blinked in my mind's eye. I saw one that would calm the mountain and settle its overheated belly, restraining its fiery claws.

And I saw something else in my head.

The blood I needed. The blood the lykill required. The knowledge froze me.

I needed heartblood.

And not just anyone's.

Jakob jerked Rafn away and put a dagger to his throat. "Well, Protector. Protect us. This is the blood you need, isn't it? Or are you as insane as you seem? Do you even know what you're supposed to do?" He faced the crowd.

"She is going to get us all killed now. She doesn't even know how to do the magic."

People gasped and cried out as the earth roared and the mountain's smoke thickened.

He was right. I hadn't known. Not until now. Not until the Redbook had shown me.

I was a sham, a fool, an idiot. I was no Protector. I hadn't realized the Redbook's lykill required different blood for different actions. So far, it had asked for none or simply some of my own or a splash of another's. Nothing like this. Nothing so…specific.

Liv pulled my cloak, near strangling me. "Starling! Do something! You know what to do. We are here for you."

Jakob's knife bit into Rafn's neck and the power in me sang. Jakob shouted over the eruption. "You need blood from someone born under your sign! That's why it was down to me or Rakel. You didn't even know, did you? Fix your mistake, seithr. I'll kill Rafn now and you can end this and save us. You said you were our Protector. Protect us!"

Rafn met my gaze and gritted his teeth. "Do it, Jakob."

"No!" I lunged for them as others shouted, "Protect us!"

Hands pulled me back and Liv put her mouth on my ear.

"Take me," she whispered. "Not the Raven. Not your Raven."

My heart beat drummed in my ears.

"Go to the docks!" a man called out, pointing toward the fjord. "To the boats!"

"We'll never make it," Father snapped, his eyes wild.

Mother herded two crazed children away from a new crack in the ground.

"Just take me, Starling!" Rafn shouted.

The tendons and muscles in his forearms stood out as he held onto Jakob. He was white as a ghost, but there wasn't any fear in his eyes. Benedikt was on his knees beside me, lost.

It couldn't be the Pea Finch. She was too good. Too kind. So much better than me. I would not take the Raven. He was so wise, beyond his years. Snowfallen needed him. But Snowfallen needed a Protector, too.

I looked at Liv. She stood, calm, arms by her sides, lip trembling just a little, but her chin held high.

Some people grabbed what they could and ran toward the docks, shouting for us to escape to the sea.

I ignored them all and dragged my blade across my throat.

"Starling!" Rafn tore away from Jakob.

Blood spooled from my body like I'd hidden a skein of red wool inside my flesh. I dragged my carver through the fluid, power sustaining me.

Liv started to tug at me, Mother pulling her away, crying and saying something over and over.

A shudder ripped through me. The angry mountain roared, and red fire spouted from its mouth.

The jarl shouted my name. Father did too.

Black ash swallowed the sun and the blue sky.

The air was bitter and tasted like bones.

The ground shook, and we fell, shouting and weeping all around. With a resounding snap, a crack opened in the glacier cave's arching entrance. Not a stone's throw away, white steam blasted from the black rocks with a scream.

Liv caught me as I fell.

"You are the Protector now," I tried to say to her. She lowered my head to the earth.

Black and white rings floated in front of my face.

Rafn wept over me, his beautiful face contorted and his lips whispering. "No. No. No. Not like this. Not yet."

Rock quaked under me. The acidic air choked, the heat seared my lungs, and a numbness grew in my throat only to slide down my chest, into my fingers and toes.

With a shaking hand, I wiped blood from my throat. I grabbed Liv's hand and pressed it against my bone rings. She screamed. My bone rings sang. The world dropped into memory. Everything went black.

THE DARKNESS SWEPT me away like a night wind, cold and sure and drawing me to places far, far away.

I searched for Ulla.

Eagle. Are you here? I didn't want to be alone in this thick and inky emptiness. *Eagle?*

But no one answered.

I was alone in the dark.

WHAT WAS HAPPENING BEYOND ME? Had it worked?

MAYBE THE ANGRY mountain's liquid rock poured fire over my body and the bodies of my friends. Maybe the smoke tangled in Rafn's black braids and the heat turned him to ash. The mountain's red tears burned my parents. Liv's pretty eyes went blank, and her skin bubbled and snapped into nothing. We were returned to the ground and I was glad Ulla wasn't here to see it, to live it, to die this way.

I could've saved them if I'd realized it all sooner. I could've given myself and saved them if only I'd asked the right questions, if I'd beaten the truth from Fellriki, from the ignorant jarl.

Now I understood Jakob's comments during the final feast.

He had known. I'd needed the heartblood of someone born under the same sign as me, the Protector. He had known it all along.

If only I had asked him.

CHAPTER THIRTY-TWO

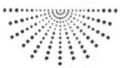

Bryn's eyes shivered, then went still, and the breath went out of Rafn. Her blood soaked into the patchy ice and black rock, then rose again to form a line. The dark ruby fluid pooled at Liv's feet, soaking the edges of her boots. The blood on the girls' joined hands melted into Liv's skin. She inhaled sharply. The Starling's bone rings shimmered oddly and grew smaller, smaller, smaller until only red welts marred her tiny, beautiful fingers.

Rafn's ribs pinched against his lungs. This wasn't happening.

The volcano snarled. A thread of orange popped into the blackening sky.

Over half of Snowfallen was gone, down at the boats, headed for the open ocean. The other half were here, kneeling by the hatchlings, praying to all the gods, the stars, and even their ancestors.

Lowering Bryn's hand gently, Liv inhaled as the two

magical rings grew from her own slim hands. She took up her carver and faced the angry mountain, raising her palm to the sky. Closing her eyes briefly, she began to work her new magic.

The Finch's whole body shook. She paused to dip her blade in the Starling's blood again. Slashing, sweeping, she finished the lykill.

The earth stopped rumbling.

The ash and smoke hung, suspended, in the air. Then, like the world was tired, the orange rising above the volcano's lip, the flakes of gray everywhere, the smoke, all of it eased to the ground. A haze cloaked the sky, the mountain, everyone's faces, and the very air.

Rafn rubbed his eyes, not sure what he was or was not seeing. He fought to expand his lungs and lost the battle.

Rakel's smooth, but shaking voice broke the silence. "It worked."

Rafn pulled a breath in. He bent over the Starling's still body. Touched her forearm. Her warm forearm.

His heart jolted.

Her skin wasn't cold yet. Her chest, it moved. Didn't it? Or was it only his heart wishing and tricking his smoke-clogged eyes?

"Liv!" His words were torn and prickly. "Finch!"

Everyone had gathered around the new Protector, an arm's length of respectful distance away.

"Finch! The Starling. She isn't dead. Not yet. What can you do?"

Rafn couldn't see anything but her crown of brown

and silver braids. She turned toward his voice and the small crowd parted. Her bottom lip trembled.

"It's okay, Liv. If you don't have anything to help her. It's not your fault. It's..."

A tear scorched its way down his cheek and fell off his chin.

Liv smiled sadly, turned, and arched her carver, making short gouges in the earth. A furred muzzle broke the symbol and a warm-blooded something crawled out of the ground.

"Skoffin," the Finch said. "Will you find my friend's soul and bring it back to her?"

She went silent as the fox? cat? leopard? stalked the space marked by magic. Liv cocked her head, then looked to Rafn.

"He must eat a secret."

Rakel and Agust leaped forward and stammered little lies, small things.

Rafn held up a hand to stop them. "I have a secret to sacrifice."

CHAPTER THIRTY-THREE

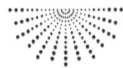

Voices flickered at the edge of my hearing.
A light blinked.
An animal gnashed at my throat.

Stop, I tried to yell. *Please. Stop. I'm sorry. If I could give it all to peaceful, wise Liv sooner, I would. I would do it all differently. No need to torture me now. The knowledge of my mistakes, my arrogance is punishment enough. To know that if I'd respected Liv's gentle, ungreedy nature, that this could all have been different...*

Power lay in the willingness to live without it.

I knew that now.

Then the pain jerked me from the darkness and spat me back into the light.

CHAPTER THIRTY-FOUR

Liv smiled down at me, her face stained with ash and tears. Her hand rose and in it was a bone needle and thread.

A flash of gray and black and white spun around us. It smelled musty, like a grave. I could just make out a muzzle, pointed ears, and two differently colored eyes.

The skoffin.

Rafn spoke softly, quickly, his gaze flicking from my face to the creature. "...give my secret to save her, little beast. My mother left me for another family, one she found during her wandering, in a far-off isle. And I hate her for it. And I hate myself for wanting to wander too."

My body shivered and a heat grew inside me.

"She is here," Liv said. "Our Starling is here. That's enough, Raven. And I thank you."

It was then I noticed the rock beneath me lay still and solid. The air had cleared mostly, showing streaks of bright blue against the ashy clouds.

Rafn, my parents, and the jarl leaned over me.

"Is she?" Rafn choked on a sob and ran a hand over his mouth, his simple family ring catching the inconsistent light.

The skoffin continued its spinning, around and around us, above us.

"A minute more, please," Liv said to the fox creature. She brushed a hair away from my cheek and I saw the Redbook's bone ring flash from her first finger.

"What is this spirit?" the jarl asked, eyeing the skoffin.

"He is the Master of the dead. He called her back for us. It's a rare gift and one he won't repeat within our lifetimes," the Pea Finch said. "He has a special affinity for Brynja."

The fire at my throat made it difficult to untangle their words for meaning.

"The skoffin is also strong-willed. It's how he can do what he does."

"Like knows like," Rafn whispered as he looked at me.

Liv drew a rune over my wound with her cool fingertip. The pain leeched away as the skoffin slowed and sat beside Rafn.

"There." Liv grinned. Her hair lay in messy strands down her face and over her shoulders.

I sat up, and Mother shoved everyone away to hug me. She cried into my hair. "My Starling. My Starling. Don't you ever do that to me again. Never."

Father wrapped his arms around both of us as best he could. "Our brave girl. My brave daughter. I'm so sorry."

A hand touched my back. I looked behind me to see Rafn patiently waiting his turn.

CHAPTER THIRTY-FIVE

The sun glittered overhead, warming my shoulders, as I carved a Growing lykill into a vineyard post. We needed ice wine to raise a drink to our Pea Finch, the strongest of us all.

Almost a full year ago, she had become our Protector and Snowfallen had never been more peaceful.

Now, Liv worked beside both our sets of parents, drawing large lykill in the ground, urging the soil's nutrients into the new root growth. Her carver moved with a sweeping confidence I'd never noticed in her.

"But she always moved like that, didn't she?" I said aloud as her father and mother each cut one finger and pressed their blood into the black dirt.

Rafn looked up from the Deadbook where he'd been writing his latest saga with a new quill. "Yes. You and Ulla never noticed."

My throat constricted at my lost friend's name and I watched Liv, trying to keep my smile.

"I want to tell you what happened during the summer," Rafn said. "When I...began acting differently."

I met his gaze. "Of course. But only if you want to. I know the secret you told the skoffin."

"There's more." A shadow passed over his face. "Before Father told me about my mother, that she left, I announced that I wanted to take two years to wander. And he said if I was going to put my naïve passion before everyone who'd cared for me, I could just go." Rafn stared at me. "He kicked me out."

"We had no idea."

"I know." He gripped the cottage key hanging from his neck. "I stayed in the jarl's winter barn."

No one would've looked for him. The place remained empty until harvest when the jarl's slaves filled it with grain and root vegetables.

"You should've told us hatchlings, Rafn. We would've helped you."

"I didn't want help. I hated myself. I still do."

"You'd always come back," I said. "And if you didn't, well, you do it the right way."

"The right way?"

"You'd say goodbye. You'd be honest. Brave."

The sadness in his eyes tore at my chest. "You don't think I'm disloyal?" he asked.

"For being curious about the world? No, no I don't. You love our home. It's all right to want to see other places too."

"But if too many people get...curious, we could lose what our ancestors built here. Snowfallen could change forever."

"We hold on to what we want to hold on to."

He cocked his head.

"It's a choice, Rafn. Our culture isn't going to slip away if we pay attention to what we love about it and give it our respect."

He looked down, his eyes moving as he studied his clogs. "I think you might just be the smartest one on the isle."

"You're just now figuring this out?"

He grinned, then we both watched Liv work.

"Are you disappointed she is the one with all the power?" Rafn whispered, his hands sitting lightly on the book and one knee. A faint light shimmered beside him. Maybe just the sunlight through the scant clouds.

"No." I smiled truly then. "She's the only one who could stay good and negate the ridgrasil's warning. This is how it should be."

I held a fist against my heart, where it beat slow and sad for Ulla. Then a shape—tall, light—appeared beside Atli, who was grouching and pulling weeds. The shape looked at me and a face grew clear.

It was her.

Smiling at me, Ulla cocked an eyebrow, and with the toe of one faint boot, tipped over Atli's bucket of weeds. He swore, face twisted in confusion. Rafn and I laughed.

"You see her?"

"I do."

Ulla held her stomach, laughing silently. Then she was gone. And with her, a piece of me.

"Can we go to the lair tonight? With the Finch too?" I asked quietly, oddly afraid of rejection.

"Of course." Rafn stood and held the Deadbook at his side. "I'm so proud you're all right with just having... simple powers."

I carved another lykill at the base of the post, and drove a fallen leaf into it with one heel of the clogs Rafn had made for me as a joke. The vines spread out of the ground and up the post and I moved my carver, urging them into a roof of sorts, encasing us in leaves.

In the green light, I spun to face Rafn. "Simple magic is still pretty good stuff."

"Indeed." He set the book down on his cloak and took my face in his rough, ink-stained hands.

"Brynja!" Father tried to peer through my little room of grapevines. "You have work to do and you two have not yet announced any commitment so—"

Mother's tsking interrupted him. "Let them be, husband."

He complained as she dragged him to the press house.

I laughed against Rafn's chest, breathing in the scent of him, incense and old stone, and feeling the soft weave of wool against his warm skin. He put a finger under my chin and guided my mouth to his.

I pulled away before he could kiss me and touched the Deadbook, still gripped in his hand. "I shouldn't have interrupted your work. You can go back to writing that saga."

"You think I want to write songs right now? When I have this"—he waved his free hand at my face and body — "in front of me?"

"Yes, I think a part of you does."

"Not the more insistent part."

I laughed again and pulled him to the ground to sit. He put the book aside, but I nabbed his quill and held it up. "You might forget what you were about to record."

"It's an old story. I'm only rewriting it because the ink is fading." He raised a knee and leaned his mouth against my neck. "Forget what I said about Liv being the most powerful. This power you have is far more dangerous. Besides"—he glanced over his shoulder— "the Deadbook is engulfed in vines at the moment. Too bad. I'm going to have to participate in this dangerous duty instead." His lips ran a line from my shoulder to my jawbone, and my skin pebbled riotously.

A memory ghosted through me, thoughts of the first time he'd looked at me with those hungry eyes he wore now, when he'd said cities had fallen from such games.

Seated, with my legs crossed and the new grass soft under me, I raised my thin woolen dress to show one thigh.

He swallowed.

"Write your song here." I touched my skin. "So you won't forget it." I handed him the quill.

With a grin like honey, he bent to his work. The quill's tip brushed my leg, made a tiny circle, then jumped in the making of three faint lines.

"The ink is gone. Should I stop?" Rafn raised an eyebrow like the final slash of a powerful rune.

I worked hard to keep my words steady. I was trembling from tip to toe. "I don't think so."

"All right then."

It felt as though I had my own store of molten rock and slowly moving fire within my veins, under my skin, threatening to erupt under the Raven's skilled touch. He wrote five lines along my thigh. The quill's tip a pleasant bite, the occasional feather brush a gasp, and his breath hot and drawing the longing out of me like nectar from a lava flower.

"What, what does it say? Will you sing it to me?" I whispered, going back to lean on my elbows.

The crushed leaves under us smelled green and bright, and sunlight touched the line of Rafn's strong nose and one of his night-black braids. He smiled.

Running a finger along the words of the saga and bending close to my leg, to my skin, he sang.

"And to the other lands he sailed,
This Tradesman turned to Wanderer,
The terrible storms only brought him joy,
The challenge was a wonder,
To emerald shores and white cliff inlets,
He learned new tongues, found skills,
And brought them gaily to his good people,
They learned new paths and grew much bolder,
And none could but praise the Changer."

His deep, lilting voice dusted shivers over my body, my heart.

"It's about you." I traced the line of his eyebrows and the edge of his ear. His longshirt hung a fraction away from his body and I could just glimpse his strong chest and flat stomach in the uneven light.

"No. It's an old saga."

"It's still about you. Remember what you told me. Your secret. We could go."

"We?"

"We."

"You'd leave Snowfallen to make me happy?"

"I'd move mountains to make you happy. Well, I'd talk Liv into moving mountains."

A half smile skirted over his lips. His eyes gave me another question, a question that involved his hand on my thigh.

"Yes. To all."

And as I heard Liv and the rest crunching and stomping their way out of the vineyard, Rafn lay on me, his weight somehow the most wonderful feeling in the world, and kissed me like he was writing our song on my lips.

Please consider leaving a review for this book.
Review are important for readers and authors alike!

Want to read more stories set in the Uncommon World? The box set is on sale now for 99c!

http://hyperurl.co/UWseries

Want a FREE prequel to the main Uncommon World series?
(Bryn shows up in the last book, Forest of Silver and Secrets.)
Go to

~SNEAK PEEK of Alisha's upcoming Adult Epic Fantasy series~

Fate Of Dragons:
Dragons Rising
Book One

(This is a raw, unedited snippet. The complete novel will be available in March of 2019.)

THE VERY LAST human stared into the sky and prayed the dragons couldn't read her mind. Vahly didn't want the exquisite creatures to see her pathetic longing to be with them, to be them. They were so beautiful and strong. Far above, they flew in the formation of the dragonfire ritual, circles within circles, scales like the finest lapis lazuli. A coming storm's distant lightning flashed off their sinuous bodies. Vahly—the world's biggest disappointment—remained on the ground, completely powerless. She was painfully aware that, as a direct descendant of the former Earth Queen and now a woman, she should've had her own wild magic. Sadly, she was just a lump of easy-to-burn, no-problem-to-maim human flesh. Vahly would've given absolutely anything to be the true dragon daughter of her adopted mother, the lapis dragons' matriarch.

~Stay tuned for more, and if you'd like to hang out with Alisha online, find her at https://www.facebook.com/groups/EpicFantasy/ or at http://www.alishaklapheke.com~